FRAGILE
PUBLISHING

THE LAST SCARECROW

NEIL J HART

First published worldwide in 2024 by Fragile Publishing

A CIP catalogue record of this book is
available from the British Library.

ISBN: 978-0-9554832-3-3
Also available as an ebook and in audio

www.neiljhart.com

*For everyone and
everything we've lost.*

No matter what you look like,
where you come from,
or how strange your ideas may seem—
you can change the world for the better.

COUNTDOWN TO EXTINCTION

"Brave the rain or die!"

Erin could barely hear Pa's sorrowful screams above the violent winds that rocked their tiny boat. She'd seen torrential rainstorms before, but this felt different, impossible.

She threaded her plimsolls between food tins that clattered about in the hull, pounded by wave after wave of frozen needles. A yellow poncho whipped against her face. Her flesh and bones felt like they could unravel at any moment.

Pa fought against the shallows. Heaving one foot onto the shore, he lifted Ma from her wheelchair and levered her into the boat. He threw the oars to Clyde, then squirmed into position.

The old rowing boat listed dangerously.

Foam and spray arced through the air.

Erin's breath came in ragged, machine-gun spurts.

Her heart rattled against her ribs.

The rainstorm groaned, angry and vengeful.

Lightning tore the sky.

Through rain-soaked glasses, Erin turned her sharp green eyes to the farm at the top of Coldharbour Hill. The farmhouse and barns peeked through a thousand sheets of rain, surrounded by the vicious, rising tides.

Coldharbour Farm was her home, her happiness, the one thing she'd always known.

Her father's words tore at her heart again.

"Brave the rain or die!"

Her mind removed the storm clouds, replacing them with a cerulean sky and a lemon-yellow sun. She pictured Pa traipsing up the cobbled path to the farmhouse after a long day in the undulating cornfields. Ma sat by the doorway as Clyde chopped wood and Erin idled in the yawning barn door. At the brow of the hill, Pa swept Ma into a wistful embrace. They kissed momentarily, lingering, their faces inches apart.

A lump stuck in Erin's throat.

She never wanted things to change.

The universe had other plans.

Choking grey clouds suffocated the sky, edged with the black of a sickening bruise. The rain came heavier, more determined, pounding like iron-clad fists on a remote inn door.

She snapped an umbrella open. The wind tore it from her hands and sent it blustering across the waves.

Pa barked at her—angry, frustrated—but she couldn't hear anything except the needles against her skin and the scream of the wind.

Seizing the oars, Pa and Clyde launched them out to sea.

Erin's stomach somersaulted on the choppy swell.

Up, down, up, down, up, down.

Panic circled like a ravenous shark.

Rainwater filled the boat.

Ma scooped handfuls over the side.

The wind spun them in circles, lifting the boat onto the tips of the waves like an endless fairground ride.

But Pa and Clyde stuck to their task.

Arms strained.

Teeth clenched.

Hair plastered to their heads.

The rain and the dark blinded them, clouding any sense of direction.

Erin shut her eyes again.

She dragged Pa into the barn by a chequered sleeve. "What do you think of her?" she asked, dancing in circles. Her father squinted through the dim light, then leant back, staring at Erin's latest creation. His face held both terror and pride.

"She's...the best yet," Pa told her.

"Really?" Erin replied. "Scarier than Number Five? More gruesome than Number Eight?" She watched her father's reaction closely. He nodded grimly, his calloused hands stroking his salt-and-pepper stubble.

"Yes, Erin. She's the most horrifying of them all!"

Thunder rumbled in the heavens.

The temperature dropped.

Icy winds rattled Erin's bones.

The sky became streaked with veins of arctic blue.

Balls of ice catapulted through the storm. They lashed against Erin's head. Her vision doubled for a moment, blurred and anxious. Her shoulders, legs, and arms came under heavy fire. She crumpled forward, pulled her knees to her chest and shuddered uncontrollably.

Clyde jumped forward and lay across his sister, taking the worst of the giant hail on his back. The sound of it lashing against him was almost too much to bear.

Erin squinted at him between the slatted wooden seats, her quivering hands over her ears.

11

His face hung above hers, twisted in agony. He whispered something that could equally have been *Don't worry* or *Goodbye* or *I love you*, but Erin couldn't hear a thing.

Clyde loved dragons. And Lego. His room had become a shrine to both. When they were younger, Erin and Clyde would build castles and smallholdings, develop languages, a rich mythology, and a royal family of which they were Prince and Princess to a loving King and Queen. But, as they grew, Clyde turned his attention to mighty armies and terrible machines of war, while Erin focused on farming and the concerns of her Lego citizens. Clyde's warmongering frustrated his sister and he decided to play alone. Erin caught jealous snatches of his endeavours through the crack in the bedroom door. Eventually, she turned her creative flare to something else. Something... darker.

The ocean exploded as a gigantic ice boulder split the surface.

Erin's rowing boat catapulted into the air. The world flipped over and over and over. Her family went flying in all directions, disappearing through walls of spray and ice.

Entering the water, Erin's toes froze immediately. The sensation moved up her legs like the crawl of some insidious poison. She looked around, panicked, the world dark and close. To her horror, the boat had capsized. Trapping her beneath. She threaded her arms around the splintered seats and hung on with all she had.

The tang of salt and copper slithered on her tongue.

Her teeth ached from clenching.

Her body didn't belong to her anymore.

Her mother screamed.

Her father gave a strangled response.

They sounded muffled.

Distant.

Lost.

She closed her eyes and prayed that when she opened them her family would be next to her, bobbing in the dark waters beneath the capsized boat, protected from the storm.

"Just count down from one hundred, dear, and the pain will wash away," Ma said, as she hunkered in front of Erin.

Blood oozed from a nick on her palm. "It hurts so bad."

"Just count."

Erin ran through the numbers in her head.

"How did you do this?" Ma went on, dabbing the wound with antiseptic. Erin squealed. "Keep counting."

As the numbers fell, the pain slipped away. Erin glanced at her hand. A coarse, pink plaster nestled over the cut. A dull ache lingered beneath. "I caught it on one of Number Eight's rusty nails."

"Well, you're all set here," Ma said, shaking her head playfully. She planted a soft kiss on Erin's forehead. "Mind how you go."

Taking Ma's advice, Erin began to count.

100 ... 99 ... 98 ...

The deadly hail drummed on the upturned boat.

82 ... 81 ... 80 ...

Pain lanced Erin's arms, urging her to let go. But she held fast, picturing the faces of Pa, Ma, and Clyde on the backs of her eyelids.

65 ... 64 ... 63 ...

She wondered about the things that lurked in the turbulent waters below.

39 ... 38 ... 37 ...

Frightening things with razor-sharp teeth and empty stomachs.

26 ... 25 ... 24 ...

She thought of the farmhouse and the safety it offered, the barn, and the greenhouse, and the stables.

15 ... 14 ... 13 ...

And the scarecrows guarding the fields all around.

8 ... 7 ... 6 ...

A chunk of ice, the size of a human head, tore through the hull with a sickening *crack!* It missed her face by inches, vanishing into the frothy grey swell.

3 ... 2 ... 1 ...

AFTER THE STORM

Erin woke to an unusual sound.

Silence.

Spying the huge barn doors, she swung out of the hayloft and dropped to the flagstones. She crept over and stared suspiciously at the world beyond.

She could scarcely believe it.

The rain had stopped.

Part of her jumped for joy.

The rest wondered if she was still dreaming.

Crouching, she ran her hands over the uneven stones that linked the barn to the farmhouse, the stables to the greenhouse. They were beginning to dry and turn pale.

Is this truly happening?

She sat cross-legged, her back to the damp barn. Above sat a brand-new sky. One she had never seen before. Grey, blank, cloudless. It had rained for what seemed like years. To be honest, Erin had no idea how much time had passed. She'd given up counting the days long ago. There were too many other things to worry about.

"Why?" she said to the world. "Why now?"

The grey, cloudless sky stared back. Silent and still.

"Perhaps Number Twelve knows."

She pushed off the floor and headed toward the shore.

Positioned just metres from the grey water surrounding Erin's lonely island stood a wooden cross, weathered and worn by the savagery of the storm.

Hanging loosely by its bindings was a scarecrow.

Number Twelve.

The scarecrow wore a long, elegant dress made of the deepest, emptiest, blackest velvet you can imagine. Over the dress was a red pirate jacket. It had wide lapels studded with metal buttons and double-folded cuffs inlaid with gold thread and silk. Most of the coat had been splattered with mud and dirt, and it was worn at the shoulders where the scarecrow's struts warped the fabric.

"Hello, Twelve," said Erin. "I bet you're happy the storm is over. There's no shelter for you out here."

She circled the cross and checked the condition of the scarecrow. Surprisingly, Number Twelve was in good working order. Her cement-filled boots and rubber-gloved hands were still attached and, despite the dirt on her clothes, Erin could see no visible damage.

"I don't suppose you have any idea why the rain stopped?"

Number Twelve just hung there, dripping.

"Didn't think so."

Erin leant back, inspecting the huge bison skull that served as Twelve's head. One of the horns was cracked and a host of bugs and maggots and worms had taken up residence in her eye sockets.

"Scarier than ever." Erin shuddered, turning to the sea.

The grey, faceless water stretched to the horizon in every direction.

"It's weird," she told the scarecrow. "For so long the sky has been black and angry and filled with chaotic clouds. The sea seemed like some endless monster, churning and smashing and destroying everything. But now—" Erin spun in a full circle, her arms outspread, her face angled to the colourless heavens. "Nothing. A silent, grey, blank nothing." She rolled her shoulders. Her stomach gurgled. "Where are all the blues and golds and pinks and greens?"

Two pale orbs blinked into existence, hanging low in the sky. She wondered which was which. In this strange light, the sun and the moon looked identical.

"Well," she said, kicking a large pebble into the water. "What now?"

The scarecrow had no answers, so Erin trudged up the cobbled path towards the greenhouse. The lopsided structure had seen better days. Some of the panes had shattered. Thick tape held the worst of them together. More by luck than judgement, Erin had managed to breathe new life into a handful of tomatoes, cucumbers, peppers, and strawberries.

Conversely, on the damp, brown earth outside the greenhouse were two headstones.

On one hung a scythe.

The other, a pendant.

Beside them sat a plastic dragon mounted on a football helmet.

Erin stopped by the headstones and smiled.

"It's finally over," she said. "The storm is done, at least for now."

Her eyes drifted to the vast, watery horizon.

"Hopefully the oceans will retreat too."

She dropped onto her haunches and ran her fingers over

the scythe and the pendant.

"What do I do now?" she asked. "I survived the storm. I never planned for what comes next."

Like the scarecrow, the graves of her parents did not reply.

She turned to the plastic dragon. "And what about you, Clyde? Are you out there? Somewhere?" She picked up the dragon and ran her fingers lightly over its jagged spine. "I'll find a way, Clyde. And I won't stop until I find you. Dead or alive. I have to know."

She tucked her long, ragged hair behind her ears and hitched up her filthy dungarees. She left the graves behind, collecting a handful of tomatoes for her breakfast.

The farmhouse kitchen looked as though it had been ransacked by squatters. All the chairs were upended. Cupboards opened and plundered. A large oak table sat diagonally across the room while cooking utensils and cutlery lay dirty and discarded on every surface.

A maze of pipes ran through holes in the ceiling and connected to funnels Erin had strapped to the roof. Beneath them pots and pans and jars and tins brimmed with murky rainwater.

She swept some dirty plates aside and hopped on the counter. Rooting around in one of the cupboards, she pulled out a semi-devoured tin of baked beans and a pot of jam. She sliced the tomatoes and dumped everything on a chipped plate.

"Breakfast of champions."

Erin spent the afternoon lying in the hayloft staring at the grey sky and wondering if she'd ever leave Coldharbour Farm. She knew one day she'd have to—vast endless grey ocean or not.

Fresh greenhouse produce had dwindled. The tomatoes were all but gone. What few cucumbers remained were the size of shrivelled gherkins and promised nominal nutrition.

There was the odd pot of jam or chutney and some mysterious cans whose labels had worn away. Erin tried to guess what lurked inside before prising them open. She was usually wrong, but the surprise made her meagre meals something to look forward to.

She crawled to the far end of the hayloft where a small cupboard was secured with a simple latch. From inside, she retrieved a thick A4 pad covered in doodles and stickers. Flattening it on her lap, she flicked through terrifying-looking monsters and demons made from drawings and magazine cut-outs. Some pages included polaroids of these horrific creatures. Erin stood beside them in bountiful, undulating fields of ripe yellow corn and twisting green shoots, a proud beam on her face.

This was Erin's *Book of Scarecrows*.

She skimmed past her creations, pausing on Number Five with her rollerblades and basketball head, the Viking twins (Six and Seven), then Number Eight's skeletal frame and chest of horrors, and the steampunk-inspired monstrosity called Number Eleven.

Number Twelve was the most frightening of all Erin's scarecrows. Everyone agreed. No other scarecrow could make your skin crawl quite like Number Twelve.

A polaroid had been pinned to Number Twelve's page. It showed the scarecrow hanging from her cross. Erin and her entire family were gathered round, smiling and laughing. The sun low in the sky.

She ran a finger over their faces. A hollow ache murmured in the pit of her stomach, a thing far worse than hunger. Tears pressed at the back of her eyes. She fought them, shut the *Book of Scarecrows*, and curled up in the hay.

Erin dreamt of the storm. About the long black days, the biting cold, the chaotic wind, the hunger, and the rain. Always the rain. But most of all she dreamt about her family—Pa, and Ma, and her brother Clyde.

And then, Erin woke up to another unusual sound.

Talking.

NUMBER TWELVE

Erin rubbed her eyes and cleaned out her ears. For the second time that day she wondered if she was dreaming.

Voices? On Coldharbour Farm? Impossible, she thought. *There's nobody here. Well, nobody alive anyway.*

The voice drifted away, so she dropped out of the hayloft and went to investigate.

There was no one in the barn. No-one in the courtyard, the greenhouse, or the stables. As she turned to the farmhouse, a sight shocked her to the core.

No. That's absurd.

After repeatedly blinking and rubbing her eyes and pinching her skin, Erin focused on Number Twelve's cross.

Her eyes hadn't deceived her.

It was empty!

Erin pounded down the cobbles. She circled the cross several times, stared up and down the shore, and scanned the water for the missing scarecrow.

Nothing.

In a swirl of panic, she noticed a trail of muddy boot prints leading away from the cross.

Her fingers gently rubbed her temples as the most

impossible idea began to form.

No, she thought again, her brain fighting the idea. *That's impossible.*

She checked the barn and stables and greenhouse once more, then followed the footprints into the farmhouse.

Here, the voice grew stronger.

And then another!

Two voices? What in the heavens is going on?

The conversation came from the lounge. Erin shuffled through the kitchen, along the hallway, and crouched outside the door.

Steeling herself, Erin took a peek.

She swallowed a gasp and pulled away from the sight.

No. No. No. NO. NO. NOOOO!

She scampered back to the kitchen where she silently circled the table. Her hands gripped her dungaree straps. Fingers tapped the buckles. She picked up an empty baked bean can and checked the expiry date, wondering if it had come and gone.

Was she seeing things?

Was she delirious with hunger and loneliness?

Had she eaten something to cause this absurd hallucination?

Surely I'm imagining all of this? This cannot be real? Can it?

Erin took two long breaths and returned to her position by the lounge door.

She summoned all her courage and took a second peek.

Sat in Pa's favourite armchair was Number Twelve.

The scarecrow barely fit. Her enormous frame spilled over the sides. Her rubber-gloved hands dragged on the floor while her knees—which, like all her joints, were fashioned from old tractor parts—bent up to meet her boney chin.

"So," Number Twelve said. "All the humans are dead?"

"Yep, dead as dead can be," replied the other voice. "Dead as doornails, as dodos, as yesterday. Drowned, most probably. If the hail didn't bash their brains in first."

"How?"

"The Many Years Storm."

Who was the scarecrow talking to?

Erin couldn't see anyone.

She curled her fingers around the doorframe and there, on Number Twelve's broad shoulder, perched a little blackbird.

"You don't know much, do you?" The blackbird sighed.

"I'm surprised I know anything at all," Twelve told him. "I mean, what am I?"

"You are a scarecrow."

"Oh. Yes. That makes sense…what with the cross and all."

"What did you think you were?"

The scarecrow paused. "I've no idea. I just woke up."

The blackbird had a smooth coat, with bright eyes and a sharp yellow beak. Tucking his wings, he said, "Life is a desperate, impossible thing. One minute I'm inside an egg and the next I'm fighting for regurgitated worms."

Twelve sat back in the armchair. "How did all this happen?"

"How would I know? I'm not a god. Nor am I a meteorologist. I'm just a blackbird. It's a wonder I survived at all."

"But you can talk."

"So can you," the blackbird told her. "And walk and think and ask endless questions."

"It's…*curious*," Twelve said, examining her rubber-gloved hands. One was a bright yellow washing-up glove that squeaked when she wriggled her fingers. The other was covered in scales, blood-red and trimmed with black. The knuckles looked sore and engorged. The fingernails long and sharp.

"That's one word for it," the blackbird scoffed. "Another would be *strange*. Or *disconcerting*. Or downright *nefarious*!"

"Was it always this way?" Twelve asked. "Before the storm, I mean."

The blackbird flew up and perched on Twelve's huge bison skull. He turned his head to the window. Beyond the glass, a pale light stretched across the sky, punctured with flickering distant stars. It was neither day nor night, dawn nor dusk.

"It was better before," he said. "And worse."

Twelve turned her massive head to the window.

"The world was a mix of colours and sounds and smells. Some places had crystal blue skies, lush green grass, clear water, and golden sandy beaches. Other places were cold and dark. Hard, bitter places where nothing grew and no one smiled. But now, all the colours have been washed away."

Twelve shook her head. It creaked like an old door. "That makes me so sad."

The blackbird fidgeted.

Twelve reached up and took the bird in her demonic rubber hand.

A worm slipped from the scarecrow's eye socket and landed on her lap.

"This is a new world," the blackbird said, eyeing the worm hungrily. "One in which a scarecrow and a blackbird sit discussing the nature of all they have inherited."

"And all that we've lost," Twelve added, gazing out the window. "Where do *you* live?"

"Here and there," he said, spreading his wings helpfully.

"Of course," Twelve replied. "What's the world like beyond the horizon?"

"There's a place where thousands of my kind live," the blackbird explained. "We call it Clifftop. But it's way, way, way out beyond the Island of Trees."

"Clifftop," Twelve whispered. "The Island of Trees."

"The tip of a great mountain forest. Some birds swear they have seen smoke billowing from the summit. The smell of fire. The crackle of wood. But it's just stories. Stuff to entertain the chicks and fledglings."

"Does someone live there?"

"On the Island of Trees? Maybe. I don't know."

"Where else?" the scarecrow urged. "There must be more places."

"I've never been beyond Clifftop," he said, displaying his wings again. "But I've heard gulls, eagles, albatrosses, and what-have-yous muttering about strange and distant places that eclipse the rising tides."

"Perhaps other creatures survived The Many Years Storm. Maybe there are more birds out there. Or scarecrows like me."

"No one's like you."

"I can't be the only scarecrow in the world."

Erin couldn't take much more.

Three impossible things were knocking on the door to her sanity.

Her scarecrow was alive.

Her scarecrow could talk.

And—so could *birds*.

She dashed towards the kitchen and the safety of the hayloft. In her hurry, she knocked a large frying pan from its hook. It clattered to the ground causing an enormous commotion.

"Who's there?" Twelve's voice boomed from the lounge.

Erin froze. Panic flared in every atom of her body.

Twelve's cement-filled boots thundered against the wooden floor. In a flash the scarecrow's horrifying face bent around the doorframe. The bug-filled eye sockets stared directly at her.

Erin squealed with fright and bolted through the farmhouse door.

HAYBALE FORTRESS

Erin darted across the courtyard, swerving and leaping over chunks of fallen masonry. Tiles and timber crunched beneath her feet as she vanished into the thick shadows of the barn. The scarecrow's heavy boots rumbled behind her, the croak of a blackbird overhead.

Skidding right, she scampered through the low doorway to an elaborate fortress constructed of hay bales that hunkered beneath the hayloft. Erin scurried in, curled up as small as she could, and closed her eyes.

She desperately tried to picture a happier time, a safer time, a place where nothing could harm her. But she couldn't escape the possibility that one of her terrifying scarecrows had just chased her across the farm. She took a long, slow breath and then—

"It's okay," the scarecrow said.

Twelve's voice sounded higher and filled with more joy than her appearance might suggest. But a strangled quality—something mechanical, industrial, rusted—rang in the background, as though she had something lodged in her throat.

Erin peered down a corridor of hay bales.

Cross-hatched wicker sheets and bamboo canes held the structure in place.

"We're not going to harm you," Twelve said, her terrifying skull floating in the doorway.

"That's exactly what psycho-killers say." Erin shivered, shifting deeper into the fortress.

Twelve levered her broad shoulders through the doorway and reached towards Erin with her demon hand.

Erin hissed like a cat, backing up against a cardboard wall. She pulled a small carving knife from her dungarees and swiped it aggressively. The blade had dulled over time, but Erin knew it could still do some damage if wielded in the right way.

"What have you got there?"

Erin's grip tightened around the knife.

"What are you going to do with that?"

"She looks hungry. Probably planning to eat me," the blackbird said, fluttering into view. "Sooner or later we all become food. If not by predators or scavengers, we're devoured by the worms in the soil or the persistence of time."

Erin had often wondered how she would die. Old age or cancer—or a combination of the two—seemed most likely. But, during The Many Years Storm, she'd decided she would probably starve to death, or die from dehydration, or catch some airborne virus, or break her leg and succumb to the infection. There was precious little else to kill her on Coldharbour Farm. Some days she wondered what lurked in the waters all around. Would something slither up the hill one night and eat her alive? A hungry alligator or a mutant lizard? She never imagined she'd fall foul to one of her scarecrows and a morbid blackbird.

Erin waved the knife, cutting the air in weak arcs. "No," she said. "I'll use this knife to stop *you* eating *me*!"

Twelve laughed. It sounded like a waterlogged engine.

"We're not going to eat you. I'm made of wooden struts and rusty bolts and old engine parts," Twelve told her, flexing an elbow that clicked and whirred. "I'll show you if you come out. To be honest, I don't believe I need to eat at all as I don't have a stomach."

"And I only eat seeds, and fruit, and insects," the blackbird added.

He'd taken a seat on the top of the hay-bale fortress where sheets of flat-packed cardboard boxes had been laid to form a roof and crenelations.

"Although," the blackbird mused, "a human girl would be quite the gastronomic challenge. I'm not completely against the idea if I'm being honest—"

"A human girl," Twelve said, interrupting the bird's dark mutterings. "You said all the humans were dead."

"She's the only one I've ever seen," the blackbird added. "It's a miracle she survived at all."

Erin bit her lip.

Her knuckles whitened around the handle.

"I made you," she said, trembling, the blade pointing at Twelve.

"I beg your pardon?"

"Your name is Number Twelve. Or Twelve, for short, if you like."

The scarecrow tried to shift forward but her shoulders had lodged in the fortress doorway.

"Your head once belonged to Lucifer, an old bison that lived on our farm. He was a stubborn old devil. Your dress is one of my mothers. Your arms and legs were broken broomsticks and fire tongs."

She shifted slowly towards the huge scarecrow. A fiery mix of bravery and fear bubbled beneath her skin.

Twelve backed away and carefully perched on her haunches. Erin loitered in the doorway, staring at the monstrosity before her.

"And those are my Pa's boots," she said, tapping the steel toecaps with the tip of her knife. "I mean, they *were* his."

"Thank you," the scarecrow said. "You did a great job. I feel very well put together."

Erin smiled.

She couldn't remember the last time that had happened.

Twelve shot up into the air.

Her dress floated out as she spun in wide, graceful circles. "How do I look?"

Erin curled her fingers around the fortress doorway.

Her grip on the knife dwindled.

"You look…good."

This scarecrow was possibly the most frightening thing Erin had ever dreamt up. But here it was, dancing around, acting like a silly child. She had always pictured her scarecrows as the embodiment of demons. Tortured, carnivorous beasts born in the fiery pits of her twisted imagination. But this demon was laughing and pirouetting like a ballerina.

Erin stood slowly and kicked the mud from her plimsolls. Beneath her dungarees she wore a thick-knit jumper two sizes too big, the sleeves of which kept slipping over her hands.

"I'm Erin."

"And I'm…Number Twelve?"

Erin reached up and tapped a yellow birthday badge

pinned to the lapel of the scarecrow's pirate jacket.

It read: *I Am 12.*

"Yes," she said. "Twelve for short."

The scarecrow towered over her, almost double Erin's height.

"That's a strange name."

"You're a strange thing."

The scarecrow held out her red demon hand.

"Well, strange or not, it's terribly nice to meet you," she said. "I don't imagine a scarecrow has ever met her creator before. This is quite the remarkable occasion."

Pulling up her sleeve, Erin took the scarecrow's hand in hers and shook it.

Twelve's grip was more delicate than she had expected. But what surprised her more was the warmth that flooded from the rubber-gloved hand.

"And who is this?" said Erin, looking at the blackbird.

"My name is Raven."

"You look more like a blackbird."

"Not that it matters a jot, but I *am* a blackbird," he told her. "My *name* is Raven."

"Ravens are quite a bit bigger, are they not?"

"Yes. I know they are," the blackbird replied hotly. "Again… it's just my *name*."

"Why?" Erin said, shaking her head.

Raven croaked and ruffled his wings. "I think it's my sunny disposition."

"And you're…talking?"

"Naturally."

"That's not normal," Erin said. "Birds fly and eat worms. Some even sing. They do *not* talk."

"Well, scarecrows don't just come to life and climb down from their crosses either," he replied.

"Apart from the ones in scary movies," Erin said, adjusting her glasses.

"Scary movies?" Twelve said, raising her hands to cover her face. "Am I…scary?"

"Scarecrows are supposed to be scary," Erin informed her. "That's the whole point. It's in the name, after all."

Raven fluttered onto Twelve's shoulder.

"I'm…*scary*," she said, trying the word on for size.

"You *look* terrifying," Erin said proudly. "Everyone that ever saw you said so: Jimothy, Hew and Geraldine, Mr and Mrs Parsons, Postman Waylon, Auntie Magrit, even Le Dangereux found you obnoxious—and he's seen things that would turn your hair white. I made lots of scarecrows, but you were the most terrifying. For a while I never thought I'd make one more horrible than Number Eight but…here you are."

She looked at Twelve's ghastly face and smiled.

"You're truly unholy! A walking nightmare. Just as I planned."

"Number Eight?" Twelve exclaimed. "Another scarecrow?"

"Yes, you're the last of a dozen I made. You know…before the storm."

"There are eleven more?" Twelve whispered. "Eleven brothers and sisters?"

"Just sisters. You're all girls," Erin said. "Well, you've all got dresses on. Not that boys can't wear dresses, they're just dead annoying, mostly, so—"

"And Eight is almost as terrifying as me?"

"Was," Erin said. "You were stationed up here at the farm. I put Number Eight over by the mineshaft. Her cross is empty now. I guess the wind and rain took her. The other ten were spread across the lower fields. They're all gone now. Drowned, most probably."

"No," Twelve said, looking hurt. "That cannot be. One of them must have made it. One of my sisters must have survived."

Erin squeezed the scarecrow's arm compassionately.

Twelve seemed genuinely sad.

"Who can say?" Erin added quickly. "Perhaps one of them scared their way onto a passing ship or frightened a whale into giving them a ride all the way to some distant land."

Her thoughts turned to her brother. Had Clyde managed to find a way to survive, a way to stay afloat, to discover land and a new life somewhere beyond the horizon?

Twelve's rubber-gloved hands rose to cover her cracked, obnoxious face.

"I don't want to scare people," she admitted. "I want to make them smile."

"She's been outside too long," Raven grumbled. "Exposure can do awful things to the weak-minded."

Erin's daydream crumbled. "It's the head," she admitted, ignoring Raven. "Skulls are not the most welcoming, I do admit. But they are perfect for scaring away birds…or robbers, or murderers, or anyone else for that matter."

Twelve twisted and turned her head, trying to hide her face.

"And anyway, there's only me and the blackbird here. There's no one to scare."

"We should change my head!"

Erin frowned, puzzled. "What?"

"Yes! A new head, Erin. That's what I need."

"Don't be ludicrous," squawked the blackbird.

"Can you do it, Erin? Can you give me a new head?"

Erin nibbled the end of her finger.

"Please," Twelve begged.

"We could certainly try."

MEDICINE BALL

Erin dashed into the farmhouse and tore up the stairs. In her brother's bedroom, an unmade bed sat beneath a small window surrounded by posters of dragons and wizards and fantastic beasts of all kinds. Buckets of mixed Lego and action figures were stacked on the other side of the room beneath shelves cluttered with toys and an assortment of many-sided dice, playing cards, and board games.

Every other conceivable space was stuffed with dog-eared books.

Erin wriggled under the bed. She searched around in the gloom before pulling out a leather medicine ball.

"My brother's," she said, returning to the courtyard and presenting it to Twelve. "He used it as part of his training. He was going to be a soldier when he grew up."

The scarecrow studied the medicine ball and seemed suitably impressed. Erin set to work cutting two eyes and a smiley mouth into the front with her knife.

No sooner had she started than the ball began to deflate.

Erin instructed Raven to fetch whatever sticks he could find. On his return, she stuffed them through the eyes, constructing a web of scaffolding to hold the head in a perfect*ish* sphere.

"There," she said, spinning the finished head to face Twelve. "What do you think?"

"I think I love it," she said, then paused. "Is it less scary than my current face?"

"Very much so."

"Night and day," Raven concurred.

"Then let's see if it works."

"How can this possibly work?" the blackbird rambled on. "It's a miracle you're alive as it is. Taking your head off might kill you. I think your face is just fine the way it is. A scary face for a scary scarecrow. Why mess with a classic?"

"Really?" Twelve stopped. "Do you think taking my head off might kill me?"

"It does for most living things. Decapitation is a messy business."

Twelve sighed, turning the new head in her hands.

"This isn't an exact science," Erin admitted. "Who knows what'll happen." She gave Twelve a brave smile. "But doubt is the father of invention, so—"

"I don't know what that means."

"Never mind," Erin said. "And ignore the blackbird. Now, kneel down so I can remove your head."

Twelve did as she was told.

Erin's fingers worked their way about the scarecrow's neck, loosening the ties that held the skull in place. As she detached the bindings, Twelve's body went as limp as a fish, and sagged pathetically to one side.

Erin lifted the horned monstrosity and carefully placed it on the ground. Spinning the medicine ball, she positioned it over Twelve's spine, forced it down, and slipped her hands through the smiling mouth to fasten the bindings.

When she'd finished, Erin stood back, admiring the scarecrow and her brand-new, smiling face.

Something felt off, weird.

Scarecrows should be scary. Not smiling and happy and filled with joy. But who was Erin to argue with the desires of a living thing? She was merely her creator. She had to let the scarecrow make her own decisions, for good or ill.

"Twelve?" she asked, struggling to sit the scarecrow up straight. "Can you hear me?"

Twelve remained motionless.

The new head beamed absurdly, as though drunk.

"You've killed her," Raven exclaimed. "Another victim for The Endless Blue."

"Shut up," Erin bit, then turned to the blackbird. "The Endless Blue?"

Raven sighed. "It's what we call the sea and the sky."

"More a sort of Endless Grey now, isn't it?"

"You say that like it's my fault," he replied hotly. "But, yes, you're right. The colour has diminished."

Erin and Raven waited patiently as Twelve slumped uselessly against the farmhouse.

"Don't say anything," Erin said finally, raising a hand. "She's not dead. Just... immobile."

Five minutes passed.

Nothing.

"I think you'd better put the horrific skull back on."

"Fine," she said, dropping down in front of Twelve and reversing the procedure.

With the bison skull back in place, they watched closely.

Nothing happened.

Erin could feel the blackbird's beady eyes boring into the side of her head. Then, Twelve's rubber fingers began to wiggle. Her arms moved. Her legs tightened.

Slowly, she rose. Her joints—made exclusively from farmyard machinery—complained bitterly. Erin wondered if they needed oiling.

Twelve turned her head from side to side and laughed.

"It's heavy!" she said merrily. "But I love it. I love my new head so very much. Thank you, Erin. You are a wonder!"

The blackbird opened his beak.

Erin shot him a cold glare.

"Do you feel happy?" Erin asked, moving to stand in front of the failed medicine ball.

"Beyond words," replied Twelve. "Knowing that my face will bring smiles and joy, rather than terror and screams, is the greatest gift you could give me."

"It's witchcraft," the blackbird muttered to himself. "Magic of the darkest kind."

Erin attempted a smile, but sadness lingered in her eyes.

"What is it?" Twelve asked.

Erin moved aside to reveal the medicine ball. The smiling face deflated as the sticks inside withered and crumbled.

"I failed you. I'm sorry."

Twelve's hands shot to her face. Her fingers ran over her long bony jaw, bug-filled eye sockets, and massive cracked horns.

"Oh no. On no no no! What happened?"

"I don't know," Erin replied, scooping up the medicine ball and inspecting it like a mechanic would a broken crankshaft. "It just didn't take."

"Take?"

"I think your head is your head. Accept no substitutes."

"Oh my."

"I think you look awesome," Erin told her, and she truly meant it. "Ma always said that it doesn't matter what we look like on the outside. It's what's inside that counts."

Twelve centred her shoulders. "But I'm full of rusty engine parts and cement and wriggling, biting, scratching creepy-crawlies."

Erin giggled. "I cannot think of anything better."

Her laugh became infectious and Twelve joined in, chortling and wheezing like a broken boiler.

Raven fluttered about, clearly finding none of this amusing.

"What about you?" Twelve asked, between chuckles. "Can I do anything for you?"

Erin stopped laughing.

"Me? No, there's nothing you can do. There's nothing anyone can do," she said. "I'm stranded here. Surrounded by all this water." She shrugged, sank her hands into the pockets of her dungarees and scuffed her plimsolls against the flagstones. "Me and my family tried to leave the island during the storm, but we didn't make it very far."

"Your family?"

"Ma, Pa, and…Clyde."

"Like my scarecrow sisters?"

"I suppose. Yes."

Twelve extended a rubber-gloved hand and squeezed Erin's shoulder.

"There's almost no food left now," she went on. "I lived off the tinned stuff in the cupboard and anything that washed up on the shore. Rationed it out, day after day. When there was nothing else, I made horrible soups with grass and flowers.

I even ate some insects. Worms were tolerable with a pinch of salt, but spiders and slugs and beetles taste absolutely villainous."

She shivered, repulsed at the memories of meals that would have bothered the most ravenous of wolves.

"I have lots of rainwater. Filled just about every container in the farmhouse."

"There must be food somewhere," Twelve said, looking to the horizon. "There must be more people out there. Somewhere. Right?"

Erin's sadness spread through her shoulders. Her head dropped.

"Raven has been to the Island of Trees," Twelve said, encouragingly. "He's seen smoke rising from time to time."

Raven tried to correct her, but Twelve went on regardless.

"There could be people there. We should find a way to reach them. Find you some food. Maybe look for your family. And my sisters."

Erin drifted away, pacing slowly across the courtyard.

Twelve took two massive strides and caught up.

"Erin?"

"My family are dead," she said, her eyes on the ground. "Ma and Pa. Gone."

"And your brother?"

Erin stopped by the graves. "Clyde is missing."

She felt a tear burst from her eye and run down her face. There were thousands more just waiting to erupt, but Erin held them back. What good were they? Tears weren't food. Tears weren't love. Tears couldn't help her survive on Coldharbour Farm. Tears couldn't bring her family back. But they pressed on the corners of her eyes all the same, begging her to give in.

Twelve ran a hand over Erin's matted hair.

The scarecrow's touch made her flinch. She took a calming breath and coiled both hands into her long sleeves.

"Sorry," Erin said. "I've been on my own for so long."

"You're not alone anymore."

Erin closed her eyes and whispered a silent prayer.

Transported beneath the capsized rowing boat, the icy water climbed her limbs, froze her blood, locked her muscles. Ice slammed into the wooden roof as saltwater sloshed around, frenzied and deadly.

The loneliness of the moment enveloped her.

Sadness filled her lungs like choking, icy sea water.

She wanted to scream, but she scrunched up her fists and closed her eyes. She hung there, waiting for the moment to pass. Waiting for the memory to drift away, sinking into the depths, drowned like everything she'd ever loved.

When she opened her eyes again, she was confronted by her new companions.

"There is nothing for me here now," she said, smiling half-heartedly. "Tomorrow, we go in search of scarecrows!"

"And food."

"And adventure."

"And your brother!"

Erin nodded slowly.

Hope for Clyde's survival hung by the thinnest of threads.

"Tomorrow," Erin added with a devilish grin, "we build a boat!"

SCARECROW WORKSHOP

Erin woke from the strangest dreams of her life. Dreams in which one of her scarecrows had come to life and agreed to build a boat and escape the watery prison of Coldharbour Farm.

She blinked away the sleep, and focused.

Across the room, Number Twelve sat in Pa's armchair, a family photo album open on her lap.

Erin jumped.

Her dreams were not dreams at all.

They were real.

All of them.

She slunk beneath her blanket and eyed the scarecrow suspiciously. Low early morning light slithered through the window, illuminating the holes where the scarecrow's eyes should be. Insects scurried around in her sockets, desperately searching for a shadow in which to dwell. The scarecrow sat like a statue, rigid, motionless.

Was she asleep?

Before Erin could decide—

"What's sleep like?" the scarecrow asked. Her menacing jaw clacked between the words.

Erin jolted upright, still not fully awake. "That's a complicated question," she said, swinging her feet onto the cold floor. "Did you not sleep?"

"No," Twelve said. "I do not believe I need to."

"Oh."

"Perhaps I was asleep for all those years during The Many Years Storm. Perhaps I was somewhere else. Or nowhere at all. Unborn."

"Unborn?"

The scarecrow had clearly spent the entire night thinking about this stuff.

"Do you remember anything from before *you* were born?"

"No, of course not," Erin frowned. "Nobody does."

Twelve nodded.

"Do you?"

"I can feel the vast, sweeping hills of Coldharbour Farm and the invading ocean, but it's not a memory. It's just an empty darkness, something tired and aching. I can feel the wet, and the cold, and the violence of the wind. It's as though they're buried inside me, soaked into my wooden frame and rusty joints."

Erin settled on the arm of the chair and looked at Twelve's enormous bony head.

"I think eyelids would be an advantage in achieving sleep," Twelve said. "Perhaps a thick scarf, an eyeless mask, or a windowless room might do the trick."

"If you were to sleep," Erin began. "What would you dream of?"

"Dream?" Twelve said thoughtfully, looking around the room. "I'd dream of a comfy chair and a warm fire. There'd be a scattering of scarecrows, humans and birds too, laughing and joking and smiling, forever and ever and ever."

The sideboard next to Twelve was open. A selection of board games and posh-looking wine glasses—that Ma never, *ever* used—filled the shelves. There were some old school reports, household bills and insurance documents, too. In the drawers above were orphaned keys, batteries, fuses, and lightbulbs. And lodged at the back, beneath a collection of greeting cards, were the family photo albums.

Inside the one on Twelve's lap were pictures of Erin and Clyde as babies and toddlers: enjoying picnics, playing with Lego and action figures, sharing baths, cooking on outdoor fires, laughing, happiness evident in every frame.

Twelve moved through the pages, looking at the photos of Erin's life. She stopped on one of her dressed in school uniform. Erin's hair was much lighter, a shimmering blonde-brown. Tangle-free. Needle-sharp. A huge smile adorned her face. Round glasses sparkled, undamaged. She held a stack of books and journals. Most were brand-new textbooks, but one had something scrawled on the cover in black marker— *Beware! Demons Within.*

The opposite page had a picture of the Coldharbour High School Football Team—*Go Redkites!*—with Clyde in his muddy helmet and shoulder pads.

Flipping to the last page, Twelve found a photo of Pa, Ma, Clyde, and Erin.

"That's my family."

Twelve nodded.

"You look like your mother. Like Ma. Your eyes, your smile. You have similar hair and the same delightfully wonky nose."

Erin prodded her nose with the back of her hand.

"Thanks. I guess."

As the pale sun slipped between the grey folds of dawn, Twelve levered herself out of the armchair and left the farmhouse.

Erin watched from the farmhouse door as Twelve stomped about collecting timber and twine, logs and rope, panelling and cloth, and the remnants of the family boat that had washed up on the shore, splintered and broken. She positioned them in neat piles around the courtyard and studied them thoughtfully.

The scarecrow's process felt familiar. It reminded her of the way Clyde used to meticulously arrange all the pieces of a Lego set before starting the build.

Clicking her rubbery fingers, Twelve brushed past Erin and returned to the living room. On the wall, above the sofa, hung *The Haughty Jinx*. It was a painting of a mighty galleon in the midst of some chaotic war that Pa inherited from his father but couldn't bring himself to sell.

"Well," she said, laying the painting against the side of the farmhouse, "I doubt I have enough material to make something quite as grand as you, but I'll do my very best."

With Erin in tow, Twelve strode into the barn looking for more materials.

At the far end, thick shadows choked the vaulted space, sliced here and there with spears of light. As the scarecrow approached, she froze.

Something, or rather *someone*, lurked in the gloom.

"Erin," she whispered. "We are not alone."

"Nonsense," Erin replied, wondering what the scarecrow was on about. "Believe me. We are *unfathomably* alone."

"There," she pointed. "In the shadows."

Twelve called out, inched closer, but there was no response. She tried again, but still the barn remained silent. The scarecrow sidestepped across the room and lifted the latch on a small rear door. It creaked as it opened, allowing more light inside.

The darkest corners of the barn slowly revealed their odd-shaped inhabitants.

Twelve stepped back, a hand to her mouth.

"Sisters?" she whispered excitedly.

Split across thick wooden shelves were the constituent parts for a dozen or more scarecrows. A jumble sale of terrifying spare parts. A boutique of macabre mechanicals.

Seeing that every item was completely inanimate, Twelve took a breath and examined them closely. She found a number of potential heads: an upturned bucket, a dented frying pan, sacks stuffed with rags, the skull of a bear, and more besides. Each had a unique face either painted, stitched, cut, dented, or carved into it. Every eye looked suspicious, every nose twisted, every mouth broken.

They were all horrible, frightening in the worst possible way.

"Goodness gracious," she said, turning to Erin. "And I thought my head was terrifying."

Erin chuckled.

Beside this cavalcade of sinister heads sat rows of boots and shoes; poles, girders and broomsticks; metal hinges and cogs and engine parts, and all manner of nails and screws; dresses, pinafores, aprons and jackets; gloves and hats and socks and scarves.

"So, this is where I was made," Twelve said, amazed. "This is where we were all created."

Erin nodded.

"Yes. All of you. The whole dozen."

"What do my sisters look like?" Twelve asked. "Are they like me? What fills my sisters' boots and gloves? What are their heads made of? Are they all as gruesome and scary as I am?"

"You're all incredibly different."

"Did people cower and shield their eyes from them too?"

"Not as much as they did for you. You're my greatest work!"

"Do you think they all woke up after The Many Years Storm to find themselves living in this strange grey world surrounded by endless oceans and lifeless skies?"

Erin honestly didn't know.

She barely believed in the one she was talking to.

"One of them had to," Twelve said confidently. "Just one."

Erin and Twelve spent the following week creating a seafaring vessel that was, in their humble opinion, a fine representation of *The Haughty Jinx* (minus the cannons, mighty sails, and soaring figurehead which, on *The Haughty Jinx*, was a prancing black unicorn with a golden horn).

The finished boat stretched fifteen feet by five feet. The prow feathered into a sharp point with a raised bench for Erin. The aft had been constructed to suit Twelve's needs with Pa's leather armchair nailed in place. The scarecrow had removed the arms and positioned two brackets made of horseshoes on either side to house the oars. Standing proudly in the centre was a mast adorned with sails fashioned from superhero duvets and pillowcases. Finally, Twelve placed a metal bucket (destined to be the head of some future scarecrow) on top of the mast for Raven to keep lookout.

"Oh my!" exclaimed Erin, as she stepped back and admired

the boat in all its glory. "Twelve, this is amazing."

Raven swooped through the air and landed in his crow's nest.

"Excellent job."

Erin turned and gazed over The Endless Blue.

"I think it's time to see if I've given you a good set of sea legs!"

Twelve looked curiously at the wooden beams that disappeared into her cement-filled boots.

Raven shook his head.

And Erin laughed.

LAZARUS

Twelve hauled their boat down the cobbled path towards the water.

"Hang on," said Erin, scratching her chin. "We cannot launch until we've given her a name."

"A name?"

"It's tradition."

Twelve stopped abruptly, tilting her gargantuan head.

"How about—" Her fingers twitched. "Dragon? Or Drago?"

Erin took a short inhale of breath.

"Your brother loves dragons," the scarecrow went on, pointing towards the plastic figurine nestled beside her parents' graves. "Perhaps it will bring us luck in our quest to find him."

"Wait here," Erin said, running to the farmhouse.

She returned several minutes later with a carved Chinese dragon head, painted red and gold, that she'd liberated from the top shelf of her brother's book cabinet.

"It was Clyde's...*is* Clyde's," she explained, her voice catching on his name. "Father said he got it in the Far East, but I think he haggled for it in a Chinatown thrift store. Nevertheless, my brother loved it very much." Erin bit her bottom lip. "Here," she said, passing the head to Twelve.

The mouth hung open, nostrils flared. Tendrils of smoke and fire etched its cheeks. Dark eyes resonated with a foreboding, ancient knowledge.

"He's called *Lazarus*."

Nodding, Twelve strapped it to the front of the boat.

"I'll find some paint," Erin told her.

After a quick tour of the barn, she returned with a pot of white paint and adorned both sides of the ship with its name, before announcing, "I name this vessel *Lazarus* in the name of the King, and the Queen, and the gods, and the adventurous spirit of every heart that ever took to The Endless Blue!"

"Hooray!" Twelve cheered at the top of her voice. "What are your orders, Captain Erin?"

"I think it's time we set sail, First-Mate Twelve," she replied, saluting.

The scarecrow saluted back.

Raven made a victorious squawk.

Erin dashed back up the hill and filled her rucksack with the last of the tins and the remnants of the greenhouse, along with half a dozen of her favourite books. She swiped her yellow poncho from the understairs cupboard and a thick blanket from the sofa. Stopping in the living room doorway she turned and went to the sideboard. Taking the family photo and a polaroid of Clyde at his high school prom, she stuffed them into her bag and left.

At the shore, Erin leapt onto the boat. She wriggled in behind the dragon figurehead and stowed her goods beneath the seat.

Raven gazed down from his position in the crow's nest as Twelve heaved *Lazarus* across the last of the cobbles, down to the muddy shoreline, and into the calm water.

Once they were settled on the waves, and *Lazarus* showed no sign of leaking, the scarecrow hauled her long legs and heavy boots on board and took up the oars.

Twelve propelled *Lazarus* effortlessly across the flat grey ripples, moving slowly towards the small clump of land where Number Eight had once stood.

Erin turned, smiling at the scarecrow. She took the slightest glance towards the two headstones that marked Ma's and Pa's graves and uttered a gentle farewell before turning her bright eyes to the adventure spread before them.

In less than fifteen minutes, *Lazarus* drew up beside Number Eight's island.

Erin jumped expertly onto the muddy earth and turned to catch a length of rope. She fastened it around a large rock and secured the boat.

The empty cross, that stood at the other end of the island, became eerily silhouetted by the low, pale sun. Erin and Twelve strode towards it.

"Eight's gone," Raven said, landing on the cross.

"I can see that," the scarecrow replied.

The blackbird hopped around, taking in the view. "Do you think she's alive?"

"What other explanation is there?"

"Well, she could be dead," Raven said, morbidly. "Torn from her cross by the wind and the rain and flung out to sea. Or ripped to smithereens by the giant hailstorm. Or taken by pirates and held to ransom. Or—"

Raven caught Erin's eye and hushed his beak.

"She's alive," Twelve said, ignoring the bird. "Same as Clyde."

"What in the name of—?" said Erin, covering her mouth.

Beyond Eight's cross, dragged clear of the water, lay a disfigured body. Erin ran over. Her plimsolls squelched in the wet earth. Mud flew in all directions.

Sadly, for someone of her young years, she'd seen dead bodies before.

But this one was different. For a start, its head was nothing more than an orb of dirt and teeth. Skin and hair had been peeled away like the rind of a fruit.

The eyes were missing too.

A shiver rattled Erin's bones.

Her skin became cold and damp.

Raven made terrified squawks.

"The...hands," he said, finally. "Look at the hands!"

Where the skin should have been, were nothing but bones and dirt. As though the skin had been removed—like a pair of gloves.

"What is it?" said Twelve, still standing beside her sister's cross.

"Death and disfigurement. Horrid barbarism of the worst kind!"

Arriving at Erin's side, Twelve glanced at the body.

"Oh, Erin. You shouldn't have to look at things like that."

"It's okay," Erin said. "You don't need to protect me from the horrors of the world. I buried my own parents. I can't imagine there are worse things than that."

"There are always worse things," Raven said, bleakly.

"Dead is dead." Erin shrugged, gazing at the body with a mild sense of indifference. "Looks like birds or bugs or the elements have gone to work on her."

"Her?" Twelve said. "How can you tell?"

"She worked on the farm with my father. Her name was Loren," Erin said. "I'd know that pink belt and neckerchief anywhere."

She knelt beside Loren's body.

The gruesome skull stared directly at her.

The neckerchief came away easily, crusted with blackened blood. She spread it into a large square, picked off any large chunks of filth, then folded it into a bandana and wrapped it around her head.

"It suits you," Twelve said admiringly. "Very…piratey."

"I liked Loren," she said, nodding slowly and threading the pink belt around her yellow poncho. "She would always stop and talk to me."

Her mind reeled. She couldn't see a logical reason for Loren's injuries. She knew the trauma, despite being amateur at best, was too precise for birds and insects. But what kind of person would commit such a despicable act?

They returned to the cross and looked at the bindings. Each was worn and frayed like Twelve's. At the base of the cross were a chaotic collection of footprints. They led in every direction, making befuddled patterns in the mud.

Something fluttered at the base of the cross.

Twelve bent down to inspect it.

Amidst all the dirt and filth, the ocean and death and the grey skies above, she found a frayed triangle of soft fabric. It was predominantly yellow. Dotted with blue flowers.

The scarecrow stood, turning the fabric over in her rubber-gloved hands.

Erin gasped.

"What is it?" the scarecrow asked.

"That's from her dress."

"Whose dress?"

"Ma…"

"Oh, yes."

"…but, also, Number Eight."

Twelve's eyes darted back to the yellow fabric. "My sister wore this?"

Erin nodded.

"Number Eight," Twelve whispered. "They're real. All of them."

"Of course they are."

"I'm sorry," she said. "I don't know why, but my sisters hadn't seemed real until now. Until I held something that once belonged to them."

"Take it with you," Erin said, smiling. "Keep it close until the day you return it to its rightful owner."

Twelve tucked the yellow fabric into the top pocket of her pirate jacket, secured the metal button, and stomped across the small island.

"Are we leaving?" said Erin, rushing to keep up.

"There's nothing more here," Twelve said, her voice edged with sadness.

"We'll find her," Erin said. "Number Eight. She'll be out there somewhere."

Twelve looked sideways at Raven.

"I haven't said a word!"

"Good. We've had quite enough of your pessimism."

"I'm just a realist," he mumbled, before swooping into his bucket.

Twelve ignored him. "Which way now?"

Erin pointed towards the horizon.

In the grey morning light, stars glimmered magically

across oceans of sky.

"The Island of Trees, Twelve. Let's start there."

"Which way is it?"

"Follow the North Star," murmured Raven, almost bored. "It's the impossibly bright one." The tip of his wing pointed the way. "Over there."

And with that, Twelve dipped the oars into The Endless Blue and pushed away.

STARS AND DEMONS

Twelve rowed for many hours beneath the faceless sky. A ghostly moon chased a pale sun hopelessly overhead. Hundreds of bodies filled the deeper waters around Coldharbour Island, bobbing and turning like rotten apples. Not just human bodies, but the bodies of every species you could mention.

The smell was something to behold.

Erin stared at each one, whispering words of good fortune and safe travels to the departed. Raven hid in his nest, croaking directions and gibbering on about the cursed waters that surrounded them.

Small islands broke the water from time to time, like the fingertips of an ocean giant reaching for the surface. Bodies lay on the shores of each, waltzing back and forth on the gentle tide.

Erin retrieved an elegant rectangular box from beneath her seat and placed it on her lap. Opalescent light reflected off an intricate pattern of flowers and ferns inlaid with mother of pearl.

"What's that?" enquired Twelve.

"Ma's music box," Erin said, popping the catch and lifting the lid. "Clockwork, you see, so still working long after all my batteries died."

A haunting melody chimed across the open water as a morbid figure pirouetted before a concave wall of mirrors. The dancer was made from licked-clean lollipop sticks, wrapped in black felt, and secured with bent paper clips. A hardened ball of chewing gum formed its head while red pushpins served as eyes above a frightful, gaping mouth.

"Who's that?" Twelve asked.

"Lucretia," Erin replied simply. "She's not a scarecrow. Well, not like you and your sisters. The ballerina snapped off and it seemed strange to have a music box without one."

"If all ballerinas looked like *her*," Raven squawked disdainfully, "then a night at the Royal Ballet would be a hideously bleak affair."

Erin hushed the blackbird and let the music play until the mechanism wound down.

Twelve rowed tirelessly, staring up at the stars. "Where do they all come from?"

Erin looked up. "From the beginning of time," she replied sleepily. "I think."

"Do they have names?"

"I only know a few constellations, groups of stars, like Andromeda or Orion."

Twelve nodded. "How long would it take us to row all the way there?"

Erin laughed, then, quietly. "More time than we have."

"Oh."

Twelve eased back in her armchair. "How far does the water go?"

Erin sniffed. "I don't know. Not for sure anyway. The Earth's surface used to be about seventy per cent water before The Many Years Storm."

"Where did all the extra water come from?"

"The top and bottom of the world were filled with huge expanses of ice," Erin explained. "They were full of amazing creatures and beautiful landscapes, mostly untouched by humans. It looked like an alien world. But they were melting. I guess they're all gone now."

"That's so sad," Twelve said. "I'd love to have seen that."

"Me too."

Evening approached. The skies darkened. The rhythmic waves and the yawn of the oars sent Erin and Raven into dreams.

Eventually, the bleak hue of dawn bloomed across the grey horizon. Raven gazed into the sky, squawked irritably, and woke Erin. "Where are we?" he bleated. "I told you to follow the North Star. We're...*miles* off course!"

"I'm sorry. I got confused. There were so many stars."

Raven stretched his wings and took off at once. Circling above, he rose on the thermal currents until he was high enough to soar towards the pale sun.

"It doesn't matter," Erin told her reassuringly. She stretched her arms, rubbed the small of her back, and stared across the endless grey water. "We'll find our way."

"They all look the same," Twelve protested, jabbing a finger towards the stars. "They were all shining and fading, as though moving closer or slinking away."

"It's okay, Twelve. Don't worry."

"I must have followed a dozen different stars, convinced each was the North Star. I was sure that sooner or later I'd lead us in the right direction."

Raven returned in a bluster of feathers and profanity. "Turn us around," he said anxiously, an outstretched wingtip pointing towards the sun.

In the distance, a handful of black rectangular shapes hovered on the ocean's surface, shimmering with a strange haze.

"The Scrapers," Raven whispered, hunkering down inside his bucket.

Slowly, Erin and Twelve looked up at him.

Raven's face appeared over the lip. "We need to get out of here."

"Whatever for?" Erin asked, standing on the edge of the boat.

"Right now," the blackbird insisted.

"There might be people there," Erin said. "They might have food. Or…survivors."

"They might have a scarecrow," Twelve added hopefully, plunging the oars into the water and drawing *Lazarus* towards The Scrapers. "They might have Number Eight!"

"They do not have any food, or survivors, or scarecrows. Trust me. It's too dangerous," Raven said. "The stories I've heard—"

"Yes," Twelve said. "It's about time you told us these stories."

Raven ignored her. "We'd probably be at the Island of Trees by now if you hadn't steered us miles off course."

"What's so dangerous about The Scrapers?" said Erin. "They look harmless enough."

The huge dark rectangles glimmered imposingly on the horizon.

"Okay, okay," Raven said. "If you turn *Lazarus* towards the Island of Trees—that way—I'll tell you everything I know. But, be warned, you might not like what you hear."

"Deal," Erin and Twelve said in unison.

The scarecrow dipped an oar into the water and heaved the boat to port.

She rowed for almost an hour, threading *Lazarus* through the still grey waters. When The Scrapers had faded away into the sun, she hoisted the oars into the boat and sat back in her leather armchair.

"Is this far enough?"

Raven's head bobbed over the lip of his nest.

"I suppose," he mumbled. "To be honest, there is no distance you could take me from The Scrapers where I'd feel completely safe."

He fluttered down from the crow's nest and landed on Erin's knee.

"The Scrapers," he began, "are forsaken."

"Forsaken?"

"Overrun—"

"Overrun?"

"—by demons," Raven explained, his voice edged with fear.

Erin moved closer. "Demons?"

"That is what I said."

"Evil, malevolent, supernatural beings?"

Raven ruffled his feathers. "I have no other name for what they are. I've flown through The Scrapers many times. I visited with the former inhabitants, but one day everything changed. The people I knew were gone and the demons had taken their place."

Lazarus bobbed gently. The splash of water against the hull seemed to be the only sound in the entire universe.

"These demons, these…*whatever they are*…patrol the rooftops armed with arrows of fire. No bird can fly low enough to get a good look without dancing its death. They have heads, but no faces. Some walk with less grace than a scarecrow, others as nimble as a fox. They bring death to all who venture too close." Raven shuddered. "Believe me, if we'd sailed in there, they would have riddled us with arrows and condemned *Lazarus* to the bottom of The Endless Blue before we'd had time to pray for our souls!"

He took a restless breath.

"Well, if I hadn't met a walking, talking scarecrow yesterday," Erin said, "then I'd have said you were stark-raving bonkers." She ran a soothing finger down Raven's back. "But the world is nothing like before. The storm changed everything. Where do you think these faceless demons came from?"

"I do not know," Raven told her. "But they are death—walking, creeping death—and nothing more."

Erin tried to imagine a demon. A real demon. A terrifying creature with burned skin and jagged horns and glowing red eyes. Her mind zapped to the ones she'd drawn in her *Book of Scarecrows* and built from farmyard leftovers and unwanted clothes.

What did something born in the fires of Hell truly look like?

Catching Twelve's reflection in the water, her eyes darted away.

But any further thought on the matter was pushed from Erin's mind when Twelve suddenly stood, towering over the mast and crow's nest.

Ahead, a distant shape flickered.

It wasn't The Scrapers. They were miles behind.

This was something else.

"Look." Twelve pointed with an outstretched claw.

Erin swivelled. "What is it?"

"I think it's a ship," the scarecrow said. "A really big ship."

HMS FORTITUDE

Being back on the water after all that time on Coldharbour Farm frightened Erin far more than she'd realised. Like visiting the scene of a vicious crime, or climbing a terrifying mountain, or returning to a nightmare you'd just woken from. But here she was, out on The Endless Blue. She saw her parents' faces in the sun-dappled waves, their bodies swimming up towards her, their hands reaching for the surface.

But this was nothing more than a dream, a mirage.

She looked in the water for a reflection of Clyde, but he was nowhere to be seen.

She shook the visions loose.

An enormous ship glinted on the horizon like a shiny penny. Erin thought of *The Haughty Jinx* with its rows of booming cannons, masts the size of redwoods, and sails billowing in red and black.

As *Lazarus* approached, Erin's illusions were diminished.

Instead of a mighty galleon, a silent grey hulk cut the water like a giant blade. Gaping holes, dusted with soot and gunpowder, pitted the hull, as though a thousand monsters had dragged their claws down the sides and punched fiery fists clean through.

Demons, she thought.

The eerie yawn of bending metal echoed across the silent sea. The ship listed gently, gliding through the water in a massive clockwise circle.

"What sort of ship is this?" asked Twelve.

"A warship," Erin replied, pushing her glasses up her nose and straining to read the name on the hull. "HMS... Fortitude."

"What happened to it?"

"The Many Years Storm," Raven rattled immediately, as if it were the answer to every bad thing that had ever happened.

"We should go aboard."

"Agreed," Twelve added.

They positioned *Lazarus* next to the hull and Raven flew onto the deck, located a length of rope and began the arduous task of lowering it to Twelve and Erin. This done, the scarecrow tied *Lazarus* off and they both ascended.

The scarecrow seemed to zip up the rope with less effort than it took her to walk.

Erin found the climb nigh on impossible. The coarse rope cut into her hands. Her malnourished muscles burned.

Twelve peered over the edge and extended a long, helpful arm.

On deck, huge turrets sat squarely in front and behind, loaded with powerful gun-barrels aimed at the sky. Fire hoses, ropes, gas masks, and lifesaving equipment clung to the walls. Signs at every doorway issued cautions and warnings.

The ship yawned again.

Twelve adjusted her stance as the floor tilted gently.

Erin held onto the scarecrow's arm. Her plimsolls slipped on the deck.

A three-storey tower stood at midships, topped with radar, sonar and echo-locating devices, satellite dishes and brightly coloured flags and pennants. At its base was a round metal door and a large wheel. Erin gave a commendable and enthusiastic attempt at turning it. Defeated, she looked up.

"A little help?"

Twelve grabbed the wheel. It seemed to turn easily, squeaking under her rubber-gloved hands.

"I definitely loosened it."

Raven, who had been circling the tower, landed deftly on Twelve's hand.

"Looks like you're going inside," he said grimly.

Erin gave Raven a curious look. "And you're coming with us."

"You've no idea what's in there," he said. "Could be *anything*. Who knows what lurks in the shadowy bowels of an abandoned ghost ship like this."

"It's not a ghost ship," Twelve said immediately, then looked at Erin. "Is it?"

The Haughty Jinx rose in her mind. A ship of that nature was far more likely to be haunted than this enormous lump of steel.

"Just looks empty to me," she said, soothing Raven. "Like a plundered tin of mackerel. Nothing to worry about."

It sounded as though Raven attempted a tut, but it was more a throaty click. He folded his wings and crept up Twelve's arm until he sat on her broad shoulders.

Inside, a dark corridor ran the circumference of the tower. Slim ladders stretched to decks and gangways. More signs listing important safety instructions in the case of fire, attack, and submersion were peeling from the walls. Twelve idly nodded at each announcement and strode purposefully towards a ladder that stretched to the top.

"This way first," she decided. "Then we go below."

Erin swung her leg onto the first rung and hauled herself up. Three floors later, they emerged in a passageway that led to the bridge. Rows of computers, scanners, radar sensors and communications equipment faced them. Every screen, panel, and interface was a black mirror, cracked and dead.

"No power," Raven said. "This place is a steel coffin."

"How could a storm have destroyed all this?" Twelve asked. "Warships were built to survive, well, war. Only bombs and missiles and torpedoes could have caused damage of this magnitude."

Erin pressed her fingertips against the silent machines.

A large window wrapped the bridge like a huge visor.

Ragged holes—some the size of fists, others like dinner plates—pocked the shattered surface. Whatever made them had disappeared somehow, been taken, or dissolved into nothing.

Melted, Erin thought.

She traced the jagged holes, fighting the memory of the night the gigantic hailstorm had torn her rowing boat to pieces.

Behind her, Twelve examined a series of arrows, feathered with vibrant flights, that protruded from the walls.

"This ship has been through The Scrapers," said Raven.

Twelve plucked one of the arrows. It juddered between her fingers.

Raven backed away, crawling around the scarecrow's neck for safety.

Half-listening to her friends, Erin stared through the

large, shattered window. "The water seems such a long way down," she said, placing a hand on the damaged glass. "I can still remember the seaside as a distant thing, something blue and far away. A destination, a place to visit, a treat, an exciting adventure. But these past months, perhaps years, have been consumed by the tides. All I see is water, The Endless Blue, the lapping waves at the fringes of the place that was once my home." She turned to Twelve. "It destroyed everything. It stole all that I loved. It stole *everything*." She took a long, soothing breath. "Yet, you both survived."

"I'm sorry," Twelve said, lurching across the bridge, a quiver of arrows in hand.

"Whatever for?"

"I survived the storm," the scarecrow explained. "Tied to a cross beneath the angry clouds, the falling rain, the monstrous ice storms." Twelve lumbered round the consoles and stood in front of the girl. "What I mean is…well…it doesn't seem fair. It's sort of a miracle. Everyone else got washed away by the storm: your family, and my sisters, that woman Loren, and perhaps every other soul on this planet, but here I am. A scarecrow. A thing of wood and rust and dirt. Plastic hands and cement-filled boots. But, *alive*, if that is truly what I am."

"I'm glad you're alive." Erin smiled. "I'm not sure how much longer I would have survived on my own. I could never have made a boat like *Lazarus*, and I certainly couldn't have rowed it across the sea."

Twelve curled her stiff arms around the girl.

Tractor joints squeaked as she pulled her close.

"You saved me."

"You made me."

They stood, wrapped in each other's arms.

Finally, Erin pulled back.

Her eyes were bloodshot and filled with tears.

"There's nothing more up here," she said, gazing around the lifeless room.

"It's going to be okay," Twelve said, stroking Erin's knotted hair. "I suggest we take a look below deck and see what we can find in the shadows."

Raven wailed feebly.

"Excellent idea." Erin sniffed, reaching up and taking the blackbird from Twelve's shoulder. She cradled him in her hand and stroked his feathers gently.

"Don't worry, Raven. I'll protect you."

BELOW DECKS

Twelve descended, lowering herself one boot at a time into the still, silent dark. A thin column of light pooled on the floor, illuminating several metres of gangway in either direction. Beyond that, everything became shifting shadows.

Nestled in Erin's hand, Raven's tiny claws clung to her pale skin. She whispered words of comfort to the blackbird then slipped him into the pouch on the front of her dungarees.

"We'll go round and check this level," Twelve said, surveying their surrounds. "Then move down."

The gangway led to the forecastle, through bulkhead after bulkhead. Twelve and Erin took it in turns to inspect each doorway. Some opened easily, revealing sleeping quarters, meeting rooms, and common areas. Others remained locked.

Those that did open were mostly in good order, but some had gaping holes through the hull where pale sunlight burst in. These rooms were a mass of splintered, charred furniture, and fleets of colourful arrows wedged into every conceivable surface.

Twelve collected the arrows and tucked them neatly inside her pirate jacket.

Raven muttered about the demons and The Scrapers from

time to time, making Erin wonder why they had attacked this mighty ship. Surely, HMS Fortitude would have made quick work of an enemy armed with nothing but bows and arrows. The gun turrets on deck alone could have reduced them to crumbling stone and cinders in minutes.

With a circuit complete, they descended again. The darkness grew, becoming thicker, closer. The next deck mirrored the one above—a few less holes, a few less arrows—and so they proceeded down and down and down.

Raven fidgeted nervously in Erin's dungaree pouch.

The sound of the waves rustled against the side of the ship.

"We're probably below sea level now."

"It's colder down here."

Raven agreed with a mirthless squawk.

Erin shuffled carefully down the gangways of HMS Fortitude. She reached out and dragged her fingers along the cold grey hull. At midships, they entered a large room.

Twelve's footsteps reverberated noisily.

A blend of stale vegetables and disinfectant hung in the air.

Erin peered through the dim light. A floor of plastic linoleum spread between a maze of metal furniture. She smoothed her hands over the cool, wet-like surfaces.

"Aluminium."

"Metal tables and surfaces?" replied Twelve. "What kind of room is this?"

Erin smiled, but no one could see.

"The galley," she said with a grin. "It's the kitchen and mess hall. If there's food anywhere on this ship, then this is the place."

The search began.

Twelve took the high cupboards and shelves, while Erin

plundered those below. They worked their way along one wall, down another, into a small windowless room that might have served as a meat cellar or walk-in refrigerator, and finally the pantry.

Erin found two dented tins of baked beans, one of peaches, and four of tomatoes. Twelve discovered open packets of flour, rice, and lentils.

Erin rested against a table and admired their haul. Instead of finding a smooth edge, her lower back pressed against several round, uncomfortable dials.

They hissed.

Erin jumped.

She turned instantly, running her fingers up and down, feeling the familiar shape. "Ring-burners," she mumbled to herself. "This is a gas stove!"

Twelve shrugged through the gloom. "Does it work?"

"My thoughts exactly."

Erin turned one of the dials and lent forward. The sound of escaping gas and the accompanying smell registered immediately.

"Yep, seems connected."

She scrambled around looking for the ignition switch, found a dark circular button, and jammed her finger against it. Flickering shadows exploded across the walls as blue flames burst into life. Erin fired all the burners up and punched the ignition switch again and again. The stove blazed gloriously. The flames danced happily in eight perfect circles.

Raven came up to investigate.

The light and heat from the stove was a welcome treat. Erin had almost forgotten the sensation. The warming balm of heat, fire, against her skin. Her nerves jangled, as if awoken, craving the warmth of the stove.

The light illuminated packets of biscuits and crackers stored on top of the cabinets that Twelve had missed. Erin climbed and threw them down, smiling happily.

The light revealed another door at the end of the room too. Erin hopped down and waltzed off to investigate.

"Are you okay, Raven?" she asked as they approached the door, stroking the top of his soft, warm head.

"Yes," he said meekly. "Better now we can see what's going on."

"Why does the dark scare you so much?"

"I'm not afraid of the dark."

"Really—?"

"It's what the dark conceals that concerns me."

Some terrible thought appeared to cross his mind. His wings shook inside the pouch. A small squeak erupted from his hard, yellow beak.

Erin smiled happily. "There's nothing to be afraid of."

Her words became an instant lie.

Rising out of her own shadow grew the figure of a man.

Raven vanished.

A blood-curdling scream erupted from Erin's throat.

The man burst forward, arms out. His palms slammed against the preparation tables with a metallic *clang!* The sound ricocheted through the room, bouncing off cupboards and tables. Erin's head rang. Blood flecked the floor from deep cuts on the man's hands. Arrow shafts jutted from his back like porcupine needles. He shook terribly, lurched, and grabbed Erin.

Still screaming, she wrenched herself free.

The man spun and crumpled to the floor.

Twelve was upon him in seconds. "Who are you?" she said in her meanest, strangled voice, a boot to his chest.

The man wore dark fatigues. A series of stars and coloured ribbons were stitched across his left breast. He strained to lift his head.

"Beware!" the sailor groaned, his eyes wild, afraid. "Boot... hill." His voice gurgled like a drain. "Patch...work Woman." His eyes locked on to Erin, disbelievingly, fingers clawing at her. "Human...girl." His pupils rolled back in his sockets. Lips quivered. "Dark powers," he whispered, as what proved to be his last breath whistled through his teeth. "Magic and—"

Then, as swiftly as he arrived, the man was gone.

Twelve kicked him with a cement-filled boot.

His body jiggled helplessly.

"Is it dead?" came a voice from Erin's pouch.

"Yes, Raven. He's dead."

The words hung in the air. Nobody wanted to accept them.

"I think we just watched him die."

"Dark powers? Magic and—*what*?" Erin said eventually, her face cast with pale terror. "What's that place he spoke of? BootHill? Where is that? And who is The Patchwork Woman?"

The blackbird became incredibly quiet and still.

"Raven?" Twelve said.

"What?"

"Do you know what he was talking about?"

"Sort of."

"Have you been there?"

"No," he replied hastily.

Erin and Twelve exchanged looks. Their faces shimmered in the light of the gas burners.

"I just...know of it. That's all."

"More secrets!"

"Tell us, Raven," Erin urged. "Tell us everything."

"Not here," he quivered, spinning in agitated circles.

Twelve marched across the mess hall, stuffed the tins into the pockets of her pirate jacket and collected up the rest of their food in her huge arms.

"We should leave," the scarecrow said. "Before we encounter more half-dead, arrow-riddled sailors."

But Erin had dropped down beside the dead man. She ran her hands over his uniform. "Human girl," she whispered. "Why did you call me that?"

She moved slowly, nervously, one eye on the search, the other on his face. She kept thinking he was going to take one final gasp and sit bolt upright. But he just lay there, lifeless and still.

Her search produced a packet of gum, a lighter, and some photos of what she presumed were his family.

Dead and gone, she thought. *Like everyone else.*

Sneaking her hand around his waist, her fingers rubbed against something cold and hard. She froze for a moment, knowing what she'd found, considering if she should take it or not.

"Erin," Twelve insisted. "We should go."

She slipped her fingers around his service revolver and tugged it from the holster.

"We don't need that," Twelve told her. "Nothing good can come of it."

Erin's eyes were stuck to the pistol, like ants in treacle. "I want it."

"No," Twelve insisted. "You're too small."

"Exactly," she said. "I'm a small, human girl."

"It's too powerful."

"They have arrows and fire...and dark powers and magic and—" Erin tore her eyes away from the weapon to look at Twelve. "I *need* it."

"We don't."

"Well, *I* do."

Erin raised the weapon and aimed it down the galley. Her eye locked on to the sight. It was far heavier than she had imagined and filled her with a sense of immense power. Taking her finger off the trigger, she released the clip. There were three shots remaining, one in the chamber.

"My father showed me how to use his rifle," she explained, snapping the clip back into place.

"I still don't like it."

"Me either," Raven added, his beak protruding from the pouch.

Erin slid the barrel through the pink belt, the way she'd seen in action movies, at the base of her spine. She tightened the pink bandana, stood and sank her hands onto her hips.

"I'm the last girl on Earth," she said. "I was a frightened child, an orphan of humanity. But now I'm something to be feared. A survivor, a warrior, a vengeful gunslinger!"

Clyde would be proud, Erin thought. She mentally high-fived her missing brother, before nodding at the scarecrow. "You're right. We should go."

Turning off the gas stove, Twelve hurried Erin into the passageway, up endless ladders and out onto deck. Lifting the girl, Twelve swung her over the side where she clasped the rope and shimmied down.

Lazarus drifted out into the ocean.

The sun flickered on tiny waves.

"BootHill, then," Twelve said, looking towards Raven who had slipped from Erin's pocket and returned to his nest. "Tell us everything. Tell us *all* your secrets."

The blackbird's eyes blinked rapidly as though trying to find a way out of this.

"Really?" he said. "The less you know, the better."

"I think, under the circumstances, the opposite is true."

"Fine."

"Good."

"BootHill is a graveyard. A huge graveyard. On a gigantic hill."

"And?" said Erin, sensing more to his story.

Raven circled the nest several times making strange, uncomfortable noises.

"It's more than *just* a graveyard," he admitted. "BootHill is part of The Devil's Fork, three mountain peaks, each topped by gallows that overlook the graveyard."

"Gallows?" asked Twelve.

"For hanging people? By the neck?" Erin added. "Good gracious."

"I told you," Raven said. "It's a horrid place. Everything about it is dead. Dead people, dead trees, dead earth. The whole place stinks to high heaven. Why would anybody want to go there? Birds fly over it, then fly away again as quickly as they came. But, this boat, no. We'd never get away. BootHill is a dark, sickly place. It would drag us in, capture us, condemn us all!"

"Calm down, Raven," Erin said. "No one said anything about going there."

"The sailor warned us to stay away," Twelve added, pulling on the oars. "To stay away from BootHill and The Patchwork

Woman with her dark powers and her magic and whatever else."

Erin stroked the pistol.

She wracked her brain, trying to imagine what the dying sailor might have said next.

Perhaps it was better she didn't know.

Perhaps it was better she never found out.

"The Island of Trees, then?" Twelve suggested, taking everyone's minds off death and dark powers and magic and The Patchwork Woman. "Follow the North Star?"

Raven squawked an affirmation.

Twelve turned *Lazarus* about and aimed her at the brightest star in the sky.

ISLAND OF TREES

Twelve manoeuvred *Lazarus* between a tangle of muddy ridges, each covered with a mass of dark trees. Their roots, bark, and withered branches spread like a cancer, straining towards the lifeless sky.

Erin let her fingertips drag in the grey water.

Raven shivered in her lap.

Two days had passed. Erin had eaten meals of tinned beans and wholemeal crackers. She'd slept for most of the journey. When she rose from her slumber, she let Lucretia dance and the music box play, reading aloud from *The Wizard of Oz*, while fielding more questions from Twelve about the nature of dreams and origins of the stars.

Dark roots knocked against the hull of the boat like unwanted visitors.

Erin wriggled onto her knees and dried her hands on her oversized jumper.

"It's not quite what I imagined," she said, looking through the mist. "I guess I thought it'd be an island of palm trees and tropical fruit and parrots, a huge volcano rising from the centre. Like something out of *King Solomon's Mines* or *Escape from Atlantis*. But it's just the top of some inaccessible mountain."

"A darkness has fallen here," Raven said. "The leaves have lost their colour. The trees look sickly and foreboding."

The sky rumbled overhead, but there wasn't a cloud in sight.

Twelve pulled on the oars and circled the island.

High on the southern face, cutting through the black and grey wilderness, rose a spark of glorious red and gold.

Erin pointed.

Twelve nodded.

Just as Raven had said, a great fire burned. Tendrils of acrid smoke spiralled between the trees, twinning itself with the mist. Twelve dropped the oars. The boat bobbed thirty feet from the shore.

"Fire," she said, almost mesmerised by it.

"Are you afraid?" Erin asked.

"Of fire? Whatever for?"

Erin indicated the scarecrow's highly flammable construction.

"Oh."

She buttoned her pirate jacket and flexed her rubber-gloved hands.

"It'll take more than fire to destroy me."

Lazarus drifted to the edge of the island and nudged the muddy bank.

With Raven in her pouch, Erin dropped into the watery shallows. She wobbled initially as her plimsolls sank into the porous seabed.

Twelve swooped passed and hauled her out of the bog. Together they mounted the bank, striding through thick nests of trees and bowing grey-green leaves that blocked their path. The terrain was tough, even for Twelve. Erin could feel one of the scarecrow's hands positioned behind her at all times, in case she were to slip and fall.

They used the trees to lever themselves up the treacherous bank while clinging and resting against rocks and boulders. High above, woodpeckers drilled percussive rudiments. Erin pressed a gentle finger into her dungarees and stroked Raven's head. He chirped reassuringly, making Erin smile.

The hill levelled out.

The trees thinned.

The island opened into a plateau of waist-high plants, thickets, and brambles. Trees loomed on either side of a trench woven by heavy footfalls. Erin wondered what sort of feet had made these tracks and whether they were still living on this desolate haunch of rock.

Ahead, the flicker of fire and smoke, that had once been thick and strong, dwindled. Walking towards it, they emerged in a clearing. At the centre, burned logs rested against one another like a wigwam, surrounded by a circle of blackened stones.

"It's still hot," Erin said, breaking a stick off a nearby tree and jabbing the ash. She raked it sideways, revealing the orange embers beneath. "Who did this?"

A mighty *crash*, like falling crockery, erupted from a strange building hidden amongst the trees and ferns and scrub.

Twelve and Erin stood stock-still, staring at the mysterious hideout.

No light came from within. The whole place looked abandoned. A summer house in the throes of winter.

Twelve folded a web of brambles to one side so Erin could reach the door. A heavy, rusted padlock hung from coils of chains. Damp, coppery links disappeared through tiny slits above and below wooden blinds that shrouded lopsided windows.

"Looks like they don't want anyone getting in," said Twelve.

"Or getting out," said Raven, his head rising out of Erin's pocket.

"It's a climber's lodge," said Erin. "I wonder how high this was before the rain came. We are, after all, on the top of a mountain."

The scarecrow nodded, her attention on the padlock. "We should open the door," she decided. "Shouldn't we?"

"I don't like it here," chimed Raven. "Smells terrible."

Twelve looked at the blackbird curiously.

"Everything is decayed and rotten. It stinks of death."

"This place *is* strange," Erin agreed. "I don't know about you, but I feel like there's a hundred pairs of eyes on me. In the bushes, in the trees, in the skies. Do you feel it?"

"No," Twelve said, closing her fingers around the padlock and ripping it from the door. The blinds buckled and fell to the ground. The chains uncoiled and clattered at her feet. She reached forward and turned the small, iron handle.

The door creaked nervously.

Erin pulled the pistol from her belt.

"Put that thing away," Twelve told her. "You're going to get us all killed."

Erin ignored her.

Inside, comfy-looking chairs and sofas pointed at a large, welcoming fireplace. Sideboards held vases, jars, and stone sculptures. Climbing gear hung from the walls next to detailed maps and framed photos of smiling faces sat atop great mountains, beards and eyebrows crusted with ice.

In the furthest corner sat a rocking chair made of gleaming hand-polished blackwood. It faced a picture window that looked out over the edge of the mountain and The Endless Blue beyond.

The rocking chair creaked back and forth.

A dark figure hunched in the seat.

CLIMBER'S LODGE

"Hello," said Twelve, stepping boldly across the threshold.

Erin grabbed the scarecrow's wrist.

"What is it?"

"We shouldn't be here."

"Yet, here we are," Twelve replied plainly.

Something moved through the shadows at an incredible rate.

Erin gasped, the pistol raised.

Twelve swivelled.

The rocking chair creaked slowly back and forth.

Empty.

A shadow descended over Erin. It knocked her hand aside. The pistol slipped from her grasp. Twelve winced as the gun clattered across the floor, expecting it to go off. But the weapon skidded to an anti-climactic halt beside a bookcase.

The shadow grabbed Erin and Twelve and hauled them inside.

The door slammed shut.

Erin tumbled to the ground.

As the gloom thickened, Twelve came face to face with the shadow. It stood seven and a half feet, just like her, but

Twelve's horns scraped the ceiling of the lodge, instinctively stretching for extra inches.

The shadow's face moved into a splinter of warm lamplight.

Twelve gasped.

"Sister?"

The figure before her was undeniably another scarecrow. Utterly terrifying and abhorrent to behold. Dark as pitch from head to foot, as though set alight, or turned on a spit. Her clothes were similar to Twelve's. A sapphire dress emblazoned with moons and stars and wrist-length sleeves, stockings stretched over rough-cut wooden legs, workman's gloves and electric-blue rollerblades that wriggled with mud and earthworms. Conversely, a thick rainbow-coloured belt circled her waist, fastened with a shimmering gold buckle in the shape of a star.

Erin twisted onto her back and stared up at one of her creations.

She knew those rollerblades anywhere.

Twelve ran a finger over the pocket where she'd stashed the vivid yellow fabric from Number Eight's cross.

There was nothing bright and colourful about this scarecrow.

Nothing at all.

Beneath a matted black wig sat the ruin of a blistered basketball. Dirt and scum coated the uneven leather, forming a crust of blackened filth. Down one side ran a deep gash, held together with uneven staples. Eyes had been crudely cut into the ball and held open with chaotic stitching in red and blue cord. And spread lazily across her face was a broken zip with missing teeth and a rusted metal tongue.

"I'm Twelve," she said gingerly, staring at her sister's face.

In the middle of her forehead—undeniably written by a finger dipped in red paint—sat a large number. "You must be…Five."

The other scarecrow stiffened. "What are you?" she said, her voice cold and sharp. "Some kind of monster?"

Twelve's shoulders dropped. "I'm…your sister."

"Sister?" Five spat, her voice different, deeper. "Poppycock!" She wheeled away until she butted against the top of a threadbare sofa where she sat, arms folded. "You and I are not sisters," Five said. Once again, her voice had changed. "Look at you. You're an abomination. You're…despicable, horrid, a menace to the eyes!" Five studied Twelve's face. "My God. Your eyes are…wriggling!"

"If I'm despicable and horrid, then so are you," Twelve told Five, sounding annoyed. "We were made by the same hand. Born from the same mind. This is Erin. She made us."

Slowly, the girl climbed to her feet.

Five twitched. Her body bent in an unusual way. "Be gone," she screamed. "I … we … cannot bear to look at you a moment longer."

Her spine locked into place. Her arms out at right angles. The edge of Five's mouth zipped open and shut frantically of its own accord.

"Leave us alone," she bellowed suddenly, her body convulsing.

"Five?" Twelve tried, reaching out to steady her sister. "What are you—?"

"Come closer … Get away … Sister? … You *must* run … Trapped … Come to us…"

Each time she spoke, a different voice sprung from Five's terrifying zipper-mouth.

"What's happening?" Twelve whispered. She turned to

85

Erin. "What's she doing? Why is she like this?"

Erin had no idea. No words. The realisation that not one, but two of her scarecrows, were somehow alive had frozen her in place.

Twelve turned back to her sister. "Your voice. It's—"

But Five was up and spinning in frenzied circles. Her rollerblades gnawed at the wooden floor. Finally, she fell backwards over the arm of the sofa, her hands clamped to the sides of her face. Collapsing to the floor, she gibbered hysterically, all four limbs kicking wildly against walls, furniture, thin air.

Twelve bounded across the climber's lodge and knelt beside her tormented sister as dozens of voices sprung from her mouth. Furious, pleading, frail, and broken.

Someone knocked on the door.

Erin's head snapped towards the sound.

More people? she thought. *More scarecrows?*

Nervously, she approached the broken window and peered out. The campfire smouldered in the clearing, but she could see nothing else. Just shadows and the marauding forest and The Endless Blue far below.

Something moved.

A deft shift in the trees.

More activity. Left and right.

The trees were moving.

The trees were alive.

And walking towards her.

Erin's skin turned to ice. She blinked three times just to be sure then peered around the cracks in her spectacles. No, it couldn't be. A collection of figures made from branches and sticks and leaves were moving into the thin light of the campfire. They stood in a rough semicircle, each holding a vicious weapon in one hand, a flaming torch in the other.

Panic fizzed though her.

A million nightmares and a million reasons fought for supremacy.

Erin dragged a table to bar the door.

Outside, the figures became a huddle. They seemed to be talking amongst themselves. Erin stared hard, wishing she could see them more clearly. The surrounding woodland blocked the light and her cracked glasses were all but useless at this distance.

She tore herself away from the window and scanned the lodge for somewhere to hide.

"The Island of Trees, huh?" said Erin, looking down at the tiny blackbird who fretted hysterically in her pouch.

"I didn't want to come here," he protested. "Who's outside? And what in creation is that thing in the corner?"

"That…*thing*…is my sister," Twelve replied hotly across the lodge. "I'll not have a word said against her."

Raven burst from Erin's pouch and soared onto Twelve's head. "She looks unwell. Positively cadaverous."

Five juddered and heaved as though crying.

The staples on her round, blistered head grated against the wooden floor.

Twelve hoisted Number Five and placed her in the rocking chair.

Five's eyes reverberated, expanding in and out. The zipper tore across her face of its own accord, locking her mouth shut. A multitude of voices mumbled inside, desperate and morose and wailing to be free.

Twelve sank onto a wooden footstool and placed both

hands on her sister's knees. "Everything is okay. I'm here now. Me, Twelve. With Raven and Erin. Your creator. *Our* creator. She made us who we are. She gave us mismatching hands and monstrous heads and numerical names and everything. She's a human girl. Possibly the very last one."

Five's head tilted towards Twelve. She looked sad and confused.

"You're safe now," Twelve reassured her. "There is nothing to fear anymore."

Again, something hard rapped against the lodge door.

Raven disappeared onto a high shelf and hid behind an earthenware vase.

Erin scanned the floor for her pistol. "Who's outside?" she called towards Five. "Who are the...tree people?"

Slowly, Five peeled the zipper back. Broken teeth hung from her mouth like rotten towels on a dilapidated washing line. "They're...me," she said slowly, her voice calm and soft. "You might have created me, *Erin*, but I, in turn, created—*them*."

"Them?"

Five seemed to fight something in her mind. Her large, empty eyes bore into Erin. The girl swallowed hard. Sweat beaded on her forehead.

"What happened to you?" Erin asked.

Five's mouth quirked. It almost resembled a smile. "Me?" she said, her voice different, darker. "Who are you talking to? Me? ... Or me? ... Or me?"

With each word her voice changed, shading into something new.

Someone new.

Twelve moved her hands away. "Five?"

The calm voice returned to her sister's throat. "I made them. The ones out there. I wanted to get rid of the ones living inside. I wanted to give them somewhere to go. I can't keep them all in here. There's just…too many."

"Too many?" Erin said. "Too many…what?"

"I don't know," Five replied. "They're all different. Some good, some bad, some…there are no words to describe them. Do you not have them inside you?"

She directed her last question at Twelve.

"I don't know," Twelve said truthfully. "I only have this voice. I don't think there are other *things* inside me."

"They're not inside me," Five said. "They *are* me. All jumbled up. Squirming, arguing, fighting, begging to be heard. To be free."

Erin approached the two scarecrows.

"What did you make?" she said, her head tilting towards the door. "What's out there?"

"Wickermen. Nine in all. I thought that would be enough. I was wrong."

Twelve stood quickly.

Her horns crashed into the beams above, showering her in dust and splinters.

"We can help," she said.

Five shook, still fighting whatever swirled inside her tortured head.

"How many more do you need?"

Five steadied herself, then whispered, "Thousands."

WICKERMEN

The door flew open. Wickermen burst inside. A nauseous stink enveloped Erin. Rotten grass, damp, and spent fireworks. She grabbed Twelve as one of the creatures stepped towards them.

"What business do you have here?" he barked.

They were strange looking things. Each stood around six feet tall. Crudely manufactured from branches, roots, twine, and sticks. And held together with a cross-hatching of kindling, knotted grass, and dried mud. Some had adorned themselves with belts, climbing rope, and chains. Others had made clothing from the forest.

One before them wore a flowing cape of dark feathers around its shoulders.

Another, a headdress of leaves and bracken.

"We are looking for food, for answers," Twelve began, towering over them all.

"And for my brother." Erin pulled the photo from her dungaree pocket and held it up. "This is Clyde. Have you seen him?"

"No," the wickerman grunted.

"We're searching for my sisters too," Twelve added. "A family of scarecrows."

"Scarecrows?" said the wickerman in the headdress. His voice rang higher than the first, edged with menace and anger. Two rows of sharpened rocks glistened where his gums should be. He gnashed them together, adding, "We'll have no talk of scarecrows here."

"But I'm a scarecrow," she protested, tapping her yellow pin. "I am Number Twelve."

"Silence," he said, moving closer still.

The wickermen's faces were simply made. Rocks and conkers and snubs of twig served as eyes and noses. Cavernous mouths were hollowed out in the middle of their faces.

"Why do you deny us? I'm a scarecrow," said Twelve proudly and gestured towards Five, "and so is my sister."

"Ha!" the other wickerman spat. "She is a wretch. A monstrous ruin. Unhinged by the voices that call to her, day and night."

"Voices?"

"They fester inside, destroying one another, creating new ones over and over and over…or so it seems."

"That's why she is kept here. In this lodge," said the wickerman in the feather cape.

His lifeless eyes zeroed on Erin who had sunk into the shadows. The wickermen were strange and creepy. They had no right to be alive and wandering around this island. But, by the same token, neither did Twelve or Five.

Erin curled her fingers into the scarecrow's pirate jacket and closed her eyes.

She remembered building Number Five. After the sharp learning curve of the first four scarecrows, she'd finally found her groove. Hammers and nails and rusty machine parts were familiar in her hands. Erin would sculpt and build and create her scarecrows after homework was done, on long summer evenings, and all weekend long. And when she was meant to be asleep, she would sit in bed sketching ideas and costumes into her *Book of Scarecrows*. Her imagination bubbled over as she stitched the edges of Five's eyes and added the zipper mouth to the battered basketball. Erin had earmarked Pa's old Wellingtons as Five's feet, but when she came across a pair of good-as-new rollerblades on one of her reconnaissance missions to the local charity shop, everything changed. Five had been positioned in the Coldharbour lower fields, her cross fitted to a wooden, circular base that allowed her to spin on her rollerblades under the whim of the wind. How had the scarecrow come to travel this far across *The Endless Blue* and remain in one piece?

Erin felt light-headed. Surely, this was all a dream: the scarecrows, the wickermen, *Lazarus*, and The Patchwork Woman. Any moment now her eyes were going to spring open and she'd find herself nestled in the hayloft, the rain hammering down, her *Book of Scarecrows* open across her chest. But when she risked a glimpse, the wickerman in the feathered cape loomed over her.

"My name's Jack," he said, almost friendly. "At least, that's what I think they called me. Before I was…*this*."

He looked down at his body. A filthy weave of brown and green.

"Always with the past is our Jack," sighed the other with a grin. "I'm Tomas. And *you*… are our prisoners."

Erin's heart thudded as nine wickermen rushed forward, arms outstretched, gnarled wooden fingers snapping. Six of them piled on top of Twelve while the remaining three wrenched Erin from the shadows.

Twelve fought bravely, but she could not contend with so many. Three perhaps. She could definitely take three of them. Erin was sure of it.

Something cold and hard was fastened around her wrists.

"I'm sorry," Tomas said, straightening his headdress and readjusting an odd clump of dislodged earth from his torso. "It's too dangerous to stay here. You must come with us now. Out of the lodge. Before she changes."

"Changes?"

Tomas signalled to the others. They hauled Erin into the clearing. The smell of fading embers filled her head. Pain lanced her arms. Two wickermen busied themselves barricading the lodge door as they secured Erin and Twelve to a sturdy tree.

"What's going on?" Twelve asked. "What do you want with us?"

"Personally?" said Jack, circling the tree and checking their fastenings. "Nothing. *We* have no interest in you or—"

"The human girl," Tomas said, his voice ripe with baleful glee.

"But *somebody* does," Erin said, her eyes thinning.

"Pretty *and* clever." Tomas crept around the edge of the clearing and hunkered down in front of her. "There is... *someone*...who covets you. But she is not here, you'll be happy to know. As are we. She is not the sort of visitor we'd welcome back to our island."

"She has power," said Jack. His feathered cape swirled as he moved. "A dark, malevolent force."

"Yes, yes, yes," Tomas said, irritably.

"A strange, consuming force."

"Enough," Tomas snapped. "But she did come with an offer."

"They do not need to know this."

"They came looking for answers. I'm simply giving them what they desire."

"The Patchwork Woman," Erin muttered. "You speak of The Patchwork Woman!"

Tomas took a long, slow breath. His leafy headdress rustled. "You've heard of her? Yet you do not quake in the uttering of her name."

Erin fixed her jaw and stared, unblinking at the wickerman.

"Bravery counts for little, human girl," he purred, shifting so close his rotten stench made Erin gag. "She is darkness, and turmoil, and malice, and every bad thing you ever dreamt or dared to imagine."

Erin snorted defiantly.

"And she is looking for a human girl. Probably wants a companion all the way out there on BootHill."

"What did she…offer you?" Erin grumbled.

Tomas trilled and rubbed his stick hands together excitedly. He seemed to recall the memory for a moment. Relishing it, perhaps.

"She came here, across chaotic seas, beneath vengeful skies, and told us that if we were to stumble upon a human girl—which baffled us as such a thing has long since vanished from this world—then she would fulfil any wish we desired."

"Any wish?" Twelve said.

"Anything."

The faces of her family flooded Erin's mind.

Could The Patchwork Woman actually grant wishes, like the djinn's and genie's in her brother's books?

No. Of course not.

Erin shook her head, sweeping those dangerous hopes away.

"And what would a wickerman wish for?" Twelve asked.

Tomas ran a finger down his badly pruned body.

"Obviously, we cannot go on like this." He approached the scarecrow. "We want our original bodies. We want her to bring us back."

"Back?"

"Back to life!"

"And?" Erin said, a slither of hope lingering. "What did The Patchwork Woman say?"

"She agreed, as if it were no more effort to her than breathing."

"How?" Erin said. "She promises the impossible."

"Impossible?" Tomas scoffed. "She has dark power and magic—"

"So we've heard." Erin frowned.

"Of course, you're a non-believer." Tomas rose, pacing back and forth. "Take a look around. The world is different now. People are gone—well, almost—and new creatures have arisen. Scarecrows and wickermen and The Patchwork Woman and her golems, and who knows what else."

"Golems?"

Tomas laughed, dry and sickly.

"You know nothing of this world, human girl."

"I know enough."

"Our human bodies are gone. Dead and cold and washed beyond our sight," Jack said to Tomas. "No matter what The Patchwork Woman says, there's no getting them back."

Tomas sighed. "So little faith in you, Jack."

"*Human* bodies?" said Erin. "You're human? But you're made of trees and—"

"We're wickermen," said Jack. "But Tomas here believes we

once lived inside humans. As spirits, or parts thereof, or some such nonsense. And now we're here, in these bodies. Others are in mannequins, or statues, or—"

"Scarecrows!" Twelve gasped. "You think we're full of human spirits. Powered by the dead. That we're made of…*ghosts*?"

"You're up and walking about, aren't you?" said Tomas. "How else would you explain it?"

Twelve failed to reply.

"What's a human body without its soul?" Tomas laughed. "A corpse. A cadaver. Meat and bone and nothing more."

Twelve flexed her fingers and rocked back on her heels. "I *am* alive," she said, ignoring the wickerman's cackle. "I can see, and feel, and smell. I can make things, and row a boat, and protect Erin, and search for Clyde and my sisters." She stopped for a moment. An eerie silence hung in the trees. "Perhaps you are right. Perhaps we are all powered by something…unexplainable."

"What do you mean *perhaps*? Of course I'm right!"

"He's not," said Jack.

"I am!"

The other wickermen rumbled, muttering opinions to one another.

"And what about my sister? What about Number Five?" Twelve said. "Do you blame spirits for her condition?"

"Something happened to her. Something…extraordinary."

Erin shuddered. She looked across at Twelve, but the scarecrow's expression was impossible to decipher.

"What happened?" Erin asked. "What did you do to her?"

"Do?" Jack cried. "We did nothing. She's the one with all the voices inside her."

"There's thousands of them swimming around in that

abominable head of hers," Tomas said. "We were all in there once. I fought hard to get out, to find my way into this body. I don't know why I made it and others didn't. Jack was the same. We all were."

The wickermen nodded slowly.

"It's the human form," Tomas explained. "That's the key. We could jump into dead rabbits or deer or birds, but we didn't. We looked for human shapes. I guess Five knew this. Heaven knows how. That's why she made these bodies for us."

Erin looked at the climber's lodge. It was quiet inside. Wickermen remained on guard, iron bars and flames flickering in their hands.

Her head spun with Jack's and Tomas's theories. Human spirits? That made sense, didn't it? How else could she explain Twelve coming to life, and building a boat, and sailing across The Endless Blue?

But whose spirits were they?

Twelve was awfully quiet.

Erin shuffled around the tree.

The chains bit her wrists.

"It doesn't matter."

"What doesn't?" Twelve said, bending towards the girl.

"All the things you're worrying about. It doesn't matter if you're powered by human spirits. Or magic, or divine intervention, or clockwork, or anything else. It's the same with the way you look. I made you terrifying and abysmal on purpose. And you're perfect. Just the way you are."

The scarecrow tried to lower herself to meet Erin's gaze.

Her monstrous eyes wriggled with bugs and critters.

The bison's skull ebbed away, replaced by the faces of her family.

It morphed from Ma. To Pa. To Clyde.

Their faces sitting above the scarecrow's broad shoulders and red pirate jacket.

They smiled lovingly at her, eyes cloaked with a lonely sadness. But Erin's daydream was dashed by a terrible noise emanating from the climber's lodge. A noise so pained and cruel that it pulled at her heart.

And made her soul ache.

LAST HUMAN GIRL

For the second time that day, the door to the climber's lodge burst open. However, on this occasion, it flew outwards, disengaged from its hinges, and hurtled through the air. Blackened branches and dying embers spiralled in smouldering arcs when the door came to rest on the wickermen's campfire.

Five's enormous, awkward frame swooped beneath the door. Behind her crudely stitched eyeholes and zippered mouth, something glowed. A burning like tortured fire. Alive and terrible.

Twelve strained against her bindings, desperate to help her sister, but Jack pinned his mountaineering axe across her chest.

Five hurled the two guards aside. Her horrific wail tore through the trees, grinding against Erin's ribs like a bone saw.

"Move back," Tomas ordered. "Give her room."

The scarecrow staggered forward, stabbing her rollerblades into the ground. She moaned, screamed, crashed to her knees, then viciously dragged her gloved fingers down the sides of her head. She clawed her ruined, leather skin, burrowing inside to pull out whatever was causing her such distress.

"What's happening?" wailed Twelve. "What's wrong with her?"

Ahead of them, the bushes parted. Two wickermen appeared. They wheeled a static figure into the clearing and positioned her in Number Five's path.

"She's ready to deliver," Jack urged.

"Hurry! Hurry! Hurry!" bellowed Tomas.

"Deliver?" Erin said, aghast. "Deliver what?"

With her head juddering from side to side, Five crawled across the clearing. She picked and prodded the new arrival, pruned and clipped, finishing the creation, moaning and shrieking like a frightened beast.

"I don't like it. The noise. Such a horrid noise," Erin moaned. "Make it stop."

"I'm sorry. I cannot break free," Twelve replied, helplessly rattling her chains. "I'm just not strong enough."

Five's wails rose, filling the Island of Trees with their eerie timbre.

Slowly, the scarecrow moved her quivering hands away from the new wickerman. Her screams slipped away through the woods like fleeting spirits, smothered in silence.

At the treeline, wickermen shifted.

Nervous anxiety cut the air.

Jack and Tomas stood closer than most, observing Five and the latest addition to their number.

Five gathered herself, rising awkwardly until she stood tall and crooked.

The light inside her head grew. The edges of her eye sockets vibrated with heat and colour. Skeins of dark smoke leaked through the scar on the side of her head.

Her hands shook.

Her legs trembled.

Then, with no warning at all, two columns of brilliant

light, edged with golden fire, shot from the scarecrow's eyes and buried themselves in the new wickerman's chest. The light expanded, encompassing Five's entire head, becoming a single fiery beam. In turn, the new wickerman jiggled and jostled as the light enveloped its entire body.

Erin shut her eyes and wrenched herself around the oak tree, searching for Twelve's hand. The light grew and grew until the backs of Erin's eyelids had turned through red to pink to white. When she thought herself unable to take any more, the light vanished.

She dared a glimpse.

Five had collapsed. She lay at strange angles, as though fallen from a great height, shattered and broken.

Tomas signalled to the others.

Carefully, they lifted Five and whisked her back to the climber's lodge.

For a while the new wickerman just hung there, motionless. Nothing more than a smouldering human-shaped mass of fetid grass and straw. Then, like a baby bird breaking its shell and bursting forth into the world, it shifted. The latest of Five's creations moved its fingers, then its arms. Slowly, it inspected its body. Wound its head from side to side as heat rose in chaotic spiralling vapours.

"What...am I?"

The wickermen turned to one another in confusion.

The voice was not what they had been expecting.

For this was not a wickerman at all.

This was a wickerwoman.

"Put me back!" she shrieked, her voice piercing and cold. "Put me back at once!" She shook her composted arms at Jack and Tomas. "What am I?" she yelled again, her voice lower,

seething with fury. "I'm cold. I'm wet through. I'm made of…
sticks?"

"You're a…wicker*woman*," said Tomas.

She seemed to fight the word as it burrowed into her ears.

"How did I get here? I was somewhere else. Somewhere comfortable, warm. And now—"

Jack and Tomas looked at one another.

"You didn't fight to be here?"

"No," she replied. "I didn't do anything. I was there. And now I'm here."

Her eyes left the wickermen and scanned her surroundings. "Where is…*here*?"

"The Island of Trees," said Twelve helpfully from across the clearing.

The wickerwoman rounded on her. "What is *that*?"

"That's a scarecrow," explained Jack. "And the last human girl."

"A scarecrow?" she said. "But it's talking. It's…alive."

"No more and no less than you," Twelve informed her.

"And you?" she said, switching to Erin. "The last human girl? I doubt that very much. The world is full of human girls. Millions of the wretched things."

Jack shook his head. "They're gone. All of them."

The wickerwoman considered the girl as though she were a priceless antique.

"I'm Erin. And this is Twelve," she said.

Twelve tapped her yellow pin badge helpfully. "What's your name?" she asked.

The wickerwoman's face twisted. "My name?" she said finally, as though the notion offended her. "I do not know. You, human girl, choose one for me."

"Me?"

"Yes," the wickerwoman bit. Her body shook as though she might explode. "I wish to be named by the last human girl. What say you?"

Erin scanned the forest for something that might suit this strange creature. Exasperated, she turned to Twelve. The scarecrow stared intently at the animated tangle of leaves and bracken that demanded a name.

"Katherine," Twelve said suddenly. "How about Kath—?"

"No!" Erin gasped. Her skin rippled. Her belly churned. She'd not heard that name said aloud for a long, long time. Her eyes burned a hole in the side of the scarecrow's skull. "Where did you hear that name?" she asked, eyes flooded with tears.

Twelve tilted her ghastly head. "Nowhere," she replied softly. "It just came forward. Like a performer stepping into a spotlight."

Erin shook the chains irritably. The iron cut her soft flesh. She wanted to run. As far and wide as she could. Through the forest, down the muddied banks, and skim the flat, grey waters like a lightspeed pond-skater.

Katherine.

That name was not for this wickerwoman.

That name was for—

Erin couldn't say it.

Couldn't *think* it.

She searched desperately for something, anything. Her eye snagged on the pink belt around her poncho. "Loren," she said suddenly. Her mind reeled back to the memory of the belt's previous owner, the skin on her head and hands completely removed.

The wickerwoman chewed the name over. "Loren it is."

Erin could feel Twelve's dark, questioning eyes staring down at her.

"Not now," she said, shaking her head. "Some other time."

The cold iron gnawed at her wrists again. Tears stung her eyes, but Erin refused to cry. These creatures were not worthy of her tears.

Most of the wickermen escorted Loren into the forest while she peppered them with rapid-fire questions. Jack and Tomas remained, lingering on the edge of the clearing.

Twelve slammed the back of her huge skull against the tree.

"Let us go," she said angrily, looking towards the climber's lodge. "My sister needs me."

"What can *you* do?" Tomas said. "Unless you have magic that can rival The Patchwork Woman."

Twelve tightened at the sound of that name. "I'm nothing like...*her*."

Tomas shrugged and adjusted his leafy headdress. "Then what good are you?" he said spitefully. He began to leave, then changed his mind. "You're alive. But what of it? What will you do with that life?"

Twelve hesitated. "I'll protect Erin from The Patchwork Woman. With everything I have. Right down to my last breath."

Tomas sighed. "Well, that's the tricky bit, isn't it? The Patchwork Woman is the one person that can help your sister," he said. "She could save Five from her tortures. All you need do is give her the human girl."

All eyes fell on Erin.

"Never," said Twelve. "I cannot—will not—swap one life for another."

Tomas leant back and took a long, cool breath.

"I understand," he said. "But Five doesn't have one person swimming around in that ridiculous head of hers. She has *thousands*. Would you swap one life to save all of those? Or are you so selfish that you would deny every last one of those spirits the gift of freedom because of this human girl?"

"That's enough," Jack said. "Leave them be."

Tomas stared at Jack, laughed, then strode into the trees after the wickerwoman.

Jack followed, looking back for a moment before disappearing into the dark.

"I'd never do that," Twelve said crossly. "Tomas is wrong. There must be another way to save Five. I will find it, Erin. I will find a way."

"What if there is no other way?"

"Don't say that. Never say that."

Erin rested her head against the bark. She glanced up through the forest canopy and marvelled at the newborn night sky.

"Where's Raven?" she asked after a while.

Twelve angled her huge, horned head at the sky too.

"He was in the lodge. The wickermen broke in and then…I don't know what happened after that."

"I bet this has been too much for him," Erin said, dejectedly. "He's probably flown back to Clifftop or somewhere, *anywhere*. Safe and far, far away from danger. And death. And us."

Silence engulfed them.

"I wish I had wings sometimes."

Twelve snorted in agreement.

The temperature dropped. Shadows inched across the clearing. Erin slid down the tree, sitting awkwardly on the ground. "I spent the last few years wishing for wings," she admitted. "Being at the farm, stuck on that island, was almost too much for me. I had nothing. *Nothing.* Everything that once held meaning was dead or gone, yet it surrounded me, reminded me, tortured me. Some days I was too afraid to open my eyes. I'd lie in the hayloft, bury my face in a pillow, and cry and cry and cry until I was too tired to cry anymore. And then, when I felt utterly hollowed out, I'd climb to the top of the barn and stand on the edge, look down at the hard cobbles far below, drenched to the skin, with the storm raging overhead, and—"

She bent her head to her shoulder and wiped her running nose.

"I didn't think things could get any worse than that."

Twelve said nothing.

Instead, she reached out and took Erin's hand.

It quivered like a fragile leaf.

UNEXPECTED FRIEND

Light thinned across the Island of Trees. All became quiet and still.

Two wickermen stood between Erin and the climber's lodge. They looked as if they were sleeping, but, as she fiddled with her chains, their heads swivelled to watch her.

Hours slipped by.

Darkness never truly arrived.

The forest moved in eerie shadows, blocking the sky and the glittering stars that Twelve loved so much.

Erin sat on the forest floor, her arms raised above her head.

In the middle distance, wickermen marched across the woods, checking the camp perimeter, heading down to the shoreline and back. Erin monitored their routines with interest. When she'd convinced herself that she'd memorised their entire schedule, the two wickermen outside the lodge surprised her by striding off into the woods.

She shifted up the tree, confused, craning her neck to see where they'd gone. But, no matter how she angled her head, she couldn't see any trace of them.

Not one.

"They've gone."

"I know," Twelve replied. "Why would they leave us unguarded? It seems—"

Something shifted through the undergrowth.

Erin presumed it to be a nosey hedgehog or a hungry fox, but her chains went slack and dropped to the earth.

Glimmering in the faint moonlight, a silver key appeared in the hands of a caped figure. He unlocked the iron clamps around her wrists and slung them to the ground.

"Jack?" Twelve whispered. "What are you doing?"

"Isn't it obvious," he replied. "I'm getting you out of here."

"But—?"

"There's no time for questions," he said hurriedly. "Take Erin and get to your boat as fast as you can."

Releasing the scarecrow from her bindings, Jack tossed the rope and chains into the bushes like a dangerous snake.

"It's okay," he said soothingly. "You're both going to be okay."

Erin rubbed her wrists. Twelve swung a huge arm down and grabbed her hand.

"Thank you, Jack," the scarecrow said, scanning the gloomy forest. "What about Five?"

"There's no time for that now," he urged. "Nothing can be done for her."

Twelve hesitated. She glanced back at the climber's lodge where her estranged, peculiar sister rocked in her blackwood chair.

"There'll be another time," Jack insisted. "Get Erin to safety. Go. Now."

"Yes, Twelve. Let's move," Erin added, her feet already marching across the clearing.

"Oh, and take this," Jack said. "I found it in the lodge."

Twelve looked down and there, in his grassy palm, lay the sailor's pistol.

Erin took the weapon and slotted it carefully into her belt. "Thank you, Jack. But…why?"

"There's no time. None," he urged impatiently. "Just go. Now!"

Setting off, Twelve took enormous strides through the trees. Jack, the clearing, and the climber's lodge vanished swiftly with every giant bound. Erin sprinted to keep up, her hand locked inside Twelve's.

They descended the muddy banks.

Languid ripples of The Endless Blue spread out hundreds of feet below.

Twelve skipped and jumped from rock to rock, clinging to trees with her spare hand for balance.

Below, *Lazarus* waited patiently in the shallows.

Erin smiled as the boat came into sight with its dragon figurehead and bedcloth sails.

But the ripples of relief were swiftly washed away.

A cry of anguish blasted through the trees. It reverberated and grew as it caught the fleeing pair.

More voices split the night, urgent and shrill.

"Oh no," Erin said. "They've found us. They're coming!"

"Hold tight," the scarecrow ordered as she dropped onto her backside and slid rapidly towards the shoreline with Erin riding her like a toboggan. The scarecrow's knees squeaked and groaned as she struggled to steer them safely down the sharp bank.

Erin's fingers clawed Twelve's pirate jacket.

Her eyes streamed.

Branches nicked her skin.

The scarecrow groaned as a heavy projectile fizzed through the trees and struck her spine. Another flew past them and buried itself in a tree.

"Axes!" Erin squealed. "Keep going. As fast as you can!"

More came. A storm of axes. High, low, direct, precise. They thudded into trees. Disappeared into the grey-green ferns carpeting the forest floor. Looped menacingly through the night.

Launching herself into the air once more, Twelve flew past the last line of trees and landed heavily in the shallows. Erin skidded to a halt. Poncho and dungarees caked in filth, she dropped into *Lazarus* as Twelve hauled her boots out of the thick, gloopy silt. Once on board, the scarecrow stopped and turned to the sky.

"Twelve," Erin bleated urgently. "What are you doing?"

"Raven," she said. "We can't leave him behind."

"He has wings. He'll find us." Erin collected the oars and forced them into Twelve's hands. "Let's go. Now!"

Twelve pushed *Lazarus* away from the shore.

Screams and wails rang through the island. Axes and wooden spears splashed violently into the water, left and right, taking nicks out of the boat.

Erin reached back and clutched the handle of a small throwing axe embedded in Twelve's spine. It came away easily and, as she dropped it into the boat, Jack emerged at the tree line, waving frantically.

Erin squinted.

What was the wickerman doing?

He looked anxious, desperate.

Axes zoomed past his head.

"Wait!" he yelled, now wading towards them.

Twelve and Erin looked at one another, then back at the half-soaked wickerman.

"Please, wait!"

An axe spun through the trees, taking a chunk of Jack's shoulder.

"Please, Erin. They know what I did. You have to take me with you!"

CLIFFTOP

Twelve rowed away from the Island of Trees at incredible speed. The distraught cries of the wickermen and their deadly axes rang across The Endless Blue. When the island was no more than a fleck on the horizon, Twelve eased on the oars, letting *Lazarus* drift gently across the water. Erin sat with her back to the scarecrow, staring at the horizon, the sun bleeding into existence. The haunting memories of the Island of Trees shuddered through her, stirring uneasily.

Twelve was unusually quiet.

Erin looked at her. "What is it?"

"I'm worried about Number Five."

"We all are."

"Will she be okay?"

"I hope so."

"That's not very reassuring."

"There's nothing reassuring about mortality," Erin said darkly. "Living things are always one bad decision away from the abyss."

The scarecrow massaged her rubber-gloved hands. "How do you live with that? Knowing that when you wake each morning, and look out upon the world, it could be your last?"

Erin shrugged. "It's best not to, I suppose."

She wondered where this darkness had come from.

Raven's fault, she decided. The blackbird was always muttering about the bleakest, most downright morbid things. But he was gone now. Erin had no idea where.

Instead, they had Jack.

Lazarus sat lower in the water with the caped wickerman on board.

He took some time adjusting to the motion of the boat but, once settled, sat with his arms and legs knotted around the mast. It looked uncomfortable to Erin, but Jack insisted he was happier sat awkwardly on a boat in the middle of The Endless Blue than in the hands of his vengeful companions.

He shifted around the mast and faced Twelve, his feathered cape pulled tightly around his shoulders. "Where are we going?"

"North," Twelve replied.

Jack nodded. "What's in the north?"

"Raven told us to head north," she answered, pulling on the oars. "So north it is."

Jack looked at the panoramic sky that capped the world in yellow-grey bands, dotted with faint, distant stars.

"How?" he asked. "Do you have a compass?"

Twelve nodded towards the sky.

"There," she said. "I'm following that star. The brightest star in the whole sky. The North Star."

Jack seemed confused. "How does that—?"

"Don't worry about it," Twelve replied. "Raven said follow the stars, so we follow the stars."

"And Raven is *who* again?"

Erin spun, nestling up to the wickerman.

"He was, I mean he *is*, a blackbird. Friend, navigator, and speaker of dark truths."

Jack fidgeted. "A talking bird?"

Erin shrugged, an eyebrow raised.

"Whatever next," Jack went on. "And he was with you on the Island of Trees?"

"Yes," Erin said. "He hid when you came bursting into the climber's lodge. I'm ever so worried about him."

"I'm sure he's fine," Jack said breezily. "Tomas and the others have no interest in birds, even ones that talk."

Jack wrung his cape over the side. "You know, I'm incredibly grateful you came back for me."

"Well, thank you for freeing us," Twelve said.

Erin smiled at the wickerman. "Why did you help us?"

Jack took a moment to gather himself. "I feel terrible for betraying the other wickermen," he began. "But they were going to hand you over to The Patchwork Woman. Tomas is completely obsessed with this notion of being a human spirit and getting put back in a *proper* body. He would take any path, no matter how distasteful, to make it so."

Erin and Twelve glanced nervously at one another.

"We have no boats or seafaring vessels," Jack went on. "The only way to get you there would be to use your own boat. But, while they argued over which of us would be strong enough to row you to The Patchwork Woman, we made our escape."

"How could Tomas just hand me over like that?"

"I don't think he saw you as a human girl with feelings and dreams of your own. All he saw was his own, selfish ambition. His own greed. I couldn't be a part of that, no matter the cost."

"The cost?"

"This," Jack said, looking down at his body of weaved

twine, branches, and hard-packed earth. "Tomas promised us all a human body with flesh and blood and bone. This tangle of leaves and bracken is destined to wither and rot."

"Human flesh expires too."

"But time is a precious commodity," Jack said. "Like this, I have weeks...perhaps months. To be honest, I was happier in the head of Number Five, but I didn't know it at the time. If I could get back there, I would. It was turbulent and confusing, but at least it was safe. Out here, in the world, I just don't know who I am, what the next day will bring or who I can trust."

"You can trust us," Erin said immediately, putting a hand on Jack's damaged shoulder. "We're your friends. Right, Twelve?"

"Of course," she said. "And what a strange bunch of friends we are."

Twelve rowed for hours, hauling *Lazarus* across The Endless Blue.

Erin helped Jack repair his damaged shoulder. She asked him questions, told him about her life before The Many Years Storm, and listed all the scarecrows she'd made for Coldharbour Farm.

Twelve followed one North Star after the next, zigzagging across the faceless water like an enormous join-the-dots. The music box played and Lucretia danced and Erin finished reading *The Wizard of Oz* aloud and moved onto *Frankenstein*. Hours became days. The sun and the moon danced around one another. The sky shifted through shades of grey.

Erin was dozing when Twelve shot up.

"What is it?" she blurted, waking suddenly.

"A tower," said Twelve. "A huge tower of rock. With a strange black cloud circling above."

"That's no cloud." Erin smiled, standing next to Twelve.

"It's not?"

"They're birds."

"Birds?"

"Excellent work, Twelve."

"Oh, yes, thank you. Sorry, what?"

"I don't know how you've done it but I think we've found Clifftop."

A colossal tower of rock jutted out of the ocean like a lone candle on an enormous cake. Beneath the surface, outlying rocks and jagged stones nicked the bottom of *Lazarus* and splashed water playfully over the sides.

Twelve navigated as best she could through the treacherous approaches to Clifftop.

A swell of black ballooned in the air above. It moved with great speed, circling the rock, changing shape and density like a turbo-charged cloud.

"There's so many," Twelve marvelled, her head twisted back.

Some birds broke away from the flock. They swooped across the bow of the boat, squawking madly.

Erin smiled, waving as each tore past. She saw sparrows and cranes, kingfishers and eagles, seagulls and hummingbirds, toucans, parrots, owls, ibis, and hundreds more. The variety in colour, size, form, and sound made her skin fizz.

"This is amazing!"

Twelve nodded in agreement.

Jack didn't appear as impressed. He clung nervously to the mast as the birds thundered by.

"What's the matter?" Erin said, trying to pull the wickerman to his feet to enjoy the amazing display spread across the pale sky.

Jack looked down at himself, slowly untying the feathered cape from his shoulders and kicking it beneath Twelve's armchair.

"Oh. I see."

Jack gave Erin a lopsided look.

"It's not just the cape—and, for the record, I collected all the feathers from the forest floor—it's more than that." He swung his arms open. "I'm basically a walking banquet."

"You need a disguise," Twelve said.

Erin pulled the blanket from beneath her seat and swept it around Jack's shoulders. Her pink belt stretched around his waist. Pulling it tight, she fastened the blanket in place. She looked up at the crow's nest and pointed. Twelve unscrewed the bucket and handed it to Erin.

"It needs eyeholes," she told the scarecrow. "Or he'll be utterly blind."

Twelve pulled an arrow from beneath her black dress. She punctured two rough Xs into the bucket and scratched a broken smile below. Erin took the bucket and dropped it over Jack's head.

"Stinks of bird in here," he complained.

Erin stepped back and giggled.

"Perfect. You look like a homeless cyborg. Or recipient of the wooden spoon in a Tin-Man-costume competition."

"He looks less like food," Twelve said. "And that's the best we can hope for, I suppose."

"It's hot in here too," said Jack inside the bucket. His voice had become muffled and edged with a metallic twang. "Is this entirely necessary?"

Before Erin or Twelve had time to respond, a penguin

burst from the water and landed heavily inside the boat. The strange bird sprawled around, finding its feet.

The penguin was long and sleek, equal parts black and white with a thin line circling his chin. He made a throaty bleat before shaking the water from his wings and investigating the faces that bore down on him.

"Greetings and welcome," he said proudly, pulling his belly in and standing as straight as possible. "I am Cairo. A chinstrap penguin of Clifftop. Emissary to his eminence, Lord Bavorski Beetlestone, Governor of this fair isle and one true ruler of The Endless Blue."

"Hello, Cairo," Twelve said and tapped her yellow pin badge. "My name is Number Twelve. And this is Erin and Jack."

The penguin nodded at them in turn, cocking his head curiously as his eyes came to rest on the wickerman.

"Jack, huh? What kind of creature are you?"

"He's a scarecrow," Twelve said immediately. "As am I. And Erin is our creator."

This, impossibly, seemed to satisfy the penguin.

"We had another in our number, a member of your most esteemed host, but he got left behind," Erin added.

Cairo hopped onto the edge of the boat.

"Who was your other?"

"A blackbird. Named Raven."

The penguin waddled down the boat. "Raven?" he said, his voice darkening. "A blackbird? Called Raven?"

Erin shifted uneasily.

"I know that sounds silly but, yes, that's him."

"It cannot be," Cairo said, looking to the heavens. "Raven died. A year ago. Maybe more."

"Perhaps you're mistaken," she tried. "Maybe it was another blackbird called Raven."

Cairo let out a mirthless squawk. "Why would there be two blackbirds with the same name? No. The blackbird you've met is not named Raven. He's an imposter. A dark assassin. A malevolent snake that has coiled his deceitful lies around your fragile minds. His motives are clearly a matter of much dread and concern."

"How can you be so sure?" Erin asked, wondering if all birds talked in the same dark tone. "How do you know that Raven died?"

"He went to The Scrapers," Cairo went on. "A research mission, reconnaissance for our Lord, Bavorski Beetlestone. Raven did not return. Birds who do not return are birds that cannot return. Birds that cannot return are dead birds."

"Perhaps he chose *not* to return," Erin suggested.

"Impossible," Cairo spat. "Betrayal and abandonment are not characteristics indicative of the sons and daughters of Clifftop."

His tiny black eyes widened.

Erin shuddered.

"No. Raven is dead. Dead as doornails, as dodos, as yesterday."

"Raven used those self-same words," Erin said, smiling at the memory. "You sound just like him."

"Whatever do you mean?"

"The…um…" she began, "Language. Dark and, well…"

"Disturbing?" Twelve tried.

"Pessimistic," Jack suggested.

"Hopeless," Erin added. "Yes. That's it. Dark and hopeless."

Cairo sighed. "No one understands birds."

119

"What's there to understand?" Jack asked.

The penguin hopped off the edge of the boat and balanced precariously on Jack's crossed legs.

"A scarecrow?" he said, flicking his head from side to side. "You're the weirdest looking scarecrow I've ever seen. You look…malformed and corrosive." Cairo sniffed. "You're decaying, like withered old leaves, gone hard and brown from time and negligence. You're a pestilence. A walking death."

"Okay, I get it," Jack said, raising his hands.

"I see your problem," Cairo announced, eyeing the thatched, mossy fingers hanging before him.

Jack hurried his hands away and turned his bucket-covered head to the water.

"You're not a scarecrow. Well, not in a traditional sense," the penguin decided. "But it matters not. You will all perish, sooner or later."

"What is it you want?" Erin said, becoming tired of Cairo's bleak patter.

"Me?" he trilled. "Nothing. Nothing at all. *You* invaded *our* territory. Like a marauding virus, I might add. But, Bavorski Beetlestone saw your boat approaching. Seafaring vessels are few and far between these days. He has a request to make of you. Payment, if you will, for breaching his sacred waters."

"No-one owns the sea," Erin said. "Well, not anymore. All the people are gone."

"Are birds less than people?" Cairo scoffed. "These are our waters, and our skies above. None shall pass without payment or retribution."

"You own all the water and all the sky?" Twelve asked, amazed.

"Well, no," Cairo muttered. "We share it with The Scrapers

and the Blue King."

"Raven warned us about The Scrapers."

"Darkness dwells in that place. Shadows and malice. Death on feathered darts."

"You're off again," Erin said, stemming Cairo's dark spiral.

"The Blue King?" Twelve asked. "Who's he?"

Cairo moved stiffly towards the scarecrow.

"I'll let Bavorski Beetlestone himself tell you of his great adversary. For his request involves the Blue King, after all. Follow me. And mind your step. We can't have the three of you sinking to the bottom of The Endless Blue before you've made amends for this obnoxious intrusion!"

BAVORSKI BEETLESTONE

Cairo emerged from the water at the base of Clifftop where a narrow inlet led beneath a hood of rock. Twelve stopped *Lazarus* in the shadowy waters and slung a rope around a boulder.

Above them, birds landed and blasted off in thousands of chaotic patterns from the gigantic rock. Erin watched, amazed by the lack of collisions.

A squawking, scraping, beating, hungry din ricocheted inside the small cave.

The noise was incredible.

"Now what?" asked Twelve.

"Now," Cairo replied, "we climb."

Erin lent back, staring up at the spiralling heights.

She stumbled, unbalanced.

Twelve put out a long arm to steady her.

"But it's so high."

"Yes," Twelve added. "How are we supposed to—?"

Cairo looked appalled.

"Do you really expect Bavorski Beetlestone, Governor of this fair isle and one true ruler of The Endless Blue, to fly down and treat with you here, on the docks of Clifftop, like some common pirate?"

"That would be most beneficial," Twelve said.

Erin wondered just what sort of bird Bavorski Beetlestone might be. A giant eagle? A courageous sea hawk? A wise old owl? Perhaps he wasn't a bird at all.

Cairo snapped his beak. "Follow me, scarecrow."

Erin turned to Twelve. Could Bavorski Beetlestone be one of Twelve's sisters? One of her lost scarecrows from Coldharbour Farm?

The penguin hopped expertly from rock to rock, slowly ascending. He shimmied along a thin escarpment that ran around the belly of Clifftop and disappeared from sight.

"I can't go that way," Jack said, holding out his frayed hands. "Send down a basket or a rope and I'll happily meet you up there."

"Don't worry, Jack," said Erin. "You stay here. Twelve and I have got this."

Twelve didn't look convinced.

Erin bound after the penguin. She clutched the wet rock, rising above Twelve's head, and worked her way along the tiny ledge. Twelve made short work of the first few metres. Her long limbs lifted her quickly until she caught up with Erin.

Ahead, Cairo hoisted himself onto a ledge filled with nesting birds.

Twelve and Erin peeked over.

An albatross screeched at the top of her voice, making Erin slip. She hung for a moment by one hand, her skin alive with fright. Twelve grabbed her waist and launched her skyward.

The albatross retreated to her nest, snapping angrily, wings wide.

"Don't mind her," Cairo insisted, shooing the albatross

away. "Noisy so-and-so."

Erin picked herself up and looked out to sea.

They were about fifty metres up now. A small clutch of wind gathered. Erin let it brush against her fingertips and ruffle her hair.

Twelve joined them, towering over the nesting birds who tightened themselves over their precious eggs. "How much further?" she asked.

"Are you tired?" Cairo mocked. "We're only a fraction of the way. You can sleep when you're dead. That's what my mother told me!"

"But I don't sleep."

"Well, that's nice," Cairo said indifferently. "Perhaps you'll never die."

They climbed again. Round and round and round Clifftop they spun, gripping sharp rocks and slippery ledges that hung precariously over the increasingly distant sea.

On a crumbling plateau, over halfway up, Erin leant against Twelve.

"I cannot go on," she said. "I don't know how the penguin does it."

"It's mind over matter," Cairo snapped from above. "By all rights I should not be able to climb this high, but here I am, climbing. Go figure."

Something occurred to Erin. "You're a flightless bird."

"Someone's read a book!"

"Seems utterly barbaric to make a flightless bird guide us to the top. Why not use one that can fly? That would be far more sensible."

Cairo peered down at them from the next ledge.

"Sensible," he scoffed. "Just because I am not best suited for a job, does not mean I cannot fulfil it." He spun on his flippers and hauled himself higher still. "We're an equal opportunities community here."

Twelve dropped onto her haunches.

"Climb on my back," she told Erin. "I cannot carry you up, as I need both hands, but if you can hold on tight, I think we can make it together."

Erin did as she was told. She slid her exhausted arms around Twelve's neck and dug her knees into the stiff rear beams. Her feet came to rest on the scarecrow's hips.

"Do you think Bavorski Beetlestone is one of your sisters?" Erin whispered, contemplating the idea more and more the further they climbed.

"I don't know," Twelve replied, hauling them both up. "Bavorski Beetlestone is an awfully strange name for a scarecrow. What's wrong with her number? I think Twelve is a brilliant name. Says everything about me. I don't think I could be a Carrie or a Beth or a Nerina. Not even a Persephone. Those are human names. I'm a scarecrow. And Twelve is a scarecrow name."

Erin's eyes were streaming onto Twelve's shoulders by the time they emerged on the windy summit of Clifftop. A triangular area, large and flat, was whipped by a vicious wind between three chiselled pillars. Vultures perched on top of each, peering down at Twelve and Erin with hungry, scarlet eyes.

One of the vultures rustled its wings and screeched, sharp and cold.

Cairo waddled between the columns and turned to face the visitors.

Erin scanned for any sign of Bavorski Beetlestone,

wondering what sort of creature their leader might be.

Twelve eyed the panting penguin with interest. "Are you—?" she began.

"Heavens, no," Cairo replied, frowning. "Me? Bavorski Beetlestone? Ha! You'd like that, wouldn't you? A flightless bird, Governor of a perilously high column of rock in the middle of The Endless Blue. A devilish thought for a devil-faced scarecrow."

"What kind of a name is Bavorski Beetlestone anyway?" Erin said. "It's such a mouthful."

Twelve nodded.

The penguin gave them a withering look.

"You know nothing of birds, do you?"

Erin felt her face flush. "I'm sorry. I didn't mean to offend you. It's just—"

"We all have two names. Much like you humans, although *we* did it first," Cairo said. "But we use Bavorski Beetlestone's full name because he is Governor of this fair isle and one true ruler of The Endless Blue. It's the law. As old as time. As ancient as Death herself."

The penguin's eyes became lost in the distance, perhaps drifting into some primal memory, passed down through generations of chinstraps.

"So," Twelve said. "What's your full name?"

"Olaf Cairochase," he replied quickly. "Cairo for day-to-day use, you see. And up here we have Tammerin Bloodpost, Arnold Fleshmask and Horatio Bonedark."

He pointed to each vulture in turn.

"Blood, Flesh, and Bone," Erin whispered, smiling at their grisly names.

"Quite so," Cairo said.

126

"Ah, so then, Bavorski Beetlestone is just…Beetle."

Cairo shot Erin a dark look. "Never," he said, rushing towards her. "We *never* call him that. And you'll remember it well, young lady."

He straightened himself.

Pulled his wings and belly in.

Cleared his throat.

"Silence, please. Behold, Lord Bavorski Beetlestone, Governor of this fair isle and one true ruler of The Endless Blue."

The penguin swept away, disappearing theatrically behind one of the stone pillars.

A head appeared from the other side of the summit. It was not a bird's head but that of a creature Erin never imagined in all her wildest dreams would be at the summit of Clifftop.

A dog.

He had a long, elegant face and floppy ears. His body was naturally thin, white with faint dappled brown markings along each side.

As the dog emerged, a curious-looking creature could be seen on his back. He was also predominantly white, with feathers tipped black, and a bright orange face around a razor-sharp beak. His long, pencil-thin legs were bent at a peculiar angle. He seemed to be holding them up to prevent them dragging on the dusty stone.

Erin couldn't be sure but he looked like a secretary bird.

Skittish and elegant.

The dog came to a rehearsed halt between the pillars and lowered himself. His tail wagged happily in the dirt. The vultures howled distasteful noise that, in some backward corner of the world, might be considered a fanfare.

"I am Bavorski Beetlestone," the secretary bird said, his voice clipped and severe. "Governor of this fair isle and one true ruler of The Endless Blue."

Erin grinned at the pomp and nonsense of the bird's entrance.

"I'm Erin, last surviving daughter of humanity and, um, steward of Coldharbour Farm. This is Twelve. She's...a scarecrow. Builder of boats and scarer of...crows."

Twelve tapped her yellow pin badge.

"Yes. Terrifying," Bavorski Beetlestone said. "And what brings you, and this monster, to Clifftop?"

"Food. Adventure," Twelve said, ignoring the insult. "And to find those we've lost. Erin's brother. And my scarecrow sisters?"

Bavorski Beetlestone dismounted the dog and approached. "Sisters?" he said. "Who ever heard of a scarecrow having sisters?"

Twelve glanced at Erin.

"Well," the girl said. "They're not sisters in the traditional sense, but I made each of them myself, so—"

"Replicas then," the bird decided. "Nothing more."

"No. Not at all," Erin told him. "They're all incredibly different, unique in their own special way."

"Do not disagree with me, young lady," Bavorski Beetlestone snapped.

The vultures shifted restlessly on their columns.

"They *are* my sisters," Twelve insisted. "I found one of them already. Her name is Five. She's deeply troubled. I must find a way to help her."

"I do not care for the troubles of your hotchpotch, replica, mutant family."

Twelve stiffened.

Bavorski Beetlestone rounded on Erin. "And as for human beings, we thought you'd all gone the way of the dinosaurs. Brother, you say?"

Erin's eyes widened. She retrieved the photo and held it out.

"His name is Clyde. He'll be older now, but I imagine his smile will be the same."

The bird shook his head. "I have waters to watch and skies to govern. Do you think the affairs of scarecrows and human girls should interest me? There are greater matters that require my attention than your petty squabbles and desires."

"The Patchwork Woman," Twelve said.

"And the Blue King," Erin added.

Bavorski Beetlestone rocketed into the air and landed on the nearest pillar. Bone clattered to the ground with an agonised screech.

"What do you know of The Patchwork Woman and the Blue King?" he asked suspiciously, pacing in circles, wings outstretched.

"Almost nothing," said Erin.

Bavorski Beetlestone laughed.

"But we do know that The Patchwork Woman is looking for a human girl." Erin swallowed hard. "She's looking for me."

"And what does she want with you?"

"We don't know that either, but it cannot be good. She promised to grant the wickermen anything they desired, give them back their bodies, if they handed me over. They say she possesses a dark magic."

"Dark magic?" Bavorski Beetlestone scoffed. "Wickermen? What in the name of The Endless Blue is one of those?"

"Our friend Jack is a wickerman," Twelve said. "He's down there in our boat. He couldn't make it up here I'm afraid. He's not built for climbing."

Bavorski Beetlestone flicked his head. The three vultures plunged towards the sea. Moments later, Jack soared into view. He circled the rock beneath the talons of the vultures. Pitiful cries filled the air. Then he dropped unceremoniously onto hard stone.

"Jack, is it? Nice of you to join us," Bavorski Beetlestone said, kicking the metal bucket off his head. "Oh, I see. He's made of sticks and leaves and dirt. How revolting. What was the meaning of the bucket?"

Jack reached around helplessly for his disguise.

Twelve dragged the wickerman to his feet.

"He was afraid you were going to eat him," Erin explained.

"Eat him?" Bavorski Beetlestone laughed darkly. "We're far more likely to make a nest out of him."

The vultures, now back on their perches, croaked mercilessly.

Jack reached for his axe. "Stay away from me."

"Oh, calm down will you," Bavorski Beetlestone said, sounding tired. "We're not going to eat you, or make you into a nest, or use you as kindling, or anything like that."

"Then why make us climb up here?" asked Twelve.

"Cairo said you had a request," Erin added.

The secretary bird approached. "For many years Clifftop and The Scrapers have been at war," he told her quietly. "The Blue King and his infidels rose from the ashes of the human race. They claimed ownership of The Endless Blue, but the sea and the sky have always belonged to the birds. We couldn't let them take it from us. And we most certainly couldn't...

share it."

"Why ever not?" Erin said. "There's so much to go around."

Bavorski snapped his beak.

"But times have changed," he said. "The Patchwork Woman now claims The Endless Blue as her own too. We've sent spies to BootHill. Those that returned have not been the same. An ill-wind has forsaken their feathers. A strange darkness toils in their hearts."

Erin and Twelve caught each other's eye.

"She commands monsters," the bird said. "Within and without—"

His feathers shuddered beneath a rising wind.

He paced in circles, clearly upset.

"I need you to take something to the Blue King."

"Something?" Erin said.

"A gift," Bavorski Beetlestone said. "A token of friendship. Of alliance."

"What sort of gift?"

Bavorski Beetlestone looked at the dog.

"Socks."

SOCKS

The dog cocked his head and raised a curious ear at the sound of his name. "He's a lurcher," Bavorski Beetlestone went on. "Good natured animal. Loyal and friendly. A steady ride."

"Does he talk?" Erin asked, as if it were the simplest thing in the world.

"Talk?" Bavorski Beetlestone spluttered. "He's a dog. Of course he doesn't talk. He barks."

The secretary bird whistled. Two notes, low then high.

Socks replied with a solitary, cheerful bark.

"See?"

"But *you* talk," Twelve said to Bavorski Beetlestone. "And I talk. And the wickerman too. Why not him?"

Bavorski Beetlestone looked incredulous. "I cannot speak for the scarecrows and the wickermen, but birds have always been able to speak. We were talking long before the humans worked it out, long before they created fire, long before they built castles and computers and scarecrows and wickermen. We've been here, talking, since the first thing slithered from the water and spread its wings."

Socks padded happily towards Erin. She ran her fingers over his soft fur and wrapped her arms around his frail body.

"A human that loves dogs," Bavorski Beetlestone rattled on. "How utterly predictable. And," he accentuated with a raised wingtip, "exactly what I'm relying on."

Out of nowhere, Twelve launched forward and grabbed Bavorski Beetlestone around the neck. She hoisted him into the air. The vultures screamed a warning. A swarm of birds descended on Clifftop, wings wide, voices crying out.

"What do you want with her?" the scarecrow asked, shaking the secretary bird, his long legs dangling helplessly. "The wickermen wanted to give her to The Patchwork Woman. Is that what consumes your mind too? How does the Blue King fit into all this? Is he in league with The Patchwork Woman? Or perhaps he *is* The Patchwork Woman in some dark disguise."

Bavorski Beetlestone coughed and choked manically.

The scarecrow eased her grip so the bird could reply.

"No, you fool," he squawked. "Your theories—no matter how colourful—are disastrously wide of the mark. The Blue King and I became adversaries during The Many Years Storm."

More than a hundred birds crashed through the pillars and surrounded Twelve. Many of them clawed the scarecrow's arms, legs, jacket. Several more adventurous birds latched on to her head and began pecking at the worms and bugs that wriggled in her eye sockets.

"Enough!" cried Bavorski Beetlestone.

The swirling mass dissolved, leaving a blanket of feathers at Twelve's feet.

"You can put me down now," the secretary bird said calmly.

Twelve glanced at Erin, Jack, and Socks, huddled together by Clifftop's edge.

Erin gave her an eager nod.

Bavorski Beetlestone dropped to the ground with a relieved whimper. He shook his feathers and spun in agitated circles. "That was unkind and uncalled for," he rasped. "Once is a mistake. Twice is your end."

"I'm sorry," Twelve said. "I thought you were going to do something horrible to Erin. I'll never let that happen. Never. No matter the cost."

"Admirable. Highly admirable. But if I intended to hurt your friend, you'd be utterly helpless. Believe me, you and the wickerman are no match for the power of Clifftop. We are afraid of...nothing."

"Except?" Erin said, sensing Bavorski Beetlestone's reticence.

The bird eyed her curiously.

"The Patchwork Woman," Erin guessed. The bird tightened. "You *are* afraid of her."

"Fear is not something that—"

"What does she have over you?" Erin said.

"What did she offer you?" Twelve added.

Bavorski Beetlestone straightened his neck and puffed out his chest.

"We do not fear The Patchwork Woman. We fear nothing. Not shadows, or arrows, or Death herself," he said. "But The Patchwork Woman is like a thousand deaths, a plague upon The Endless Blue. We cannot overcome her alone."

His eyes shifted to the horizon.

"That's why you need the Blue King."

"An alliance. Yes," Bavorski Beetlestone said, strolling to the lip of Clifftop. "Not one that I relish, but our options are slim."

"Wouldn't you rather die than align yourself with your enemy?" Jack ventured.

"The enemy of my enemy is my friend," the bird bit, his eyes still on the edge of the world. "But, yes. Some of us would rather perish than join with the Blue King. I am not one of those. And I command here. History will be of my making, to whatever end. Now, take the dog and be on your way."

"Why should we?" Erin asked. "This is not our fight. We're just looking for food and my brother and more of Twelve's sisters. Your war is your own."

Bavorski Beetlestone spun. "That's where you're wrong, last human girl."

Erin's tongue turned to sandpaper.

"If The Patchwork Woman is truly after you, then you should care dearly about this war. If Clifftop and The Scrapers fail to defeat her, then what hope remains? If she remains alive, she will find you. No matter where you run. No matter where you hide. She is inevitable."

Erin pulled her poncho around her shoulders.

"Why Socks?" Twelve asked. "What does he mean to the Blue King?"

"The dog once belonged to him."

Erin gasped. "The dog belonged to a demon?"

Bavorski Beetlestone laughed darkly. "Whatever the Blue King is, the dog meant the world to him."

Erin's skin prickled.

"Now, be gone!"

And with that, Bavorski Beetlestone vanished over the side of Clifftop, soaring away at the head of a mighty column. The birds created a huge shadow on the ocean, as though some monstrous leviathan lurked beneath the surface.

"Come on," Cairo said, appearing beside them. "Just count to three and step off. It's dead easy."

Below, the water stretched away in every direction, flat and calm.

"Sorry? What now?" Erin said, aghast. "You want us to jump?"

"So many questions with you," he replied. "Yes, jump. The water's very deep. You *should* be perfectly fine. It's not like I'm asking you to walk the plank into a sea of ravenous sharks, or plummet onto a bed of jagged rocks."

Erin's face remained unchanged.

"I've done it hundreds of times. Look at me. I'm not dead. Well, not *yet* anyway."

Cairo prepared himself, ready to jump. At the last moment he stopped. "Not going to jump, are you?"

"No," they all replied.

Socks watched intently, his tail wagging.

"I can carry Erin down," Twelve suggested. "But I'll have to come back for Jack and Socks."

Cairo tutted. "We haven't got time for your heroics."

He whistled and threw himself over the side.

Blood, Flesh, and Bone swept down from their pillars, claws outstretched.

"Not this again," the wickerman wailed, sailing into the air.

They soon returned and lifted Socks by his collar.

"Are you sure this is safe?" Erin asked as the vulture's claws dug through her poncho, seizing her by the dungaree straps.

"Be quiet," Flesh croaked.

"Stay still. Don't panic," added Blood.

And with that, Erin was airborne.

The sensation was new, but also familiar.

It reminded her of being on the water, at the will of the elements. Thermals rushed beneath her now rather than tides and blustering winds. Flight was exhilarating, breathtaking, and a dollop of terrifying, too. They skimmed low, dragging Erin's toes through the cool water, and deposited her recklessly beside the boat.

Erin watched the vultures carry Twelve around the pockmarked tower of Clifftop. Beady eyes and beaks protruded from every nook and crevice as the seven-and-a-half-foot scarecrow with a bison's skull for a head and cement-filled boots went flying past.

It was quite the spectacle.

With everyone on board *Lazarus*, and Socks sitting with Erin at the bow, panting contentedly, Twelve picked up the oars. She took a long, cool breath, straightened her bird-pecked pirate jacket and pushed away from the rocks.

Cairo waved one of his flippers slowly from side to side in a macabre farewell. Then, as they drifted away, he rolled his shoulders and began the long climb up Clifftop once again.

THE SCRAPERS

Twelve turned *Lazarus* south, keeping the latest estimation of the North Star at her back. The sun and moon lingered low on the horizon. Erin found it hard to tell them apart.

Jack took off the pink belt and returned the blanket. He fidgeted with his damaged shoulder. The vultures had ripped through the bindings and loosened his stuffing. Finishing his repairs, he returned the metal bucket to the top of the mast.

Erin scanned the sky.

Where was Raven? And why did Cairo think he was dead?

Night bled across the sky, thin and grey.

Stars appeared. A billion eyes, a billion miles away.

Socks sat calmly beside Erin, head on her lap, tail swaying happily from side to side. She fussed him and smoothed his ears. The lurcher made contented whimpering sounds. His back legs kicked in tiny circles. Erin watched the dog drift into long, sumptuous dreams while Twelve pulled evenly on the oars. The rhythm, a reassuring sound. But, despite her exhaustion, she couldn't find sleep.

Even Jack had drifted off.

What do wickermen dream of?

Tomas's idea of wickermen being powered by human

spirits returned to her. Was there even the slightest truth in that? Looking at Twelve, she had to concede that his theory was at least possible, if not completely plausible.

"Aren't you tired?" Twelve asked.

"Nah," Erin replied. "Too much excitement."

Twelve nodded.

"That's what Ma used to say when we couldn't sleep. Normally the night before my birthday, or a big holiday, or Christmas." She looked at the huge scarecrow. "Now? I don't know. Perhaps excitement is the wrong word."

"Anticipation?"

"Worry."

They sat together, silently scanning the skies for whatever truths dwelled in the stars.

Erin smiled and felt happy.

Just for a moment.

With everything going on, she felt guilty for taking a moment and feeling something other than horror and fear and worry. But the smile endured, pondering the fragility of her life beneath the magnificence of the universe.

The sky ripened. Clear and crisp. The heavens were on heightened display, intense and mesmerising. Erin could make out faint blossoms of colour—cobalt, maroon, sage— swarming between the pinholes of light and the promise of dark.

She wound the music box and let Lucretia spin beneath the stars.

Morning arrived, bland and cold.

Erin snorted as she woke from what could only have been an hour's sleep.

The moon had shuffled below the horizon.

The stars endured, however dimmed.

Twelve ploughed the oars into the water, her current choice of North Star at six o'clock.

And then, to their surprise and relief, a collection of dark rectangular shapes materialised at the edge of the world.

The Scrapers.

Twelve had found them.

As they drifted closer, Raven's cries of distress echoed through Erin's head. But they pressed on, *Lazarus* carrying them to their fate. The seas surrounding The Scrapers teemed with dead bodies. They hung on the surface like revolting, putrefied buoys. *Lazarus* eased by, causing them to roll and slosh in the filthy water. Erin covered her mouth as a putrid stench swamped the boat. The aroma shocked Jack and Socks, pulling them from their dreams into a living hell.

The wrecks of shipping vessels and pleasure craft littered the surface surrounded by broken wood, sailcloth, and punctured inflatables. Twelve scooped a lifebuoy from the water and tucked it down the side of her armchair.

Ahead, Erin could make out a dozen huge blocks. They appeared to float on the water. The sharp edges of each were made of huge iron struts and concrete. Glass panels suspended between each reflecting the sun-smeared sea. Satellite dishes and antennae sprouted from some. Railings and ladders ran up the sides. Precarious gangways criss-crossed overhead. A web of steel and iron.

Lazarus drifted between the first of The Scrapers, cloaking the boat in a shivering shadow.

"Ashewood City," Erin breathed.

Socks curled himself on her lap, shaking nervously.

"I remember coming here. Being down…there."

She trailed her fingers in the water. Her gaze darted across the huge buildings that emerged from the depths.

Something crackled all around. Feedback, high and piercing.

"Halt, Intruder!" thundered a voice. It echoed several times, as if growing further and further away. "What is your business here?"

They looked around, searching for the source. It seemed to be coming from every direction, bouncing off glass and steel.

Twelve's attention fixed on a line of figures, silhouetted against the sun, congregated on the edge of each Scraper.

She stiffened.

Erin noticed. "What is it?" she asked.

"Demons," Twelve whispered.

The figures stood motionless.

Bows gripped in one hand.

Arrows nocked in the other.

Erin tried to count them, but quickly gave up. There were at least a hundred, undoubtedly more.

An arrow whistled through the air and thudded into the mast by Jack's head. It wobbled for a moment then juddered to a deadly halt.

Socks whined sorrowfully, burying his head further into Erin's lap.

"What is your business here? Answer me!" the voice roared again. "Answer the Blue King. Or perish!"

Twelve plunged the oars into the water, bringing *Lazarus* to a stop.

Erin scanned the dark figures. Each rooftop held a vast horde of troops, bows and arrows hovering, waiting for the order to fire. She wondered just how much damage those arrows would do. They'd most likely splinter Twelve's arms, or shatter her spine, or crack her head, or loosen her fixings in a way that meant she'd simply fall to pieces. Jack would be torn and shredded, but easily re-made. But none of that truly mattered when she considered herself and Socks. Their soft skin and delicate innards wouldn't last more than a few seconds under an arrow storm of that magnitude.

Escape seemed an impossibility.

But escape was not their goal.

The scarecrow stood, waved her long, wooden arms and rubber-gloved hands. "We come in peace!" she exclaimed. The boat listed dangerously under her weight. "We come bearing gifts."

Her voice reverberated against The Scrapers and disappeared out to sea.

"Gifts from Bavorski Beetlestone!"

"Emissaries of Bavorski Beetlestone are not welcome here," the voice said again, then paused. "What…gift?"

Erin picked up Socks and cradled the slender dog in her arms.

"Here," she said. "He asked us to return your dog."

Silence hung in the air.

"It is your dog, isn't it?"

Water sloshed against *Lazarus*.

Bows creaked high above.

"The dog was once mine," the voice said eventually. "Stolen from me by Beetle. I'll accept nothing from that turncoat. Not even the dog!"

Socks barked helplessly.

"Why?" Twelve called.

"I am the Blue King, and my word is law. These are my

waters, and my skies above. You are not welcome here. Turn your vessel around before I condemn you to the bottom of The Endless Blue."

"Why is everyone obsessed with ownership of the sea and sky?" Twelve muttered. Turning to Erin, she asked, "What should we do?"

"We're outgunned and outnumbered," Erin said. She gripped the mast with one hand and cupped her mouth with the other. "Who are you to tell us what to do?" she yelled. "The Blue King? I've never heard of you. Show yourself and let us decide if the waters should belong to anyone other than the fish and the whales and the monsters that swim within them."

Bow strings creaked in readiness.

Twelve sank into her chair and grabbed the oars.

But Erin remained still. One foot on her seat. The other on the edge of the boat. Her hair rippled beneath her pink bandana. The pistol, tucked into her belt, shone in the morning light.

"And who are you?" came the voice once more.

"A warrior. A fearless gunslinger," Erin shouted. "The last human girl!"

"Human...*girl*?" the Blue King said. "Impossible. You were all destroyed in The Many Years Storm. A new breed has arisen."

"A new breed?"

"Demons," whispered Twelve helpfully.

"Mannequins," the Blue King replied. "We awoke beneath the turbulent, chaotic skies. Our eyes opened, our minds filled with knowledge, our bodies flooded with life!"

"Mannequins?" Erin said. "Like the ones in shops—?"

"Never again!" boomed the voice. "We are the new breed.

We are alive. And these are *our* skies and *our* waters!"

The volume of the Blue King's voice rattled the mast and set the sails fluttering.

"Be gone now, little girl. The last of your kind has been driven from this world," he said. "We have no time for your meddling. If it is humans you seek, then the last woman dwells on BootHill with her ghosts and monsters."

"BootHill?" Twelve said, rising in her seat. "You speak of The Patchwork Woman."

"What of her?" the Blue King replied.

"Bavorski Beetlestone sent you this dog as a token of goodwill, an alliance against The Patchwork Woman."

"No one can destroy her," the Blue King barked. "Not me, not you, not Clifftop."

"But together—" Erin began.

"Enough!" the Blue King raged. "Follow the lights. Bring the dog."

THE CRYSTAL TOWER

Lazarus followed a series of red flashing lights. They reflected on the steady ripples of The Endless Blue, pulling them deeper and deeper into The Scrapers.

An imposing office building of steel and glass rose high above the rest. Pa had taken Erin here to collect the deeds to Coldharbour Farm when she was six years old. Apparently she'd waited outside eating ice cream with Ma and Clyde, but Erin had no memory of that day.

Shadows ran at strange angles down the enormous tower. The exterior was riddled with concave indents of various sizes, glass cracked and split where The Many Years Storm had done its work. They reminded Erin of the surface of the moon.

Six feet above water level, where a flat glass wall had once been, was an opening.

Two figures stood either side looking down at *Lazarus* and her crew. Both were shop mannequins, their skin reflective and smooth, devoid of hair or features. The contours of their faces appeared and vanished in light and shadow. They were dressed in human clothes beneath waterproof overalls and jackets. One had a powerful bow and a quiver of arrows slung across its shoulders. The other held a seven-iron golf club and

145

a large wrench.

The one holding the bow had leather gloves and heavy, steel toecap boots. The other wore pink slip-on shoes and had painted its face with lipstick and eyeliner. It gazed covetously at Erin's pink headband before falling in next to the other.

Both figures beckoned them to enter.

Twelve raised Jack on to the ledge. He and Twelve both helped Erin and Socks clambered into the tower. While Twelve hauled herself out of the boat, Erin gazed around an abandoned open-plan office. Cubicles ran down one side like a series of rabbit hutches, intersected with photocopiers and floor-standing printers. Busted strip lighting dangled from water-stained ceilings. Hard-wearing floor panels overlapped beneath their feet. Across the room were several private offices, hidden behind partition walls and venetian blinds. Abstract paintings hung pointlessly between ransacked filing cabinets and stationery cupboards.

Damp and stale coffee invaded Erin's nostrils.

The mannequins took off across the office, walking awkwardly.

Erin followed her friends, trailing in the mannequins' wake.

They passed a lift, the doors prized open. Erin peered into the well. Several feet down, water churned in circles. Above, the shaft rose more than a hundred feet towards a boxcar whose cables looped below like sleeping snakes.

Twelve grabbed Erin's shoulder and hurried her away from the edge.

The mannequins marched into a cold, stone stairwell. They trooped to the top, eight storeys in all, finally emerging into a vast open-plan penthouse.

Piles of broken furniture edged the space, forming a barricade. Rows of mannequins lined the room, each adorned with distinct clothes and weapons, their faces a mix of colours. Some human tones. Some psychedelic. Some appeared to have defined themselves as male or female, but many were androgynous. The mannequins looked fragile, crudely put together, but their weapons looked vicious and hungry.

Erin stopped.

Her hand reached for Socks.

The dog whined quietly as blank mannequin faces turned towards them.

Their heels clicked to attention.

At the end of the room sat a throne made from office chairs, steel drawers, air-conditioning pipes, keyboards, and multicoloured cabling. Perched on top, one leg crossed at right angles, sat a figure dressed in blue from head to toe.

The Blue King!

He was concealed beneath a cobalt-blue all-in-one leather biker suit with flashes of white trim. His feet vanished into a pair of blue riding boots, his hands hidden inside sapphire driving gloves. A motorcycle helmet in more than a dozen shades of shimmering blue covered his head while a dark visor hid his face, a slim gap visible over the bottom lip.

He held no weapons that Erin could see, but was well-protected. She wondered what possessed him to demand so many guards. The idea of The Patchwork Woman formed in her mind. She tried to picture the strange woman that dealt in dark magic and impossible promises, but there was no time for such daydreams.

Beside the Blue King stood an imposing mannequin. Light reflected off her golden plastic skin, twinkling like a million stars. Red-and-white streaks had been painted across her cheeks while black nail polish coated her deep, lifeless eyes. Atop her head, a series of nine-inch nails jutted skywards. An industrial mohawk.

"Welcome," said a young man's voice, as he rose from his throne, "to the Crystal Tower and the Court of the Blue King."

The mannequins turned through ninety degrees—some moved more easily than others—and snapped their feet in unison.

The Blue King walked slowly between his troops.

Twelve towered over the Blue King but he showed no sign of intimidation, for it was his surroundings, his mannequins, the smell, and the eerie silence between his words that really held the power.

The golden mannequin followed at close quarters.

"What kind of *thing* are you?" the Blue King asked.

"Thing?" Twelve replied. "I'm a scarecrow. Made by the hands of the last human girl. Are you not afraid?"

The Blue King made a sickly, gargled laugh.

"And what are you?" Twelve fired back.

"I am the Blue King," he roared theatrically, quickening his step as he moved within inches of Twelve, Jack, Erin, and Socks. He tilted his helmet up. The mannequins shifted into attack formation. "And this is Harunara. Head of my army and greatest warrior."

Harunara wore a silk dress around her long frame, concealing a deadly blade.

"Are you not afraid?"

Erin squinted at the thin aperture beneath the Blue King's visor but was unable to discover what kind of creature lurked within.

"I am not afraid," Twelve told him. "Not of you, anyway."

The Blue King bristled. He edged away from the scarecrow and circled slowly. He brushed past Erin and swung to face the wickerman.

"Interesting," he said. "You're new. Different."

"I'm a wickerman."

"Of that I have no doubt."

"I was born of a scarecrow. Made by her very hands."

"Scarecrows making wickermen? The world is stranger than anyone could imagine."

He turned his attention to Erin. "And you?" he said, with a new wave of confidence. "Do you fear me? Do you fear The Scrapers? The might and power of these waters? The dominion I govern?"

He tilted his head to one side, searching for her eyes.

"We came to deliver Socks…and Bavorski Beetlestone's message of allegiance."

Twelve inched behind Erin as she spoke.

A rubber-gloved hand came to rest on her shoulder.

"An alliance against The Patchwork Woman. Whoever and whatever she is."

Erin looked up at the dazzling blue helmet.

"Yes, yes, yes," the Blue King said. "It's all very well for Bavorski Beetlestone—for *Beetle*—to send me his empty promises of alliance. This would not be the first message he has sent talking of such things. But perhaps it will be his last."

The Blue King turned to look at the pale lurcher circling his feet.

"The dog, however, is a nice touch."

"Socks is yours then?" Erin said.

The Blue King nodded. "We were companions. Long ago."

"It seems particularly odd for a mannequin—an articulated doll with no heat, smell or emotion, nothing *human* at least—to have a dog as a pet," suggested Twelve.

Socks made a series of desperate noises while rubbing his snout against the Blue King's leg, who lurched into Twelve's personal space. Helmet pushed back on his spine. Black visor directed at the scarecrow's skull.

"Is that so?" he whispered.

Twelve bent down.

Helmet and skull came together.

"Prepare the elevator!" screamed the Blue King, spinning away.

Harunara waved the mannequins into action.

Twelve rocked back and turned to the bewildered faces of her friends. "Elevator?" she said. "But we're already on the top floor."

"That's right," the Blue King said, arms outstretched, his voice playful. "If we cannot go up, then we must go—?"

"Down?"

He snapped his fingers. "To the merciless bottom of The Endless Blue!"

SUBMERGED

Erin jumped as the mannequins' heels slammed together. The sound echoed across the room once, twice, then died. The plastic soldiers turned one hundred and eighty degrees and marched past the Blue King's throne, filing into ranks beside a wide service elevator.

"Follow me," ordered the Blue King.

Erin was first in line, studying the Blue King as he walked. He had a lilting gait, a touch uneven, and bounced in a way she found curious. The other mannequins moved in a regimented, symmetrical, mechanical fashion. She slowed and let Twelve and Jack pass.

Jack's walk was a stomping, shuffling march; his feet taking short, powerful steps.

The scarecrow's gait was large and unwieldy, as though each time she moved she had to compensate for a hundred unknown variables in her cockeyed construction.

Erin smiled.

Twelve was truly unique and utterly weird.

She skated forward and watched the Blue King again.

Her heart quickened.

He wasn't built in a factory.

Or a soggy woodland.

Or an old barn.

He was made somewhere warm, and delicate, and cradled with love.

That walk was undeniably—*human*.

The realisation hit her like a gut punch.

She felt like crying.

For so long she'd been the only one.

The last one.

And now here he was.

Another human.

A man.

A boy.

A King?

Every emotion she possessed spun inside.

Then, a new thought hit her.

Clyde?

Her legs turned to jelly. Her vision doubled.

It couldn't be.

Erin grabbed hold of Twelve.

Could it?

The first human she'd met since The Many Years Storm and it was her long-lost—presumed dead—brother? The cruel, unrelenting world she'd known for so long could never allow that.

But, what if…?

Just… what… if…?

At the elevator doors, the Blue King faced his guests. "I'm going to show you something extraordinary," he announced. "Something that only a select few have been privy to."

He nodded to Harunara who turned and pressed a small,

round button. The elevator doors juddered, then stuck in their runners. Two mannequins yanked them back.

The Blue King peered into the elevator shaft. He wobbled comically on the lip of the chasm before righting himself.

"Just kidding," he professed. "Sturdy as granite."

He beckoned to Erin.

She approached cautiously, expecting to see the same square of water sloshing around some hundred feet or so below. But there was no water to be seen. Just an endless chasm swallowed up by shadows.

Erin looked back at the man, at the boy, at her...*brother*?

"Where's all the water?"

Twelve and Jack glanced over her shoulder.

"Well?" Erin asked again, trying to see through his infuriating visor.

"Hyperbaric...water...pressure...something-or-other. I don't know." He shrugged. "Inexplicably, the lower floors of this building are watertight. And this is the only way in or out."

An elevator boxcar rumbled into view and hissed dramatically.

The Blue King stepped inside and signalled for them to follow.

Erin shot a concerned look at her friends, but Twelve had already launched herself into the elevator and started jumping up and down.

The boxcar complained bitterly.

"Be careful!" the Blue King erupted, pointing to a sign.

Max Weight Limit 800kg.

"The elevator isn't indestructible."

"How much do you think I weigh?"

The Blue King tightened. "I've no idea. You could be made of pig iron for all I know!" He rushed out of the elevator and took Erin's hand. Despite the gloves, his touch was soft and warm. "It's quite safe," he assured her. "As long as the scarecrow doesn't start jumping again."

"I was trying to prove how safe the elevator was," Twelve said.

"And what a great job you did," he replied, not turning to look at her. "Erin. Come with me. I've got lots to show you."

Jack joined Twelve inside the boxcar, inspecting a panel of buttons on the wall.

Erin ran her eyes over the long line of strangely attired mannequins. Harunara stood closest of all. Their odd, blank faces looked through her. Their weapons glinted menacingly.

Nodding gently, she reached down and lifted Socks into her arms.

"It's okay, boy. Nothing to fear."

The boxcar juddered as they jostled inside. The metal walls were buffed and scratched, the red rubber floor indented with a spirograph of wheel tracks and hardened bubblegum. Twelve wrapped a long arm around Erin's shoulders. Socks whined nervously.

"Would you like to do the honours?" the Blue King said to Jack.

"What do you mean?"

"There," the Blue King said. He pointed to a button at the bottom of the panel where rusty screws jutted from each corner. A patina of dark green lingered around the edge. The remnants of the number 3 were still visible.

The wickerman held out a peculiar finger of twig and twine. As he pressed gently, the button eased into the panel, glowing with yellow light. The doors squeaked shut, blocking out the ominous sight of Harunara and the army of mannequins.

For a moment nothing happened.

Then, the sensation inside the elevator changed. Erin felt like she was back on board *Lazarus* or stood high on the deck of HMS Fortitude. Floating, unhinged from the world, but this time she floated hundreds of feet above...well, she didn't know what. What was down in the depths of The Scrapers? What did the Blue King keep at the bottom of The Endless Blue?

Another light appeared on the panel.

This one was behind the number 70.

It, too, had been pressed far more than the others.

The elevator groaned, hissed again, then dropped.

Erin's stomach did somersaults as the elevator plunged through the interior of The Crystal Tower, moving much faster than any elevator should. For a moment, she thought the cables and counterweights had failed, and they were descending to a watery grave.

She took a long breath, her eyes glued to the numbers on the panel.

58 ... 57 ... 56 ... 55 ... 54 ...

Down and down and down they went.

41 ... 40 ... 39 ... 38 ...

The buttons blinked on and off with flickering light.

24 ... 23 ... 22 ... 21...

Suddenly, Erin was underneath the capsized boat, counting down. She couldn't help it. The numbers brought it all back. She closed her eyes, but the memory endured, clear and sharp.

15 ... 14 ... 13 ...

She felt the cold water against her skin. The sickening

sound of ice smashing against the hull. The wail of her mother's stricken voice. Her father's despair.

9 ... 8 ... 7 ...

The boxcar rattled. Erin clung to Twelve. The numbers tumbled in her head.

The boxcar hissed. Slowed. The cables yawned horribly.

5 ... 4 ... 3 ...

Ping!

RISE OF THE MANNEQUINS

The Blue King swept into the room on level three with a bold familiarity. Shards of reflected light danced all over his blue biker outfit, flickering strangely, coating every surface. Erin followed him, arms outstretched. The light played on her plastic yellow poncho, mesmerising and magical.

But something wasn't right.

The atmosphere in the room felt thicker, closer, as though gravity had been dialled up a notch.

A huge window of toughened glass circumnavigated the entire room. It was like the window on HMS Fortitude, but fifty times bigger. And beyond, nothing but blue.

Here, hundreds of feet beneath the surface of the water, lived the colour she remembered. The rich, deep blue that she'd swum in, played in, glimpsed in memories, and captured in a hundred polaroids.

The Endless Blue hadn't gone.

It was here, mere inches from her fingertips.

Light shifted through the water, casting pirouetting spectres and zigzagging demons. Faces appeared in shadows and bubbles and ripples. She fought to keep the memory of the capsized boat at bay, but it pressed in, demanding her to remember, to feel it all.

"Amazing, isn't it?" the Blue King said, slouching against the glass.

Erin swallowed the memories down.

"The Endless Blue."

His voice sounded different.

Higher, younger, far less serious.

She turned from the window. Instead of looking into his dark visor, she found the Blue King calmly holding the helmet between his wrist and hip.

She gasped.

The Blue King was human.

And he was a boy, a year or more older than her. Pale and freckled, with dusty hair hanging over his eyes. He looked familiar, the shape of him, the angle of his jaw. Was it Clyde? Had she forgotten his face after all this time?

She pulled the photograph of Clyde from her pocket.

A hard fold cut through her brother's face, the image bent and crumpled from their adventures. She reached to touch the boy's cheek, but he smiled coyly and took her hand in his. "My name is Marshall," he told her. "Sorry about all the…"

Words formed in her mouth but got no further than her tongue.

His skin felt warm, clammy.

Erin struggled to stay on her feet.

Marshall slipped his hand away as the dog came bounding towards him. "Socks!"

He dropped to his knees and wrestled playfully with the dog. Socks yapped and yipped, overcome with excitement. Marshall made odd, baby-like noises that the dog seemed to respond to.

Erin wiped a tear from her cheek. A strange mix of emotions swelled in her belly. Anger and disappointment that she hadn't found Clyde. But hope too. Hope that, if this boy could find a way to survive, her brother could too.

"Oh, Socks. I've missed you so much," Marshall went on. "How are you, boy? Did those horrid birds treat you okay?"

"Their leader used him like a horse," Twelve revealed.

"How dare they! How dare Bavorski Beetlestone use poor old Socks as a beast of burden. He's hardly a Doberman or a Great Dane. He's not built for such things. Justice Raventhorne would never have treated Socks so cruelly."

"To be honest, Socks didn't look like he minded," Twelve added.

"Justice Raventhorne?" Erin said, confused.

"Bavorski Beetlestone's predecessor," Marshall continued. "Justice Raventhorne and I had an alliance, an agreement. We kept to ourselves for the most part. He had the waters in the north and the skies above. We patrolled the waters surrounding The Scrapers and the southern skies. But when Justice was overthrown, Bavorski attacked. Thousands of birds swarmed The Scrapers. We lost many. His vultures took Socks. Bloodthirsty, wretched things!"

Erin felt her stomach churn again. "Justice Raventhorne. That's his full name, isn't it?"

"I suppose so," Marshall replied.

Erin bit her lip and looked at Twelve's enormous head and slithering eyes.

"Raven," she said, her voice a ghostly whisper, "was Governor of Clifftop."

Twelve shifted awkwardly. "That blackbird is riddled with secrets."

Erin struggled to piece everything together. So much had happened while she'd slept in the hayloft and cooked worms and collected endless pots of rainwater. Shaking the past from her mind, she focused on the Blue King. "So," she said, "what's your story? How did you survive The Many Years Storm? How did you become...a King?"

Marshall led them across the room to some threadbare sofas. Beyond, doors led to a kitchen, a cloakroom, and a games area complete with pool table, dartboard, and air hockey machine. Managerial posters encouraging *Positivity* and *Achievement* were pinned to the walls in black plastic frames.

Marshall dropped onto one of the sofas and crossed his legs.

"Well?" Erin said, agitated. "How did you manage to survive all this?"

A shadow crept across the boy's face. "It's a miracle I survived The Many Years Storm. Sometimes I wish I hadn't. Sometimes I wish I was out there, floating, drowned like all the others. Sometimes I wish I was free of...*this*." His cold eyes scanned the room. "I watched them all die. *Everyone.* Some people I knew, but most were strangers. Their deaths were no less traumatic.

"When the city flooded, hundreds of people retreated to The Crystal Tower. Socks and I were among them. The rising tides forced us to climb every week as floor after floor was taken. The higher we climbed, the less space remained. People began turning on one another, forcing women, children, the elderly, and the weak out onto the roof. A handful of us hid from it all, but we could hear it happening. We could hear the yelling and the screaming. And then the ice storm came. It pounded on the sides of the building and silenced everyone on the roof. And still we hid."

Erin trembled.

"Eventually it was just me and Socks hidden in a cloakroom on the sixty-sixth floor. Others went in search of food and survivors and never returned. I wrapped myself and Socks in as many coats as I could find, burying us in the deepest, darkest corner of the cloakroom. Days passed. Eventually, hunger got the better of me, so I ventured out. It was strangely quiet and empty, despite the torrential rain and hail rattling against the windows and the monstrous waves below. I stood for a time, staring out into the new grey world.

"Across the water, in another skyscraper, a war was raging. There were hordes of people fighting. More and more of them on every floor. At first, I thought I was seeing things, my hunger causing illusions. There were humans fighting, sure. But they were not fighting each other as they had before. They were fighting mannequins, animated plastic humanoids from the shopping malls far below. The mannequins were merciless. Powerful and deadly. Fuelled by some tremendous force, something ugly and vengeful. They were beating the humans back. Herding them towards the edge of the building. Throwing them down into the churning water.

"As the humans slipped beneath, more mannequins surfaced, floating on the water like rafts. Some people tried to hang on to them, but the mannequins were too strong. They threw down cables and air-conditioning tubes and hauled their own to safety, letting the humans drown."

"My God," said Erin. "You must have been terrified."

Marshall nodded. "But they were in another building. They didn't know Socks and I were here. For a time I thought it'd stay that way. I was naive. A few days later I noticed groups of mannequins launching themselves into the water tied to photocopiers, office chairs, and filing cabinets. It was the most peculiar sight I'd ever seen. I thought they were trying to drown themselves in the wake of what they'd done. But, as I hid in the shadows and watched, the mannequins surfaced holding all manner of objects: golf clubs, hammers, baseball bats, wrenches, bows and arrows."

"They'd gone on a supply mission," Erin said, almost unable to believe it. "This is incredible."

Marshall pulled Socks close.

The dog whimpered.

"The next bit was the worst. The mannequins fired arrows tied to long cables and started zip-lining across, infesting every building. Once they were inside, they started constructing walkways out of ladders and desk legs and network trusses and central heating pipes. Socks and I hid in the cloakroom, buried ten coats deep, our hearts pounding. I was convinced they'd find us and discard us into the ocean. If I'd been on my own, then perhaps that might have happened. But I had Socks. I had someone to fight for. Someone to protect.

"Hiding was getting us nowhere, so I threw the coats aside and looked for a way to walk amongst the mannequins without raising suspicion. That's when I saw this." He looked down at his blue biker overalls and dazzling helmet. "If I could hide the fact that I was human, I might be able to move freely through the buildings. Look for a way out of this nightmare. Escape, survive somehow.

"As I emerged from the cloakroom in my disguise, several mannequins were immediately drawn to me, weapons raised. I nodded at them, as calmly as I could manage, and then, despite my quivering legs, walked purposefully to the stairwell. To my relief, they returned to their scavenging and let me go.

"I decided to make my way to the roof and look around. I passed more mannequins on the stairs, but they paid me little notice. On the roof, everything changed. There seemed to be one mannequin ordering the others around. She caught sight of me the moment I stepped out."

"Harunara," Erin whispered.

"She confronted me as rain and hail bounced off her hard plastic body. I remember thinking that this was the end, that Harunara was about to launch me into the churning waters. But, at that moment, a huge warship appeared on the horizon. The mannequins panicked, running to and fro across the rooftops, desperately trying to organise themselves.

"The warship crashed against the skyscrapers, shaking the buildings to their foundations. Harunara fixed her gaze on me. I couldn't tell what she was thinking but I knew I had to do something. I had to take action. I had to join the mannequins or my fate would be sealed. I began barking orders, lining up the mannequins with bows and arrows along the edges of the buildings.

"Below, the warship looked in a bad state. There were huge gashes along the hull. The windows to the bridge were shattered. It seemed deserted but I ordered the mannequins to fire anyway, saying I could see people inside armed with guns. A volley of arrows punctuated the ship. Some hit the deck, others went into the bridge, but most vanished through holes in the hull or into the water. I screamed *Victory!* and the mannequins waved their weapons in the air. Harunara came to me and dropped to one knee, her head bowed, her weapon placed flat across her palms. She called me her King, her Lord. She called me Your Majesty, Your Excellency. But I'd done nothing. The ship and its crew had already been destroyed by something else. The storm most probably. I'd got lucky. The luckiest boy alive."

Erin and Twelve and Jack sat staring, mesmerised and bewildered.

"And then?" said Twelve.

Marshall's eyes drifted away. "Then she named me. The Blue King."

"Why?" Twelve asked, getting carried along with the story.

"Because of his clothes," Erin replied helpfully.

"Oh. Yes. Right. Of course."

"And Socks?" Erin asked.

"They accepted him as mine," Marshall said. "Even went to the bottom of The Endless Blue to retrieve tins of dog food. Perhaps there's something human inside the mannequins. Something good. Buried."

Erin couldn't decide what was worse. Her tragic story. Or Marshall's. But this wasn't a competition. Everything was tragic. Everything was horrible and broken. Or so it seemed.

The world made no sense. Mannequins and scarecrows and wickermen and The Patchwork Woman all strangely alive and embroiled in an enormous war for the seas and the skies.

How had she managed to drop herself right in the middle of it all?

Should she have grieved for her parents, abandoned all thought of finding Clyde, and stayed on Coldharbour Farm until it was time to join them?

She focused. Shook her cowardice aside. One way or another she would find her brother, get home to Coldharbour

Farm, and live out her days drifting around the farmhouse, snoozing in the hayloft, and building scarecrows in the barn.

She put an invigorated hand on Marshall's knee.

"We need to get you out of here," she told him.

Marshall raised an eyebrow. "Really? How?"

"It's time for the Blue King to fall!"

NON-BELIEVERS

Erin lingered on the sofa after Marshall finished his tale. She played the story back in her mind, amazed the boy had survived through such horror and torment. Harunara, the golden mohawked mannequin, bothered her something rotten. She was trouble. Big trouble. If they were to break the Blue King out of his own fortress, then Harunara would be the biggest obstacle. That, and the hordes of mannequins at her back.

Raven came to mind.

Justice Raventhorne.

Governor of Clifftop and one true ruler of The Endless Blue.

That was the craziest part of the whole story. Erin struggled to get her head around it. Cairo had insisted Raven had been killed over The Scrapers. Did Cairo lie? Or did he genuinely believe Raven to be dead and gone?

She turned to Jack. "That's one hell of a story."

The wickerman played with his feathered cape. "Unbelievable," he said. "Mannequins rising up from the depths. Murdering humans. Preparing for war. The anointment of a King." He shook his head. Grass shavings drifted to the ground. "I thought the world was strange enough with wickermen and scarecrows. But now, well, I just don't know. It's lunacy. All of it."

"But you saved us from Tomas and his plans with The Patchwork Woman," Erin told him. "You made the world a better place. A kinder place."

Jack pulled the cape over his shoulder and sank his chin to his chest. "I suppose," he replied. "But now we're here. A situation possibly more dangerous than dealing with The Patchwork Woman herself."

"I'll get us out," Erin said. "But I'll need you. Every last twig and branch, leaf and blade."

Twelve stood beside the large windows, staring into The Endless Blue. Erin rose, straightened her poncho and dungarees, and joined the scarecrow.

Beyond the glass, the world glimmered in a thousand shades of blue.

Erin traced the long shadows of The Scrapers as they fell on the water. Below, for the first time, she saw the high street where the mannequins had pillaged their weapons and clothes. A supermarket on the corner displayed *Sale Now On* and *Everything Must Go* banners. She saw a sports store, a delicatessen, a toy and games shop, and an abundance of clothing retailers.

Schools of fish in every colour fizzed past. They spun in looping arcs, diving to the high street and rocketing towards the surface.

Something else moved in the water.

Something at the bottom of the ocean, in the middle of the high street amongst the benches, and concrete trash bins, and oversized planters.

It wasn't fish or whales or marine life of any kind.

Twelve shifted to get a closer look, smacking her bony head against the glass.

Erin giggled.

"What's that down there?" Twelve asked, tapping the window.

Erin stared harder. Slowly, the image came into focus. Her hand shot to her mouth. If she wasn't mistaken, they were mannequins. Hundreds of them, maybe more. They were waving, struggling, their bodies buried beneath piles of scrap metal and office furniture.

"They're The Non-Believers," Marshall said, appearing beside them.

"The...what?"

"Not all the mannequins agreed I was their King. Not all believed we should be drowning humans in the water. Harunara had them tied to heavy objects and thrown off the side."

Erin stiffened. "But..." she said. "They're alive."

"They're mannequins. They have no lungs—much like scarecrows or wickermen—but yet they live. At the bottom of the sea. Trapped. Forever..."

Erin spread both hands against the window.

Her forehead pressed gently against the cold glass.

Marshall nodded. "Unless you have a frogman suit or diving gear."

"I can go one better than that," she replied.

Erin busied herself around the Blue King's sanctuary, collecting a curious mix of items, and piled them on the sofas. Wedging the boxcar open with a metal waste bin, she spent a few minutes crouched on her knees examining every inch of the elevator.

Marshall approached tentatively. "Um. What are you doing?"

"Getting you...us...everyone...out of here."

"I see. Great. But...how?"

"I'm not entirely sure. I mean, I know what I want to do, but I've no idea which parts will work. Some may be more successful than others. There's a lot of parameters."

"That doesn't fill me with confidence."

She stood and faced him. Her tangled hair fell over her broken glasses. She flicked it away impatiently. "This is going to be risky. Extremely dangerous. Nigh on impossible. But what other choice do we have?"

Marshall paled, then smiled. "Tell us."

"Gather round."

As she laid out her plan, a sense of disbelief filled the submerged room. Body language turned from eager excitement to fearful reluctance. The task ahead was simultaneously simple and complicated. Relatively speaking, Erin, Marshall, Jack, and Socks had the simple part. Twelve was not so lucky, but there was danger on all sides.

"We're all going to die," said Jack, rustling in his seat.

"Why don't we just stay down here?" Marshall added. "I'm sure I can continue the Blue King charade for a while, get us something other than dog food to eat, and work out a safer plan. One that avoids death by drowning, evisceration, burning, or blunt-force trauma. I'm pretty sure I'm going to scare myself to death somewhere in the middle of your chaotic plan."

Erin knocked him playfully on the shoulder.

"Some kind of King you are."

"I think it's a wonderful plan," Twelve told them. "Erin will save us all. She created me and look what an amazing job she did."

Erin's cheeks turned scarlet.

"She made twelve of us. A dozen scarecrows to govern the hills of Coldharbour Farm. One of her scarecrows went on to create nine wickermen and a wickerwoman. I built a boat and sailed it from one side of The Endless Blue to the other. This is *not* how our story ends. This is just the most dangerous—most exciting—chapter yet. I, for one, cannot wait to see what comes next." Twelve sounded as though she believed most of the words in her speech. "I'm not afraid to die," she added. "I just don't want to. Not yet anyway."

"You've got lots of living to do," Erin told her. "I know it. I believe it."

"Faith is a daring leap into the dark," Twelve said.

"Embrace that Raven energy!" Erin told her, then turned to the boys.

They looked less than convinced.

"Prepare for battle!"

Erin helped Jack and Marshall strap metal piping over their arms and legs. She fastened padded chair seats to the front and back of Marshall's torso and fitted Jack with a corrugated office trash can from armpit to knee.

In turn, they assisted Erin into her makeshift armour.

She placed Socks inside a rucksack and padded it with thick coats and scarves from the cloakroom, leaving a space for his head to poke out the top. For now, he sat watching as Erin handed out the weapons she'd accumulated.

There were two wooden-handled knives from the office kitchen which Jack taped to either end of a pool cue. Marshall swung a large frying pan in one hand while gripping a rolling pin taped to a pizza slicer with the other. She stuffed handfuls of forks into the belt of his biker overalls. "Auxiliary weapons," she told him, then stuffed more cutlery into the top of his boots.

Jack swished his pool cue bayonet back and forth, checking the balance.

Erin stood and admired them both.

"Now you look like a King," she told Marshall. "Armed, armoured, and ready for war."

Marshall spun to face the wickerman.

"Kneel," he commanded, his mouth quirking.

Jack hesitated, then obliged.

"I pronounce you Sir Jack of…um, where are you from?"

"The Island of Trees."

"Sir Jack of the Island of Trees."

He tapped the exposed twigs and moss on Jack's shoulders with the tip of his pizza slicer rolling pin.

"Rise, Sir Knight."

Erin lifted the Socks-shod rucksack and hoisted it onto Marshall's back. Socks let out a cheerful yelp and licked his master's ear. Marshall tried to reach back and stroke the dog, but his armoured limbs were heavily restricted.

"I can barely move," he complained.

"You'll move less if you're riddled with arrows," Erin told him.

"Where's *your* weapon?"

Erin raised a finger. "Hang on."

She went to Twelve. The scarecrow was staring thoughtfully through the window.

"Are you okay?"

"I'm ready," Twelve replied. "As ready as I can be. I've not done anything like this before."

"None of us have."

Erin pulled the pistol from her belt.

Everything became real.

Hyper-real.

Until that moment, Erin's plan had just been words. Words that she'd formed into pictures in her head. Frightening scenes from a bedtime story or a horror movie or the battle games she'd played with Clyde on the bedroom floor. Scenes that were distant. Safe. But now, holding the gun, those scenes came racing towards her.

This was happening.

Now.

She forced the cylinder open. There were four rounds in total. She'd need them all and then some.

"You'll do fine."

Twelve rolled her shoulders. They squeaked horribly.

"I won't rust, will I?"

"There won't be time."

"I won't drown, will I?"

"You don't breathe."

"Will I die?"

Erin's reply didn't come as fast.

"Not today," she said eventually.

Tucking the pistol back into her belt, she wheeled a freestanding photocopier beside the scarecrow, daisy-chained power cables around the machine and handed the other end to Twelve. The scarecrow wrapped it around her waist half a dozen times before asking Erin to fasten it in a complicated-looking knot.

"Good luck," Twelve said. "It's been—"

"No goodbyes," Erin told her quickly. "I'll see you on the roof."

Returning to the sofas, Erin secured a felt bag of pool balls to her waist and lofted the second pool cue above her head like a javelin. She wrenched a fire extinguisher from the wall, swung the red cylinder onto her back and wedged it between her shoulder blades and the makeshift armour. The extinguisher's rubber cord and nozzle hung across her chest. White powder burst into the room as she gave it a satisfying test.

Time froze.

Anticipation thickened.

The deep breath before the plunge.

Erin pressed her back to the elevator and looked at her friends. And what a strange group of friends they were. The Boy King and his dog. A wickerman in a feathered cape. And the kindest, most ghastly, seven-foot scarecrow.

Was this the last time they would all be together?

No.

Twelve would make it to the roof.

She had to.

Everything depended on it.

It was time.

Everything was set.

Without warning, the elevator *pinged* and the doors began to close. The small metal trash can used to wedged them open was crushed and spat noisily into the room.

Erin tried to force her hand between the closing doors, but it was too late.

Above, the numbers on the panel quickly rose from 3 all

the way to 70, lingered, then began to drop again. A wave of panic sloshed in Erin's gut.

"Someone's coming down," Marshall said.

"Up against the wall," Erin ordered.

Marshall and Jack obeyed. Across the room, Twelve waited. Silhouetted against the radiant blue beyond the window, the scarecrow stared at her friends and the elevator door. It seemed to take forever. Finally that menacing *ping!* arrived.

The doors rattled open.

Gold flecks danced across the room, spinning like a mirrorball.

Harunara emerged.

She stalked forward. Her black eyes glistened. In her hands hung a skipping rope studded with morning stars. She wore a tight, black cocktail gown, a split running to the hip.

"Where are the others?" she hissed at Twelve, sweeping forward elegantly. "Where is the Blue King?"

Erin crept silently, leading the others into the boxcar.

"Gone," Twelve told Harunara.

"Gone?" She laughed. "There is only one way in and one way out."

Behind her, Jack slipped. His mossy arms pinwheeled, grabbed for Marshall, then clattered against the back of the elevator.

The golden mannequin pivoted.

Her dress bloomed.

"What is happening, my King?" she said, inspecting the blue overalls beneath his crude armour. Her black eyes drifted up to where his dazzling helmet should be. In its place was Marshall's pale, freckled face.

"Imposter!" she screamed.

The deadly skipping rope shook wildly in her hand.

"Now what?" Marshall mumbled, dropping the helmet over his head.

Erin punched 70 on the panel.

Then aimed the pistol at the enormous window.

"All hell's about to break loose," she told him, and squeezed the trigger.

BATTLE FOR THE CRYSTAL TOWER

The bullet whistled towards Twelve. There was no danger of it hitting her, but she seemed to sense the aftershock, the way the air moved around it.

At first nothing happened.

The window appeared to swallow the bullet.

The glass had survived floods, battleship attack, and unbelievable water pressure.

What good was one tiny bullet?

The pistol quivered in Erin's hand.

Gunpowder swamped her senses.

But, as everyone watched, tiny cracks developed and spread like icy veins. Then, splintering into a billion pieces of every conceivable shape and size, the window shattered.

Time became fractured.

The air pressure changed, morphing into something alien, terrifying.

A rectangular block of water pressed into the room.

It smelt strange. A mix of chemicals, salty and stagnant.

Harunara's screams were swallowed by the roar of the ocean. Chunks of ragged glass battered against her body. Her long golden arms whirred demonically as the water engulfed her and Twelve.

Erin stuffed the gun into her belt and frantically hammered number 70 on the elevator panel. A thin, vertical wave jetted into the boxcar as the doors squeezed together.

The boxcar shuddered, rocking horribly.

Water hammered on the outside, streaming in through air holes and worn fixings.

But the boxcar rose.

4 ... 5 ... 6 ...

The elevator took them up. Slowly at first. The cables and counterweights complained high overhead. Water pooled around their feet. The elevator accelerated. Churning water chased them up the elevator shaft, deafening, disorientating.

13 ... 14 ... 15 ...

Marshall tried to speak, but his voice became lost. Instead, he grabbed Erin by the arm and they huddled together in a corner, fear of the unknown crawling across their faces like the bugs in Twelve's eye sockets.

28 ... 29 ... 30 ...

Socks disappeared into the rucksack, yelping frantically. The pressure built. Water poured into the rattling boxcar at an alarming rate. Erin found herself forced towards the ground as they were propelled ever upwards.

45 ... 46 ... 47 ...

Erin tumbled, taking Marshall with her.

Jack collapsed face first into the waist-high water.

59 ... 60 ... 61 ...

Something changed.

The boxcar felt detached, light, airborne.

The torrent pushing them up must have reached water level and spilled out, flooding the Blue King's throne room on the seventieth floor.

But the boxcar continued to climb.

"We're going too fast!" Marshall screamed, his fingers gripping her tight.

But she smiled, full and wicked. "The faster the better!"

Twisting metal screeched and wailed.

Sparks and steam billowed into the air.

Rocketing upwards, the boxcar tore the cable housing apart, erupted through the top of the lift shaft and catapulted through the air. Erin, Marshall, Jack, and Socks tumbled end over end like underwear in a drier. With a sickly crash, their tiny metal transport landed, rolled onto its back, and came to a screeching halt.

Everything hurt. Motion sickness came in steady waves. But there wasn't time to assess the damage. Erin and Marshall detangled themselves and helped Jack to his feet.

Head still spinning, Erin reached up and threw the doors open.

A dozen mannequins stared back.

It was hard to tell what the mannequins were thinking as they gazed down into the battered boxcar. Their Blue King stood crushed between a girl and a wickerman, all of them clad in metal piping and office furniture with crude weapons in their hands.

The mannequins turned to one another, as if waiting for a command.

Erin seized the moment.

She plunged her thumb onto the fire extinguisher nozzle. Foam and powder exploded into the air. The mannequins stumbled back, dropped their weapons, faces coated with thick white gloop.

Erin vaulted out of the boxcar as screams erupted all around. She quickly helped the boys out and, with her feet safely on solid ground, she scanned the rooftop. There were more than a dozen mannequins nearby. Half of them were disorientated, while the others stood on the perimeter, staring questioningly into the shattered remains of the lift shaft.

Jack's trash-can armour reverberated like a steel drum as an arrow embedded itself in the corrugated metal.

"Move!" Erin urged, sending a fresh arc of white foam skyward.

Arrows filled the air.

Most flew wide. Others struck armour or disorientated mannequins. Erin loosed more foam, creating a battlefield of chaos and confusion.

Jack and Marshall moved ahead, attacking each mannequin as they struggled through the fog. The wickerman's pool cue whirred menacingly, creating skeins of white cloud and dust. The knives on either end slashed at the nearest foe but bounced off without inflicting damage. He thrust the weapon forward again, a direct hit to the chest, but the mannequins kept coming.

Long, plastic fingers clawed Jack's arm, tearing the aluminium piping.

The wickerman crumpled to his knees. He swung the pool cue venomously. It connected with the mannequin's knee joints. Instead of ricocheting off as before, a burst of intricate metal parts exploded across the roof.

The one-legged mannequin collapsed to the ground, dragging itself on its chest. Rising, Jack stepped over the stricken creature and brought the pool cue down on both elbows.

Direct hits.

The mannequin came to pieces.

Jack kicked it onto its back where it writhed and fought like an upturned tortoise.

"Go for the joints," he yelled to Marshall.

The Blue King spun away from his attackers, his armour nicked and scratched.

Holding the frying pan like a shield, Marshall deflected incoming arrows while he swung the pizza slicer rolling pin in wide circles.

Jack jumped into the melee, taking one of the mannequins out with a deadly strike.

Erin circled them, hosing the enemy with her fire extinguisher.

She'd made her way to the edge of The Crystal Tower and took a nervous glance over the side, praying *Lazarus* was waiting below.

"We're on the wrong side!" she called to the boys.

The foam and spray and the airborne boxcar must have muddled her sense of direction.

Marshall was engaged with two more mannequins while dozens approached from behind.

Erin sank her hand into the velvet bag at her waist and retrieved one of the pool balls.

She took aim and launched it as hard as she could. It sailed wide of the mark and disappeared out of sight. She grabbed another. Bullseye! The pool ball clattered into the shoulder of a mannequin as it prepared to strike. The creature spun like a top and dropped its weapon. Marshall swooped low and destroyed its knees with his rolling pin.

More pool balls filled the air as reinforcements arrived.

Erin drove a few back but, before long, Marshall and Jack became surrounded.

Erin zigzagged across the rooftop, nozzle in hand. Plumes of white foam sprayed in chaotic bursts. As she launched the last of her projectiles—the shiny black eight ball—her fire extinguisher choked, spluttered and died.

Mannequins closed in.

One kicked Marshall in the knee, sending him to the floor.

Jack roared and swished the pool cue at any that approached.

But his valiance was for naught.

They were overrun.

It was over.

Dozens of mannequins raised their blades and nocked their bows.

Jack shook his homemade spear once more before standing over Marshall, who grimaced on the floor, hands clutching his knee. Socks let out a sympathetic yelp of his own. His head popped out of the rucksack, looking to soothe Marshall's pain.

Erin slammed the heel of her hand against the fire extinguisher nozzle.

It rasped and spluttered.

Utterly spent.

Hordes of mannequins crossed the metal walkways from other Scrapers.

Jack dropped his shoulders.

His weapon too.

Erin's hand went to her belt.

The pistol.

But what good were three shots against a hundred enemies? She scanned the edge of the building again, then the water, then the top of the ruined elevator shaft.

Where is Twelve? She should be here by now.

Then, as Erin's heart yearned for her friend, a pair of golden hands latched onto the rim of the elevator shaft and a vicious, mohawk head appeared over the lip.

Erin swallowed a scream.

Harunara stood before them.

Soaked from head to toe.

Battered and broken, but still alive.

She strode towards the once Blue King and ripped the helmet from his head.

The mannequins roared at the sight of the boy beneath, angry and vengeful.

Harunara threw the blue helmet over the side.

She raised a golden fist above her head.

And declared, "Long live the Queen!"

GOLDEN QUEEN

The plan had failed. Erin knew it.

Everything they had fought for was gone. What came next? Would the mannequins tie them to chairs and tables and boot them off the side of The Crystal Tower? Or perhaps they'd enslave them. Turn Jack into kindling. Make an example of the once Blue King. Haul Twelve up from the bottom of the ocean and hang her from The Scrapers as a warning to whoever or whatever might drift into their deadly waters.

Erin's gaze fell on the golden skinned, black-eyed mannequin. Part of her arm hung at a strange angle. Dents and gouges pocked her head. But here she stood.

Alive.

Victorious.

Erin's stomach rumbled with something other than fear and anger and frustration. She propelled herself forward, arms flailing, fists clenched. But she made it no more than six feet before mannequins in balaclavas and high-vis body warmers lifted her into the air.

"I'll kill you!" Erin screamed, shaking wildly beneath their grip like a tortured puppet. "I'll destroy you! I'll take you apart, one piece at a time, and personally sail your dismembered parts to the four corners of The Endless Blue!"

Harunara laughed cruelly. She hopped down from the remains of the elevator shaft, stalked over and pressed a cold, wet hand against Erin's face.

"No, my child," she said softly. "It is you who will be destroyed."

"Where's Twelve?" Erin snorted. "What did you do with her?"

Harunara fussed with her busted elbow joint, snapping it back into place. "The one with the ridiculous head and concrete shoes?" she said casually. "You need not concern yourself with her anymore."

Erin's strength faded.

Her breath became ragged.

Vision blurred.

"Take them to *my* courtroom," Harunara ordered. "I'm sure they'll enjoy witnessing the coronation of the Golden Queen before being sacrificed in my honour!"

Erin clattered to the ground.

Every ounce of energy evaporated.

The mannequins grabbed her dungaree straps.

"And these two," Harunara barked, flicking a wrist towards Jack and Marshall.

But only a handful of mannequins moved.

"What's wrong with you? Seize them!"

Erin stared at the mannequins as she was dragged towards the stairwell. Her plimsoll heels juddered on the roof. The fire extinguisher rattled against her spine.

"Well?" Harunara screamed.

Something felt wrong.

Not wrong.

Different.

It was only now, with the frenzy of battle swept aside, that Erin noticed the new mannequins. For the most part, they were naked, not wearing jackets and hats and make-up and jewellery like those that lined the Court of the Blue King. They stood in pools of water, their shiny bodies coated in shells and barnacles.

A shot of hope spiked her chest. "The Non-Believers!"

In the blink of an eye, they turned on the Golden Queen, reducing her faithful mannequins to nothing more than spare parts. Thin tendrils of dark light spiralled from each as arms and legs and mannequin heads were ripped from torsos and dumped at the feet of their Queen.

Harunara gripped the side of her damaged head. "Fire!" she shrieked. "Fire at will!"

Archers rushed to the edge of The Scrapers, their weapons raised.

Erin batted several dismembered mannequin limbs away and scrambled across the roof, grabbing Jack and Marshall. The Non-Believers formed a circle around the three friends as hundreds of arrows launched into the air with a resounding *whump!*

Silence fell, but for the pounding of Erin's heart.

Arrows kissed their zenith, then fell.

Desperate thoughts ran through her.

Was this the end?

How much was this going to hurt?

She still had three shots in the pistol.

Should she use them now to blow Harunara's head clean off?

Deadly darts descended, littering the rooftop. Non-believers dropped. Limbs clattered and spun, riddled with steel shafts and colourful flights. Brilliant white light drifted from the mannequin's bodies, arcing speedily towards the sky.

Jack stumbled over fallen bodies. He grabbed Erin for balance. Several arrows had pierced the trash bin around his waist. Another sat in his shoulder. A fourth in his head. More fell. The sound of their impact reverberated against Erin's bones.

"Jack," she yelled. "Are you okay?"

"I'll mend," he told her, pulling the girl close and slinging an arm around Marshall. "But we need to leave. I'm not sure we can take another volley."

The Golden Queen had stalked to the edge of The Crystal Tower and was negotiating a metal walkway across the watery chasm.

"She's getting away."

"Let her," Marshall said. "She's too strong for us."

Erin hated it but she knew he was right.

There was only one person who could tackle Harunara.

"Where is she?" Erin asked them. "Where is Twelve?"

Neither Marshall nor Jack could answer.

"I cannot bear it," she wailed, picturing the scarecrow trapped, destroyed, ripped to pieces at the bottom of The Endless Blue. Was the scarecrow…dead? She had to know, one way or the other. Perhaps they could find some scuba-diving equipment, or fashion an underwater breathing apparatus, or risk an impossibly long, lung-busting breath.

Marshall yelled.

Erin could barely hear him.

He shook her wildly, pulling her from her impossible daydream.

"Now," he screamed. "We have to go now!"

The Golden Queen raised her arm, signalling for the next wave of arrows. But before she could order their release, two rubber-gloved hands gripped the metal ladder by her feet. A massive head emerged, covered in seaweed, eyes wriggling with sea worms, baby crabs, and anemones. The scarecrow pulled her dripping body up the ladder, wobbling dangerously as she fought for balance.

Erin's heart leapt, soared.

Her soul sang.

Number Twelve is alive!

A tsunami of hope drenched her.

An emotion so powerful that she almost collapsed to the ground.

Harunara shook both arms in the air, screaming her frustration. "Fire, I said. Fire at will!"

A handful of arrows *thwocked* into Twelve's sodden limbs. She staggered under the impact, swaying from one cement-filled boot to the other, struggling to stay upright. More arrows looped high, passing over the scarecrow, heading for the roof.

Erin's heart beat frantically.

Number Twelve is alive! My friend is alive!

But great danger swirled all around.

Marshall grabbed Erin's arm again, yanking her away from Twelve, away from the falling arrows. The Non-Believers shielded Erin and Marshall from the next deadly storm. Jack stood with them, taking untold damage, grass and roots flying in all directions.

Erin squinted over his shoulder. Twelve was balanced precariously on the metal ladder between The Crystal Tower and the nearest Scraper, blocking the Golden Queen's escape.

Fire arrows zipped towards the scarecrow.

Some skimmed, missed, but a dozen or more bit.

Harunara cracked her vicious skipping rope at Twelve. Lacerations tore the scarecrow's fiery pirate jacket. Twelve smashed both rubber-gloved hands into Harunara's face. The Golden Queen wobbled, her plastic feet unsure on the thin, slippery rungs. Twelve charged, battering Harunara again and again, her torso dancing with flames. The golden mannequin tripped and fell. She clattered against the ladder, arms and legs dangling over the sides. Twelve pounced, landing on the Golden Queen. Her cement-filled boots creaked as the makeshift bridge sagged under her weight.

Dark smoke rose from the scarecrow's jacket.

The ladder juddered and jerked.

Rungs popped from their sockets.

With nothing left to support her, Twelve fell. Her hips clattered against Harunara as they both went somersaulting over the edge.

"No!" Erin screamed, breaking cover and sprinting towards the side of The Crystal Tower. Jack and Marshall dashed to her side.

Before them, the metal walkway was bent and yawning. In the middle hung Number Twelve, her rubber-gloved hands locked around the fragile ladder. Below, with golden fingers clasped to Twelve's cement-filled boots, Harunara climbed eagerly.

"Kick her!"

"Shake her!"

"Fight her!"

Twelve looked over at the three friends and then up at her hands.

Harunara was up to her waist.

The walkway creaked and buckled, dropping them closer to the water below.

"No," Erin whispered. "Don't you dare!"

Twelve hung on.

Flames licked her jacket.

And Harunara climbed.

"It's over," the Golden Queen spat. "Soon you'll be nothing but ash and dust."

"Never," Twelve told the mannequin, through a swirl of smoke. "It's never over. I may burn. I may smoulder and scatter to the winds. But someone or something will always endure. The humans came and went. The scarecrows and mannequins and wickermen have risen and, one day, we too shall perish. But something will remain. Something will survive. Something good. Always."

More Non-Believers surfaced far below. They began scaling the broken extremities of The Scrapers like determined, vengeful spiders. Archers struggled to fire more arrows, were brought to the ground, torn to pieces, and thrown to the sea.

"It *is* over," Twelve said, as Harunara wailed, "for you."

Hanging by one hand, Twelve threaded her red demon fingers through Harunara's metal mohawk. She tore the mannequin away, holding her out over The Endless Blue. The Golden Queen bucked and kicked, screaming atrocities and merciless vengeance.

But Twelve seemed calm.

Her ghoulish head tilted in the direction of her friends.

And, in a single, triumphant motion, she ripped Harunara's head clean off.

Her elegant golden body went careening down and down

into the water. Rising Non-Believer's swarmed around the headless remains. They snatched and clawed. Ripped and thrashed. Dissolving her body, like liquid gold, into The Endless Blue.

Harunara's dark light drifted past Number Twelve.

Fire and smoke engulfed her jacket.

She dragged herself onto the damaged walkway.

Stood.

Held Harunara's decapitated golden head aloft.

And roared like a lion.

JOURNEY HOME

Twelve carefully negotiated her way onto The Crystal Tower as the last of Harunara's mannequins were slung into the sea. She rolled back and forth until the flames died and the smoke began to clear. Stopping on her back, the scarecrow took a deep breath, relaxing every joint and tractor part and mechanical device in her body.

Erin took the Golden Queen's head from her grasp and raised an eyebrow. "You shook her head clean off."

"Well," Twelve replied. "I stopped working when mine came off."

"Your head is your head." Erin nodded knowingly.

"Accept no substitutes!"

Erin placed her own head on the scarecrow's smouldering chest.

The pirate jacket was scorched with patches of charcoal and soot, the stitching frayed and torn, buttons loose or missing.

"I thought you were dead," Erin said. "I thought I'd lost you."

Twelve reached down and stroked Erin's ragged hair.

"No such luck," she joked. Then, more earnestly, "For a time I thought I was done for. The water made things a hundred times harder than I ever imagined." Her massive head fell against the ground. "I feel…tired."

Erin sat up, her eyes staring into Twelve's wriggling hollows. A starfish had attached itself to the side of the scarecrow's head.

"But…" she said. "You never get tired. You never sleep. You don't need to eat or breathe or…anything. How can you—?"

"I don't know," Twelve began. "I'm just exhausted. Everything hurts."

Erin wondered if Twelve would finally find sleep, perhaps dream, and restore all the energy she had lost rescuing The Non-Believers and battling Harunara at the bottom of the ocean and atop The Crystal Tower.

Time was the only true healer.

That, and a reconditioning overhaul in Erin's Scarecrow Workshop back on Coldharbour Farm.

A sudden pang of homesickness shook her. It was strange and surprising. She'd spent her entire life there, been trapped there during The Many Years Storm, buried her parents there, longed for her brother, and prayed for escape. But now, having been away for a time, she pined for her barn, her bedroom, her toys, her scarecrow spare-parts repository, and every memory that Coldharbour Farm conjured.

"Where's your badge?"

Twelve tapped the spot on her chest where the little yellow pin badge had lived for so long. "Oh no. Where is it?"

Erin sighed. "It's gone."

"Gone?" Twelve said. "It can't be. It was right here."

"Don't worry."

"I could go back down and fetch it?"

"No," Erin told her. "Not in your condition."

"But—?"

"I have more."

"Where?"

"Back home."

"Home?"

"Yes. I want to go home."

"What about Clyde?"

Erin bit her lip. "I'm not giving up on him. I'd never do that."

"But, why…?"

"Look at us," Erin said. "We're beaten and battered. Barely alive. We need to regroup." She turned to Marshall and Jack and Socks. "Do you want to come and live with me?"

Socks yipped.

Marshall nodded. "Sure. Where?"

"Coldharbour Farm. There's plenty of room for all of us. Twelve can have my parents' room, you can take my brother's for now, and Jack can live in the hayloft. It's dead comfy and snug. Pirate's honour."

The wickerman smiled. "Sounds wonderful. A real home."

He looked as though he had been pulled through a bush backwards. Arrows protruded from every square inch of his body. The metal armour was split and battered and his feathered cape torn beyond belief.

"I'll put you back together the moment we arrive," Erin said. "I'll make you as good as new. All of you."

She turned her attention to the scarecrow. "And once we're all good as new we'll find my brother and every last one of your sisters."

"Promise?"

"I promise, Twelve. Cross my heart. Hope to die."

The scarecrow squeezed Erin's hand.

"Can you move?" she said. "Can you take us home?"

"Of course," she said, hauling herself to her feet. But, as the scarecrow reached full height and stared into the middle distance, she began to sway. Then, to Erin's horror, she clattered against the stone roof of The Crystal Tower.

"Twelve!"

"I'm okay," the scarecrow mumbled, rolling onto her back. "I just need to rest."

Erin stroked Twelve's arm, then stared across The Endless Blue. "But how will we get home?" she said, almost to herself. "I don't want to spend another minute here."

"I'll take us."

She looked up.

It was Jack. "Just patch me up and I'll take us all back to Coldharbour Farm. I can row. I may not be as strong as the scarecrow, but I can get us there. Keep the North Star at our backs, right?"

Erin plunged her arms around the dishevelled wickerman. "Really?" she said, her eyes filled with joy. "You're strong enough to take us all the way home?"

The wickerman nodded, poked some of his stuffing back inside, and ripped the arrows from his armour. "I don't see why not."

Erin tended to the wickerman while Marshall and Socks raided The Scrapers for food and provisions. They returned with cans and non-perishable goods from kitchens and staffrooms across the city. Lowering them onto *Lazarus*, Marshall took a seat at the very front with Socks perched half in the crow's nest.

The Non-Believers carefully abseiled Twelve into the boat,

positioning her arms and legs either side of the mast, her massive head cradled by the sails. Erin sat with her back to the mast, the scarecrow's rubber-gloved hands on her lap.

Behind them all, Jack took the oars in his green fingers. Most of his stuffing was back where it should be, and Erin had even tied her pink bandana ceremoniously around the top of his head.

"Sir Jack of the Island of Trees," she announced. "Take us home."

The sky darkened, the same way it had for many years without becoming night. *Lazarus* moved slowly through the water. The stars twinkled in the heavens far above. Erin stroked Twelve's rubber-gloved hands when she was awake and curled into them when she slept. The journey seemed to take far longer than she'd hoped. Perhaps it was Jack's rowing style. His pull on the oars was shorter and weaker than Twelve's, but they were moving towards home.

Pale light filled the world, then faded.

Erin set the music box playing while she finished *Frankenstein* and took it in turns with Marshall to read aloud from *The Adventures of Pinocchio*.

Another day passed.

"Twelve?" Erin said. "How are you feeling?"

"The same," she managed, her head bent, her living eyes directed at the sea. "I do not know what has come over me. I have always been so strong and tireless, but now—"

"It's okay," Erin comforted her. "Just rest. We'll be home soon."

Jack's arms worked at the oars, pulling them onwards.

"Not far now," he told her, pre-empting Erin's questioning eyes.

She was sure Jack didn't know how much further it was any more than she did, but it was comforting to hear those words.

Not far now.

Coldharbour Farm.

Her sanctuary.

Her home.

Not far now.

Socks coiled himself into the crow's nest, making peculiar snuffling noises as he slept. Erin lay with her eyes closed for a time. She wondered what Socks dreamt of. A place to run, to sleep, to play. And a bone the size of a mannequin leg to chew on, no doubt.

As sleep wove its threads across Erin's mind, her fingers lost all feeling. Her face became taut. Her heart slowed. Forcing her eyes open, she was confronted by a swirl of blue streaks that spun and undulated in chaotic patterns around *Lazarus*.

She stuffed her frozen hands into the pockets of her dungarees. She looked at Twelve but the scarecrow was fast asleep, her skull crystallised with ice. Jack pulled on the oars but his rhythm had become slow, his twigs and bracken coated in hoarfrost.

Erin glanced across the water. Blue streaks spread now, growing, becoming an all-encompassing fog. She stood and lifted Socks from the crow's nest. The poor dog shook terribly. His teeth chattered inside his long, elegant snout.

"What's going on, boy?"

Socks whimpered a chilly response.

"What is this?" Marshall stammered. "Do you live in the North Pole or something?"

And then—Jack froze.

Lazarus drifted through the gathering mist and came to a disorientating halt.

The water settled.

A sheet of grey glass.

Erin eyed the fog. "What are you?" she said aloud. "Some kind of localised weather anomaly?"

A shape whipped past the boat, trailed by an icy gown of mist and fog.

"What the—?" Marshall erupted.

"Did you see that?"

"See what?"

The fog tumbled over and over until it bloomed into a horde of disembodied faces. They floated around *Lazarus*, mixing into one another, eyes and mouths stretching and bending in the icy fog. Fingers shot out. They clawed the edge of the boat. Crept onto the deck, reaching for Twelve and Jack.

"Get away from there!" Erin screamed, fighting them back with frozen limbs.

The fingers swept towards her.

"Didn't you hear me?" she yelled defiantly.

The fog fingers passed over her skin. They were colder than twice frozen ice-cream, or Clyde's hardened snowballs that he stored in Ma's deep freezer, or the knuckle-splitting paper-round Erin had endured one bitter winter.

A cacophony of strangled voices refocused her attention.

Help us …

She reached for Marshall, huddling close for warmth and protection.

"Who are you?" she said, looking around.

We're lost …

"Wh-what are you?"

Let us in …

Marshall's lips had turned blue. Ice formed on his eyebrows. "So cold," he whispered, his eyes wide with pain.

Untethered … Outcast … Lost

"Marshall," Erin said, wrapping her freezing arms around the boy. "I think they're spirits."

"What…like ghosts?"

"Like the ones inside Jack and Twelve and Number Five." Erin nodded. "We need to get out of here."

Afraid … Abandoned … Alone

"Agreed. But…how?"

Help us … Lost … Let us in

"We'd love to help you, but we can't," Erin said, addressing the faces in the fog. They looked sad, forlorn. "Our bodies still hold spirits. There's no room for anyone else."

Afraid … Abandoned … Alone

Erin wondered who they were. Or who they'd been. Where they'd lived, who they'd loved, how they'd died—

Of course, that was it.

"They're dead," she said to Marshall.

"Well, yeah. Obviously," he replied. "I mean, their bodies are."

Erin frowned. It made her skin hurt. "Can spirits die?"

"I don't know. I always thought they just, you know, moved on."

"Moved on. Yes, that's right."

Help us … Hopeless … Homeless

Erin turned to the faces. "You've not been abandoned or

outcast. The bodies you lived in are dead and gone. It's quite normal. Death…" Erin fought the cold and the school of sorrowful memories just waiting to surface. "But you're free now."

Free …

"Free to leave."

The faces in the fog hung around Lazarus in silent contemplation.

Dead …

Free …

"Yes. Free. There's nothing to keep you here anymore. You're as free as the wind!"

The spirits seemed to exhale as one. A joyful, contented sigh. They spread, merged, thinned into colourful skeins, pirouetting around *Lazarus* before rising into the night sky.

Jack crunched forward, his foliage thawing quickly. The oars almost fell from his grasp. "What just—? Was I—? Did I fall asleep?"

"No," Erin said. "It's okay, Jack. Keep rowing, if you can. Take us home."

"Aye aye, Captain."

Twelve barely stirred. The ice on her skull melted, forming a puddle on the deck.

The sea opened before them, dark and empty.

Erin squeezed the scarecrow's hands tenderly.

The music box played.

Erin found sleep.

And dreams.

Clyde always arranged his action figures into armies. Good guys positioned under his bed to represent the Rebel Base on Yavin 4. Bad guys cloistered under a black umbrella by the bedroom door. Erin passed her brother a handful of Gamorrean Guards, Klingon Warriors, then Shredder and Skeletor to complete the battlefield.

"What are they fighting for?" she asked.

"Dominion of the galaxy," Clyde answered plainly.

Erin crawled over to the good guys. He-Man sat proudly on Battle Cat at the forefront of the lines. At his back, Optimus Prime, Spiderman, and a selection of droids and Redshirts were ready to lay down their lives for the freedom of the galaxy.

"Is there no chance of peace?" she asked. "Surely, there's room in the galaxy for everyone."

Clyde turned to her, his face different, darker. He grabbed Darth Vader and thrust him headlong into the rebel troops. "No, Erin." He smiled wickedly. "It's already too late—"

Erin woke with a start.

The world felt dusty and cool. Starlight glimmered on the ocean like a million fireflies doing backstroke. She looked into the sky. The North Star shone brighter than all the rest, clean and clear.

Her skin tightened.

The music box had almost wound down. Its haunting chimes were weak and isolated. Lucretia juddered in rough, graceless circles. Her red pushpin eyes stared menacingly.

Erin snapped the lid shut.

What was the North Star doing in the sky ahead of them?

It should be at their backs.

Pulling her legs in, she sat upright and peered across the water.

A large body of land approached.

Coldharbour Farm?

It couldn't be.

Straining through the cracks in her glasses, she tried to make out the farmhouse, the barn, the greenhouse, and the cross where Twelve had hung during The Many Years Storm. But, as they drew closer, she could see none of those.

Instead, the land looked barren and lifeless.

Long gritty shores met the rippling tide. Beyond, rising from the earth like broken teeth, were thousands of mottled, cracked gravestones. Uneven dunes spread towards a run-down chapel. At the top of the hill stood a curious-looking Scaffold, a ring of rope swinging from a right-angled crossbar.

"Jack?"

No answer.

"You were meant to keep the North Star behind us," she said, climbing over Twelve and placing a foot on one of the oars. "Turn us around. This place looks dreadful."

Jack flicked her foot aside and pulled harder.

"Jack? What's going on?"

Lazarus passed through two smaller outlying hilltops, each mounted with the same strange Scaffold then juddered to a halt on a shingle beach.

The wickerman dumped the oars overboard.

"This isn't Coldharbour Farm!"

"That's right, human girl," he replied, grabbing Erin by her dungaree straps. "This isn't your cosy hide-away home with your books and your toys and your scarecrows."

Jack dropped onto the shore.

Erin struggled to get away.

A figure emerged from the moonlit graveyard.

He wore an elaborate headdress.

"Hello," Tomas said. "You took your time."

BOOTHILL

Erin kicked and squirmed like a trapped animal, desperate to prise Jack's fingers from her dungarees. Tomas ran a bramble-entwined finger down her cheek. "The last human girl is finally here," he whispered close to her ear.

Erin's heart quickened.

What was happening?

And where was *here*?

She shot a look at Twelve. She badly needed the scarecrow at her side, but she was in no condition to repel the wickermen right now.

Marshall's head appeared over the lip of the boat. As realisation dawned, he exploded into life, grabbing his rolling pin and staggering through the shallows towards Jack and Tomas.

"And what do we have here?" Tomas said, knocking the boy aside. "Don't tell me we have another human survivor. A boy, no less. My cup runneth over!"

Wickermen flooded the beach, forcing Erin's and Marshall's arms into metal restraints.

They seized Socks, who yelped helplessly, and toppled Twelve into the water. They dragged the exhausted scarecrow up the beach. Her boots dug trenches in the wet sand.

Jack stood shoulder to shoulder with Tomas, straightening his damaged cape and adjusting his stuffing. "I'm sorry," he told Erin. "I am. Truly. But I cannot live the rest of my life in...*this*."

Something black and shiny crawled out of Jack's chest. Repulsed, he flicked it onto the ground, and crushed it with his heel.

"There's nothing wrong with you," Erin told him. "You're perfect—"

"—just the way I am, right?" Jack bit in a sing-song voice. "Grow up, Erin."

"You don't have to do this."

Tomas laughed.

"I do," Jack went on. "Once I deliver you to The Patchwork Woman, she'll put me back in a human body, and all this horrid business will be long forgotten."

"That's not your dream," Erin reminded him. "That's Tomas talking."

"That's where you're mistaken, little girl," Tomas said, kneeling beside her. The stench of his fetid construction invaded her nostrils. "That dream was never mine. It was Jack's. Always Jack's. The Patchwork Woman's promise to return us to our human bodies was his idea, and his alone. Jack made believers of us all."

Erin ground her teeth.

Tomas's hand snaked down Erin's back and pulled at her belt.

"Get off!" she screamed. "That's mine."

Before she could stop him, Tomas stood back admiring the pistol.

"Goodness me," he said. "Didn't your parents warn you not to play with firearms?"

"Give it back."

"Hardly." The wickerman laughed. "You could do some real damage with this thing. I know just the person to hold on to it. For safe keeping."

"How could you do it?" Erin yelled at Jack, summoning every last ounce of strength. "How could you betray me? Betray us all? After everything!"

Jack rolled his shoulders. "It's not personal," he said. "This is war. And I plan to survive."

The wickermen lifted Erin to her feet. Jack and Tomas walked in front, the rest manoeuvring Twelve and Marshall behind. The earth changed beneath her plimsolls. The wet sand retreated, replaced by a parched, arid dust. Erin glanced back to see Twelve stumbling over blackened branches. Two wickermen held her long, tired arms. A weary look hung on the scarecrow's face. A rusty, grinding wail bled from her mechanical joints.

The wickermen muttered among themselves, dark and uneasy. Erin tried to listen but only the occasional word registered.

"Jack … Patchwork … Girl … BootHill."

Twelve stumbled and almost collapsed.

"What's wrong with her?" Tomas said.

"She's exhausted," Jack replied.

"But she's a scarecrow. I thought they had boundless energy with no need for food or rest."

"There was a battle," Jack explained as they walked. "While we fought on the roof of The Crystal Tower, Twelve went to the bottom of the ocean to rescue The Non-Believers. She scaled The Scrapers and defeated Harunara on the rooftop. It appears events took it out of her."

Tomas rounded on his companion. "Do I detect... sympathy?"

"No," Jack replied spitefully. "Of course not."

"You didn't...make *friends*, did you?"

Jack grabbed Tomas by the shoulder.

"No," he said, pushing the wickerman away. "I tricked them all. I gained their trust, played on their kindness, made them feel sorry for me. *Then* I betrayed them." His eyes left Tomas and fell on Twelve, Erin, and Marshall. "Friends? We were never friends."

"Good," Tomas said, moving away. "Because what must come next would be almost impossible if you felt anything at all."

Jack strode up the hill after Tomas, his ragged cape billowing ominously.

Erin dragged her feet up the broken path. Gravestones and strange burial monoliths sprouted from the ground on either side. A dirty wooden fence, eroded by saltwater, lay collapsed to her right. Pebbles crunched beneath her plimsolls.

The sky seemed darker here than anywhere else across The Endless Blue. The sun paled away towards the horizon where it would sleep for a handful of hours. Night—a dull, hazy gloom—advanced across the sky.

Ahead, the path split.

One track led to the summit of BootHill, where the Scaffold loomed, mean and imposing. They took the other, towards the chapel.

"Everyone inside," barked Tomas.

"What are you doing to us?" said Erin. "Twelve, are you okay?"

"You should be more worried about the coming moments of your own life."

What did that mean? What was there to be afraid of? The Patchwork Woman? Was she here? Erin refused to be afraid of something she had never seen, never experienced, never understood. What kind of woman was she anyway? A witch, a magician, a sorceress dealing in the black arts?

She looked back at the three hills and the Scaffolds at their summits.

"The Devil's Fork," Jack said, sidling up beside her. "The very tip of BootHill. Most has been lost beneath the water… like your Ma, and your Pa, and your precious brother, Clyde."

"What's the hold-up?" snapped Tomas. "I want them inside."

"Jack," Erin whispered. "Don't. Please, this isn't you. I know it. Just—"

"Stop," he said quietly, raising a single gnarly finger. "Just stop. I like you. All of you. But I like me more. I *have* to do this."

The door to the chapel opened.

Marshall stumbled inside.

The scarecrow followed.

Erin stopped in the doorway.

Her eyes found the wickerman's.

"Inside," Jack commanded. "You do *not* want to keep her waiting."

THE PATCHWORK WIDMAN

Sackcloth plunged over Erin's head. It smelt damp and itched her face with every movement. As she knelt on the hardwood chapel floor, Jack tied her hands around a splintered column. Pain swelled between her shoulders. Hunger rumbled and clawed her stomach like an oil-deprived engine.

Erin shivered.

Her skin prickled.

Something felt wrong.

Very wrong.

She'd sensed it the moment they'd stepped on BootHill.

The lines of abandoned graves, the cloaked hilltops, and the Scaffolds.

A hollow, ravenous darkness encompassed everything.

This was a forsaken place.

A place dealing in death and punishment.

Nothing more.

Beneath the sackcloth, amidst the pain and discomfort, she could think of nothing but those she held most dear. Of Twelve and Marshall and Socks. Of the love she felt for Ma and Pa. For her lost brother, Clyde, out there somewhere—she hoped—fighting to find his way back home.

But this was a forsaken place.

Death and punishment.

Nothing more.

Why would BootHill be any more lenient to her? To Marshall, Socks, and Twelve? It wouldn't. It couldn't. That's all this place was.

Death.

Punishment.

Nothing more.

This was the place where the dark things dwelled.

"Are you okay?" she called to her friends. "Where are you?"

"I'm here," replied Marshall, to her left.

"Erin. I'm okay." Twelve was ahead, somewhere in the middle of the chapel.

Wickermen scurried to and fro, muttering among themselves.

Mixed with the damp odour inside the sackcloth, came another.

A putrid, rotten stench.

Erin almost gagged as the aroma enveloped her like a shockwave. She inched back and forth to escape the stink, but her bindings held fast. Disorientated by the sackcloth, she slipped and twisted awkwardly. A stab of pain roared across her spine. Angling her body to help relieve the discomfort, she squirmed on the ground like a fish out of water.

The floor carried the more palatable scent of rotten wood and dead leaves.

With her ear pressed against it, she could hear the subterranean scurry of rodents and insects and stubborn, enduring life. Life that had refused to accept the doctrines of BootHill. Life that had refused to slip silently into the night.

Life that had found a way.

Perhaps hope remained.

Just a sliver.

Her fall shifted the sackcloth, revealing a ragged tear where she could view the room. Morning shadows spread across the chapel floor, vibrating with the heat from a small fire at the centre. Positioned around the flames were six rough-cut tree trunks.

Two were occupied.

On the first sat Loren, the wickerwoman. She wore a battered pale Stetson and a thick leather belt studded with rhinestones and bloodied feathers. Tomas stood behind her, whispering something in her ear.

The other person wore a long, dark cloak that pooled on the dusty floor. It was made from squares of dark material, each about the size of a human hand, crudely stitched together with coarse thread. Bunched, uneven, lopsided.

"Patchwork," Erin whispered to herself.

The figure rose as Twelve staggered helplessly into the firelight and slumped down on one of the tree trunks.

"The scare—crow," the figure in the patchwork cloak said, drawing the word out as though savouring it on her tongue. "I hear impressive things. Skills I would have at my side, should you prove trustworthy. You built a boat and sailed The Endless Blue. You rescued a wickerman, sought an accord with Bavorski Beetlestone, and fought your way out of The Scrapers, taking down Harunara and her mannequins for good measure." Her voice was undeniably female but rough and sore, like her tongue was made of sandpaper. "You're a one-scarecrow army, Twelve. Can I call you Twelve? I feel like I already know you."

"That is my name," she said. "Although, I lost my pin badge so you'll have to take my word for it."

The woman laughed drily.

"A simple-minded creature, aren't you? A battering ram. All grunt, no finesse. But useful in a tight spot, I'll grant you."

"And you're The Patchwork Woman, I suppose."

Sinking her hands into deep pockets, her cowled head rose atop slim shoulders. The woman took a breath. "*My* name?" she said. "Yes. Some call me The Patchwork Woman. It sounds…*imposing*, yes?"

She bent her head to one side.

Her neck cracked horribly.

Erin winced at the sound. The swirling stench returned to her nostrils.

"What do you want with us?" Twelve asked.

The Patchwork Woman sniffed. "You? Nothing much. However, I do need warriors. You'd definitely qualify. But every part of me screams a warning. Can you be trusted, Twelve? You wouldn't betray me, would you?"

"What makes you think I want to fight for you?"

"If not for me, then who? The birds, the mannequins…the *girl*?"

Erin felt The Patchwork Woman's gaze settle on her.

"Harunara's mannequins have been overthrown. Bavorski Beetlestone and the Blue King have settled their dif—" Twelve tried.

"Ah, yes," The Patchwork Woman said. "The dog. Socks, isn't it? What a ludicrous name. A creature that was once stolen as two colonies battled for ownership of The Endless Blue. But now the mutt is returned. An olive branch. A peace treaty. A union of the sky and The Scrapers against a mutual foe."

Erin wondered how The Patchwork Woman knew all of this.

Dark magic? Arcane sorcery? Foresight? She caught a glimpse of Jack loitering at the edge of the fire, his foot raised on one of the trunks.

Of course. The liar. The turncoat. He'd told her everything.

"Why do you want to destroy them?" Twelve asked.

"Me?" she replied. "You must get your facts checked."

"Facts?"

"I do not seek war and destruction," The Patchwork Woman explained. Her hands slipped from her pockets and spread down her legs.

Erin's gaze shot to the woman's hands.

Instead of being smooth and plain like her own, they looked malformed. They were predominantly pale, but several fingers were much darker, as though scorched over a ferocious heat.

"All I want is the world," she went on, her head angled at Twelve again. "The quickest way to end a war is lose. The wickermen—and Loren, here—were smart enough to acknowledge that. I promised them all manner of riches for their immediate surrender and allegiance. A return to their human bodies. A rebirth. A dream that I, too, am searching for."

"A rebirth?" Twelve managed.

The Patchwork Woman's gaze fell on Erin again.

"No!" Twelve whispered. "Leave her be!"

The Patchwork Woman hissed.

Her body quivered excitedly.

"Erin. The last human girl. And she's all mine."

A strangled scream lodged in Erin's throat.

Twelve rose. "Never!"

She pulled a handful of arrows from beneath her ruined pirate jacket and launched herself through the fire. Flaming logs tumbled in all directions as Twelve plunged the arrowheads into The Patchwork Woman's chest. They slipped through her clothing and embedded themselves in whatever lurked beneath. Twelve crashed backwards, exhausted. She landed awkwardly, rolled through dust and fallen roof beams that cracked and split under her monstrous frame.

The Patchwork Woman took three long paces then vaulted into the air. Landing deftly, she straddled two tree trunks, looming menacingly over the fallen scarecrow.

She grabbed the arrows and tore them from her chest.

"As I thought," she said, throwing the flights aside. "Untrustworthy. Deceitful. And false."

And with that, she pulled a cord at the top of her embroidered cloak.

The garment parted like a curtain.

And dropped to the ground.

Erin's screams bubbled on her lips.

The Patchwork Woman's name had nothing to do with the dark, fragmented cloak that covered her from root to leaf.

The truth was a horror beyond anything Erin could imagine.

SKIN

The Patchwork Woman stood naked in the firelight, an embroidered catastrophe of mottled, hairless flesh. Erin trembled as she took in the full terror of her distorted form.

Each segment—large, small, pale, dark, grey, tattooed, infected—was tethered to the next with coarse stitching. The flesh had frayed in places, the stitches pulled apart where skin was broken, inflamed, raw, and crumbling.

But most horrifying of all was The Patchwork Woman's head.

Made of a dozen pieces and held together with the same ghastly stitching, it was uneven, unbalanced, as though it might topple at any given moment.

Like a landslide of spoiled meat.

She had no mouth, not in a traditional sense, just long black stitches that ran horizontally over a pair of mismatched, bloated purple lips.

Her eye sockets were torn, ruined holes, as though someone had taken a sharp fingernail and gouged them out in a roaring hurry. Behind swirled nothing but shadows.

Erin turned away, disgusted. She closed her eyes and saw the body of Loren, the skin on her head and hands removed.

Bile rose in her throat.

Her head spun.

Even in the darkest watches of the night, in her most devious scarecrow-designing phases, Erin could never have conceived a creature quite like the one that stood before her.

An abomination.

An ungodly ruin.

Impossible to behold.

"Am I not beautiful?" The Patchwork Woman roared. "Am I not everything you imagined I would be?"

"What *are* you?" Twelve said.

The Patchwork Woman straightened, her corrosive arms spread wide.

"I am the last human woman!"

Twelve struggled onto her knees.

"I see derision in your eyes," The Patchwork Woman said. "I see fear, and confusion, and repulsion. I know my skin is worn, damaged, and riddled with corruption. It's cold and fragile. It splits. The stitches break and itch and burn. But no longer. Soon, I will have a complete skin. A skin smooth, young, and supple. Not cobbled together from a hundred others. One that will not splinter. One that will not break. One that will last me forever!"

Twelve thrust a cement-filled boot into the ground and launched herself to full height. With The Patchwork Woman standing on the tree trunks, their eyes locked.

"What *are* you?" Twelve said again.

"Twelve," Jack warned, raising a hunter's axe. "Leave her. You have no idea what she can do."

Twelve didn't see the blow coming.

One second she stood, eyeballing The Patchwork Woman.

The next, she hit the ground, consumed by dirt and dust. Wickermen leapt upon Twelve, hog-tying her wrists and ankles. The Patchwork Woman swept the long black cloak over her shoulders, hiding her abhorrent form. She said nothing, merely glared at Twelve, then turned for Erin.

A strong hand clasped the back of Erin's poncho and dragged her to her feet. A fresh wave of pain flooded her frail body. Pinned to the column, hands held her in place as her knees trembled and promised to fail.

"Take it off," The Patchwork Woman ordered, her voice a venomous whisper.

A dim glow filtered Erin's vision as the sackcloth slipped away. She sucked down a lungful of air, swallowed hard, and steadied her shoulders.

Jack, Tomas, and a handful of wickermen lingered by the doorway. The others surrounded Twelve's hog-tied body. Loren stood close, hat back, chewing nonchalantly, her thumbs tucked into her belt either side of Erin's pistol. Her strange green fingers caressed the cold steel. To her left, Marshall knelt beside another column, his hands bound, his head covered in sackcloth.

"Child," The Patchwork Woman hissed.

Erin could barely bring herself to look.

"The last human girl."

She examined Erin from top to toe before snatching the broken glasses from her face.

"You're not exactly what I would call beautiful, but definitely not unattractive."

Marshall murmured something incomprehensible and rattled his chains.

"Silence," The Patchwork Woman rasped, snapping her

fingers. Loren clipped Marshall across the top of the skull with the butt of Erin's pistol. He sank to the floor.

"Leave him alone!"

The Patchwork Woman rounded on Erin, sinking to eye level.

"You're smaller than I'd hoped too," she said, revealing a hand of divergent fingers. Fanning them across Erin's face, she added, "But you'll grow. One way or another."

The Patchwork Woman threw her hood back, displaying the full horror of her rotten, stitched face.

She moved close.

Erin now understood the true horror of that repulsive smell.

"As you can see," she added, through her bulging lips. "This skin has deserted me. It's time I shed it and took a new one."

Her eyes swarmed Erin's body.

"A complete one."

Horrors snaked through Erin's mind, dark and deadly.

Shaking, she collapsed.

Wickermen raised her clean off the floor.

Pain tore through every muscle.

"As I explained to your...*friend*, the scarecrow, I've come to tolerate my name. But not for much longer. Soon I'll be... someone else."

Erin quivered, almost unable to comprehend the thoughts poised on her tongue.

"And you want...my *skin*?"

"Very good," The Patchwork Woman replied. "Go to the top of the class."

"That's madness."

"The question is, how do I remove it in one complete piece? Do I cut slits in the bottom of the feet and peel it upwards? Or do I remove your scalp and drag it down?" She rocked her revolting head from side to side, tapping her chin thoughtfully. "Why don't you choose?" She pressed a rotten, yellowing finger against Erin's cheek. "A last request. A final wish."

Erin bared her teeth. Her nose wrinkled. "Go to Hell!"

The Patchwork Woman laughed darkly. "A noble, fighting spirit. That's more than can be said for that pile of timber and rusty cogs." The Patchwork Woman's face brushed against Erin's. "Every last drop of fight seems to have been drawn from your scarecrow."

Erin fought uselessly.

"I'm afraid she's no use to you anymore. She's no use to anyone. The scarecrow is done. Probably best I put her out of her misery."

"Liar," Erin bleated. "You can't kill Twelve. She's—"

What was Twelve? A scarecrow? A sister? A warrior? A friend? Yes. But more than that. Much, much more.

"She's immortal," Erin erupted.

Was that true? Erin didn't know, but neither did The Patchwork Woman. Whether it was true or not, Erin wanted to believe it. She *needed* to believe it.

"Immortal?" The Patchwork Woman spat, a cruel laugh caught in her throat. "Impossible."

Erin rallied. "She's a scarecrow. The greatest scarecrow I ever created. She's made of wood and metal, not flesh and blood. She's built to last. Built to destroy the likes of you!"

The Patchwork Woman froze. "You...made her?" She turned on Jack and Tomas. "Who failed to tell me this?"

The wickermen looked accusingly at one another.

"You built the scarecrow and brought it to life?" Her morbid face lowered towards Erin once more. Her back arched into the air. "So," she purred. "Your worth has increased a thousand-fold."

The Patchwork Woman swept around the room.

Wickermen shied away.

"I need an army, Erin. One that is stronger than all the birds, and all the mannequins, and every last thing sent to oppose me!" Her long cloak swirled as she moved. "I need a true, loyal army. One that will protect me and my new skin! And you—" she snorted, clutching Erin's face in her rotten fingers "—will give it to me!"

Erin's instinct was to deny her, but something hatched in her mind. Something that might save them all. Something that might *literally* save her skin.

"I can't do it here."

"There's no such thing as *can't*," The Patchwork Woman rasped. "Everything can be achieved with time, patience, practice, or manipulation. The only decision you must make is whether you *will* or *will not*."

The Patchwork Woman tilted Erin's chin towards her.

"I *will not* do it here," Erin conceded.

A warm sensation rippled through her tired body.

"If not here," The Patchwork Woman said, her rancid eye holes thinning. "Where *will* you do it?"

"Coldharbour Farm," Erin told her. "There, I will make you the greatest army The Endless Blue has ever known."

"Coldharbour Farm?"

"Yes," Erin smiled. "You have to take me home."

THE SWARTHY STRANGER

Outside, a headwind gathered. Dust dervishes waltzed across the dried, cracked paths of sprawling graveyards. Rot and corruption filled the air as angry purple fissures bloomed across the sky.

Erin slammed against the side of the run-down chapel.

Wickermen clutched her tightly.

The Patchwork Woman headed for the water.

To Erin's surprise, a thin, elegant schooner bobbed gently in the shallows. Made of dark wood and inlaid with slivers of turquoise and cobalt, the resin hull shone brilliantly in the pale moonlight. Three black sails rippled excitedly, calling for adventure.

Emblazoned along the hull in sparkling silver was the name *The Swarthy Stranger*.

It was by far the most beautiful boat Erin had ever seen. She wondered how *The Swarthy Stranger* had survived The Many Years Storm when all others had been smashed to smithereens and condemned to the trenches of The Endless Blue.

But now was not the time for questions.

She had to get the plan straight in her head.

There was time.

But was there enough?

Geographically, Erin had no idea where they were. She wondered how long the journey back to Coldharbour Farm would take. Days? Weeks? The longer the better.

Two strange figures dropped a rope ladder over the edge of the elegant boat. The Patchwork Woman boarded a nimble skiff, crossed the water, then slowly climbed aboard.

Marshall burst through the door of the chapel.

Jack's hands gripped his shoulders.

"Take that sack off his head," Erin urged.

"The Patchwork Woman's orders," Tomas replied, shrugging.

"You're pathetic. You know that?"

"Says the girl in chains," he sneered, shouldering her aside. "Bring them both!"

Marshall appeared at her side, urged towards the shore by strong, evergreen fingers. "Are you okay?"

"Peachy," Marshall mumbled beneath the sackcloth. "What's going on?"

"They're putting us on a boat and taking us to Coldharbour Farm," she explained. "I haven't seen Twelve. She must still be inside."

"Enough chatter!" cried Tomas as the wickermen hauled the skiff onto the beach. Once settled on the shingle, he ordered Erin in. Tomas sat opposite and signalled towards the schooner.

Erin turned to BootHill. The entire area swarmed with shadows and gravestones and nameless, horrible shapes. She stared at the chapel, expecting to see Twelve emerge.

But the chapel remained silent.

The door firmly shut.

Erin was ordered onto *The Swarthy Stranger.* She clambered over the gunwale and onto a solid, slippery deck. The Patchwork Woman had disappeared below, but two new shapes dominated the quarterdeck. Both appeared to be naked, shiny, the colour of clay. Their eyes shone like rubies through the gloom.

"What fresh Hell is this?"

"Golems," Tomas told her, climbing aboard. "Monsters of clay. Eyes of crimson glass. One, a hulking glutton. The second, a rakish wisp. They were built hundreds of years ago inside the chapel. Some believed they were made to guard BootHill against ghosts and malevolent spirits. Others say they led the souls of the dead beneath the hill. Either way, they're alive now and sail with The Patchwork Woman."

Voices yelled from the beach.

Erin's attention was ripped from the golems.

The remaining wickermen had lit fire-torches and were returning to the chapel. With one quick movement, flames spread from their hands to the frail wooden building, turning it into a deadly inferno.

"No!" Erin screamed, mounting the gunwale. "Twelve's in there. You'll kill her!"

She prepared herself for the drop, for the cold water, for the sprint back up the hill, and the searing blaze. But before she moved an inch, Tomas grasped her, holding her back.

The tinderbox chapel took quickly. Fire and flame wreathed the structure, curling around windows and doorframes. Devouring and consuming. The roof yawned and buckled, collapsed, pulling the walls with it. A dust cloud erupted. Molten embers danced and died in the moonlight.

Erin wailed.

Long and sorrowful.

But the wickermen did not stop there.

Making their way to the shoreline, they approached *Lazarus*.

"No!" Erin screamed. "Not our ship!"

But they paid no notice.

Fire licked *Lazarus* with wicked fiery tongues.

Twelve's leather chair blistered and bubbled. Sails rippled with sickly sparks. Flakes of blackened ash floated into the sea. The hull burned bright and vibrant one minute, a charred husk the next. Even Clyde's dragon figurehead was not spared. It smouldered ferociously then dropped head first into the wet shingle.

Erin screamed, burying her face in her hands.

Tomas finally let go, laughing cruelly.

She collapsed to the deck, swaying on her knees as she fought back her tears.

An ill wind swept across *The Swarthy Stranger*. It brought the smell of fire and ash. A smell that invaded every sense Erin possessed. She pictured Twelve at the centre of the chapel surrounded by a ring of fire. She saw the ceiling fall onto the scarecrow, engulfing her. Twelve's heart was strong, but her wooden limbs were no match for the consuming blaze.

Erin forced the image down.

Deep.

Her hands shook.

Blood boiled.

Hope faded to a pinprick.

A vicious crack pulled her focus.

The Swarthy Stranger's sails whipped dangerously in the gathering wind. Weather at BootHill was more evident than at

Coldharbour Farm. There, a breeze was something to behold, like an eclipse. But here, the world was different. What had caused it? Geographical location? The tilt of the planet? The Patchwork Woman's dark magic?

Marshall's sack-clothed head appeared over the side of the schooner.

He struggled to climb on board, searching desperately for something to hold. Erin steadied herself, clutched his arm, and gave directions. Soon, he crouched beside her, swaying gently with the motion of *The Swarthy Stranger*.

"What's happening?" Marshall bleated. "Something's on fire."

Erin dared a glance back at the shore. "They burned it."

"What?"

"*Lazarus...*"

Marshall gasped.

"...and the chapel. It's...gone."

"But," he said, "Twelve was inside."

"Why?" she screamed at Tomas, pointing at the shore. "Why did you kill her? She'd done nothing to you. Nothing. All she wanted was to find her sisters and live her life daydreaming in an armchair at Coldharbour Farm!"

"What's done, is done," the wickerman replied coldly.

"That's not an answer."

"I don't care."

"The sackcloth," she roared, her entire body shaking. "Take it off."

"No," the wickerman replied. "The Patchwork Woman's orders. I already told you."

Marshall groaned.

"He cannot wear that thing forever!"

Erin's fingers reached for the knots that secured the bag over her friend's head.

Tomas lifted her into the air.

"Put me down!" she wailed. "Take that bag off his head. This is inhumane!"

Landing awkwardly against a barrel, she rolled onto her side.

"Stay put, human girl," Tomas ordered, then disappeared below decks with Marshall.

Erin's hands pumped into fists. Fire coursed through her. She shivered and tightened as emotions came again and again like the rain during The Many Years Storm.

She took quick breaths.

Her chest burned.

Nose streamed.

Eyes fought to remain dry.

There was a time to fight, but this wasn't it. Patience. Planning. There would be time for retribution. Revenge. She pushed her emotions away, promising to draw on them when the moment was right.

She sank her elbows onto the gunwale and forced herself to stare at the gloom and desperation of BootHill. "Twelve," she whispered. "Dearest Twelve. You can't be dead. Not yet. You've got so much living to do."

The remaining wickermen were now clambering onto *The Swarthy Stranger.*

Loren arrived last.

Black sails caught the wind.

Something moved on the shore.

Erin's eyes shot towards it, hoping desperately to see the scarecrow wading towards them. But it was someone else who paddled after them, whining sorrowfully.

Socks!

"Stop the boat. We have to go back!"

Loren stood beside her now, looking at the forlorn lurcher. The wickerwoman said nothing, just folded her arms and watched as *The Swarthy Stranger* slipped further and further out of the poor animal's reach.

Eventually, Socks circled back to the shore.

"What do you want?" Erin said, her heart aching as she watched the paddling dog.

Loren shrugged. "Nothing. Just taking in the view."

Erin fidgeted. A million questions bubbled on her tongue.

"What do *you* want to know?" Loren said, teasing Erin's curiosity.

"Nothing," she said, crossing her arms defiantly.

"As you like."

Loren turned, sighed, and shuffled across the deck.

The Swarthy Stranger passed between The Devil's Fork. Scaffolds stared down with malicious intent.

"Wait," Erin said, trailing after her.

Loren stopped. Her fingers stroked the pistol in her belt. "Well?"

Erin opened her mouth to speak, but nothing came. There was too much. She didn't know what to ask first. Loren sighed agitatedly and started towards a low door beneath the quarterdeck. Above, the two clay monstrosities stood at the ship's wheel.

Erin followed the wickerwoman into the captain's cabin, a small room with comfy armchairs pointed towards a series of portholes. A drinks cabinet and a bookshelf lined one wall, the other housed an antique desk covered in maps and instruments for reading the stars. There were communication radios, an echo-locator, and radar equipment piled up at one end of the desk. Cables slithered onto the floor.

Loren dropped into an armchair. "Well?" she said again, stretching her legs and crossing them at the ankles.

"Who is she?" Erin managed, taking the other chair.

"The Patchwork Woman?" Loren said. "The stuff of nightmares, wouldn't you agree?"

"I don't know," Erin said. "I've seen so many terrible things."

"Believe me." Loren smirked. "You'll see far worse before the end."

"My skin," Erin said, her voice a fragile whisper. "She wants my skin—"

"—for her own," the wickerwoman finished, unfazed. "You cannot help but notice that hers is frayed and damaged. The stitches cannot live with the salty sea air. Corruption swims through her, like monsters in The Endless Blue. But yours…"

Erin pushed the sleeves of her poncho up to the elbow and ran her fingers over her pale, cold arms. The skin prickled under her touch. She felt sick. Not the churning sickness of a stomach ache, but a sickness that covered every inch of her flesh and every molecule inside her too. A repulsion. A nauseating vitriol.

Something dark moved in her mind.

"What's underneath?" she said. "What's under the patchwork skin?"

Loren shifted uncomfortably. "I do not know."

"She's not human," Erin told her. "I can tell in the way she moves. I knew the Blue King was not a mannequin because of the way he walked. The same is true of her."

Loren laughed. "Silence, child. You know nothing."

Erin sat back and watched the wickerwoman.

"What is it?" Loren croaked.

"Nothing," Erin replied. "Do you actually believe you've got a human spirit buried in there somewhere?"

"It's not buried," she replied hotly. "I am a human spirit. This *foliage* is just a vessel."

"And you believe she'll put you back in a human body once she wears my skin as her own?"

"Of course. Why wouldn't I?"

"Why *would* you?" Erin asked, exasperated. "Because she made a promise? And you trust her?"

Loren gazed through the portholes.

Beyond, grey water separated them from The Devil's Fork like a giant slab of concrete. An endless parking lot. The islands had faded. Columns of smoke from the chapel and *Lazarus* had all but vanished.

"I trust no one," she said evenly. "Least of all the last human girl and her tricky questions. The Patchwork Woman *will* deliver me a human body."

Loren thrust herself out of the armchair and strode to the door. Placing a hand on the frame, she turned. "And if she doesn't, I'll take one for myself."

With Loren gone, Erin watched as shadows swallowed The Devil's Fork.

Twelve was still there.

Somewhere.

On BootHill.

Dead?

Alive?

Erin didn't know. But she remembered Twelve's words.

It'll take more than fire to destroy me.

The scarecrow had survived so much already.

This wasn't the end.

"I'll come back for you," she whispered. "In a day, a week, a month, a year. It doesn't matter. You don't need food or water. Nothing can kill you. You're *immortal*, aren't you?"

Erin spun the word over and over and over again.

"Nobody I love is ever going to die. Not again. Not ever again."

She returned to the deck and curled up on the forecastle. She slept in shifts. Her mind dragged her into nightmares that forced her to wake, sweating, shivering. But *The Swarthy Stranger* was a swift berth, fast and true. No sooner had the sun clawed its way across the sky and sunk to the horizon, than Coldharbour Farm came into sight.

Erin wrapped her fingers around a brass rail on the gunwale and pulled herself up. She saw the farmhouse. The barn, the stables, the greenhouse, Twelve's empty cross, and the graves of her parents.

This was not the way she had hoped to return.

As a captive of The Patchwork Woman.

As a sister without a brother.

As a broken, terrified girl.

But, despite everything, it felt good to be home.

DIRTY DOZEN

Flecks of crystal blue twisted through the shifting grey skies. A gentle breeze scurried across the flagstones, blowing dried leaves and dirt towards the shore.

Erin walked up the hill, passing Twelve's cross. She marvelled at the differences in the sky and the wind in her wild hair. Part of her wondered if the world was changing again, fixing itself. Or had it always been this way? Had she been away for so long that she'd forgotten?

The Patchwork Woman stood in the courtyard, admiring Coldharbour Farm. "It's nice here," she said. "In a bleak, homely way. I'm going to like it."

"This is *my* home."

"And now it's mine."

Erin's hands balled into fists.

"So," The Patchwork Woman said, "where do you make the scarecrows?"

Without a word, Erin led her to the barn.

The Patchwork Woman stalked back and forth before sheets of metal, engine parts, nuts and bolts and screws, wooden struts and beams, clothing, saws and drills and mallets, and every item that Erin had etched or beaten into a disturbing face.

She crossed her rancid arms. "Is this all?"

"Yes," Erin said, adjusting her glasses. "I can probably make ten scarecrows. A dozen at the most with the parts I have. Is that not enough?"

The Patchwork Woman swept close. "Would you consider twelve scarecrows an army, little girl?"

"My Ma once told me that a person who fights for something they love is worth a hundred hired hands."

The Patchwork Woman snorted and whipped her cloak tight around her repulsive body. "Can you make them love me?" she said, eyeing the hotchpotch, odds and ends, brick-a-brac collection of spare parts.

"Love you?"

"Yes, love me. I want to be adored!"

"Ye-es." Erin smiled slowly.

"Truly?"

"They will love you as only a child can love a mother."

The Patchwork Woman's shoulders widened. Her head tilted high, proud.

"You will be The Mother of Scarecrows."

"Yes," the woman hissed. "Yes, I will."

Erin bowed her head. "As you wish."

Snapping her fingers, The Patchwork Woman swept past Erin, heading for the farmhouse. "Then let it begin!"

Erin spent her days and nights working tirelessly.

Bending.

Sawing.

Hammering.

Soldering.

Creating.

When sleep finally took her, Erin collapsed in the hayloft. She twisted and turned in nightmares about the different ways The Patchwork Woman might remove the skin from her bones, the plight of Number Twelve, Marshall entombed in sackcloth, and the poor abandoned Socks on BootHill.

The barn became Erin's home. A sanctuary away from The Patchwork Woman and the wickermen. They left her alone for the most part, going about their own business, preparing Coldharbour Farm for whatever was to come.

The golems stood guard either side of the yawning barn door.

Erin had heard of golems before. Her brother's dorky fascination with Dungeons & Dragons and Terry Pratchett's *Discworld* had paid dividends. They didn't chat much, just stood and stared. But, when asked a direct question, they tended to answer. The large one called himself Hank, the thin one, Shun. They sounded more like nicknames than birth names.

Erin wondered who had built them, named them.

Hank and Shun didn't know.

Erin positioned her new creations against the back wall of the barn, between the hay-bale fortress and her creation station. They were functional, but lacking the personality, time and care her original dozen had been given. Erin desperately tried to eke out another three from the remaining scraps, but materials were becoming scarce.

Was this army of scarecrows enough to buy time, to stave off her inevitable death and torturous skinning? She shuddered every time she thought of it, finding a new compassion for the sufferings of rabbits and chickens and pigs.

Everything seemed so bleak.

Insurmountable.

Impossible.

But every memory of Number Twelve rekindled the spark. Nothing was impossible. *Something will survive. Something good. Always.* Slamming a hammer into a scarecrow's shoulder socket did her a power of good.

Erin could only control what was in front of her.

Her fight was here, now, in the barn.

Buying time.

Saving their lives.

Leaving the barn and striding across the courtyard, she could feel the burn of the golems' red eyes on the back of her neck like laser-targets. The courtyard buzzed with activity. Wickermen constructed a platform on the far side. Others were hauling huge logs off *The Swarthy Stranger* and positioning them in a large circle. It reminded Erin of the large cookfires she'd built on camping trips with Ma, and Pa, and Clyde.

Lookout towers had been erected at each compass point to scan the water. Fences stood along the shoreline between each tower, topped with coiled barbwire.

Erin darted through the industrious wickermen as they fortified the island. She scowled at Tomas and Jack, and entered the farmhouse.

The Patchwork Woman had taken up residence in the living room. She clearly liked it in the same way Twelve had. The only change she had made was the ceiling. There simply wasn't one. She'd ordered the wickermen to remove it, creating a lofty space like a royal court.

The Patchwork Woman sat on Erin's parents' bed, surrounded by broken furniture and crumbling masonry. She seemed to be entranced by the painting of *The Haughty Jinx* that dominated the opposite wall.

"Inspiration," she said, as Erin hung in the doorway. "For your adorable sailboat, right? I can see it now. You must have spent months building that thing. Shame it burned so fast."

Erin swallowed hard.

"Twelve built *Lazarus* actually."

The woman laughed. "A scarecrow built a seaworthy vessel. Whatever next?"

"Twelve has levels that you could never understand," Erin said. "She is a very surprising...person."

And Twelve *was* a person, a real person. Even though she'd been made of inanimate objects and brought to life by— well, Erin wasn't sure what, she was definitely real. As real as anyone she'd ever met.

The Patchwork Woman swung her legs off the bed. A medley of skin and stitches flashed into view before she concealed them beneath her dark gown.

This was the first time Erin had seen The Patchwork Woman's feet. What lived at the ends of the woman's legs were not feet in a traditional sense but more akin to slippers. She had no toes. Not one. Just rounded blocks of patterned skin and disgusting black stitching.

"It's rude to stare."

Erin didn't care. "I need more parts for the army," she said, curling her hair behind her ears.

The Patchwork Woman waved her on.

"I'll be upstairs. Collecting...things."

"Make it quick. The wickermen have lots to do today. I don't want you under their feet."

Erin nodded and swept up the thin, wooden staircase,

moving swiftly into her bedroom. She darted to the bedside cabinet, dropped to her knees and pulled the bottom drawer out. Hidden beneath were two plastic pouches stuffed to the brim with red reels of paper, each punctuated with hard, black dots.

The contents had once belonged to Clyde who'd secretly stored them on a shelf that he believed Erin couldn't reach.

He was mistaken.

Erin's father had forbidden her from playing with the paper-reels, saying they were too dangerous for a young girl. So, when the coast was clear, Erin had sneaked into Clyde's room and removed a reel here, a reel there, stockpiling her own arsenal. However, once The Many Years Storm struck, she'd inherited the lot. Her treacherous cunning and thievery had been for nought.

She turned one of the pouches over.

A tattered, faded label clung to the reverse.

Cap-Gun Explosives. Handle with care.

CAP-GUN EXPLOSIVES

Returning to the barn, Erin carefully stashed the cap-gun explosives at the bottom of a cake tin filled with nuts and bolts. She'd also collected two dozen wooden struts from beneath the beds, a handful of coins, and a stack of old newspapers. In the farmhouse basement she'd fetched a woven wash-basket and filled it with the one thing her father had forbidden her from using on her scarecrows: the Coldharbour High School American Football kit—a team he coached on the weekends—complete with shoulder pads and helmets.

It had taken several trips to transport all the sports equipment, but the effort excited Erin to see it piled in the barn stinking of stale sweat and teen spirit.

"Go Redkites," she muttered, inspecting one of the scarlet jerseys.

She turned to the angular frames of the new scarecrows and considered each one. Picking the sturdiest-looking monstrosity, she slung a pair of shoulder pads over its head.

"You can be the quarterback," she decided.

She scrunched up handfuls of newspaper and, after dousing them in motor oil that she'd used to lubricate their joints and hinges, packed the torso to bursting.

Next, Erin carefully threaded the reels of cap-gun explosives through the oil-soaked newspaper, being sure to leave an end poking out at the top of the spine. Concealing the makeshift explosives, she slipped a large scarlet jersey over the top, silver numbers shimmering on the front and back. She did the same to the other scarecrows, stuffing oil-soaked paper into their chests and wrapping them with cap-gun explosives.

Next came their heads.

Initially, they were a mix of colourful balloons inflated inside sackcloth, demonic faces drawn on the front with marker pens. Erin untied the balloons and let them deflate, refilling each with gasoline that she syphoned from Pa's tractor. This done, she slipped them back into the sackcloth and placed a battered helmet on top.

She took a moment to admire her latest creations.

They were scarecrows, for sure.

Redkites, indeed.

But they were something else too.

Undercover resistance fighters.

Berserkers.

Born to fight. Born to burn. Born to die!

She felt a little sorry for them, but they were not alive. They had no words, no feelings, no personalities. They were just numbers on football jerseys. A dirty dozen.

11, the Kicker.

18, the Quarterback.

23, 25, 39, Defensive Backs.

43 and 47, Linebackers.

50, the Centre.

80, 82, 85, Wide Receivers.

And 89, the Tight End.

Everything was set.

All she had to do was bring them to life and make them fall in love with The Mother of Scarecrows? If Jack and Tomas were to be believed, wickermen and mannequins and scarecrows were animated with human spirits.

Where was she going to get those?

She prayed for a miracle.

The same one that had brought Number Twelve into her life.

"I'd quite like to keep you all," she told them, fussing their jerseys. "But, like you, I have no choice."

Sighing, she returned to her workbench and laid out the coins she had collected in the farmhouse. She frowned at the mishmash of currencies, but that hardly mattered. Most were the size of a penny, two considerably larger.

Taking more cap-gun reels, she wound them round and round and round until the pennies were the size of golf balls. The larger coins got a double helping. Once finished they were big enough to play an explosive game of tennis. She encased each ball in a layer of tape to hold the explosives in place, then carefully hid the pennybombs at the bottom of her toolbox.

She positioned the last one.

Clang!

Grabbing her body, Erin inspected it for burns and missing limbs, but there were none. She spun, shaking, wondering what had caused such a noise.

There, in the middle of the courtyard, Jack and Tomas and the other wickermen were dragging a cast-iron, roll-top bath across the cobbles.

Erin dashed outside. "What are you doing with the tub?"

Tomas ignored her, barking at the others.

Jack stepped towards her. "Orders from The Patchwork Woman!"

"I figured as much," she replied, raising an eyebrow. "But for what? Are you planning a hot soak under the stars?"

"Very droll," Jack said. "I fear I would not survive such an ordeal. And don't get any ideas."

The option of boiling the wickermen alive hadn't occurred to her before. Now it was all she could think about. Their leaves and grasses and moss and bracken would wither and blanche while the water turned into a deep brown gloop of bubbling dirt.

She ran her hands down her goosepimpled arms.

A sickening thought clawed her bones.

The wickermen manoeuvred the roll-top bath into the middle of the courtyard where the huge pile of logs were neatly stacked, like triple-cooked chips in a posh restaurant. They placed the bath on top and secured it carefully. Saucepans and jars and biscuit tins filled with rainwater—that Erin had spent months collecting—were now being used to fill the bathtub.

Memories of Ma flash-boiling tomatoes and red peppers so she could easily remove their skins and blend the innards into soup consumed her mind.

By the time the iron-clad, roll-top bath sloshed full of rainwater, the world had sunk into twilight. Erin would have loved to stand and take in the sight, but the events before her stole the moment. Instead, she ignored the horrors of the roll-top bath and worked on her new scarecrows, adjusting their jerseys and helmets, checking the homemade explosives were safely hidden inside.

The Patchwork Woman stomped through the farmhouse

door and inspected the gigantic construction.

The wickerwoman followed, thumbs tucked in her belt, cowgirl hat casting a shadow over her face. The bath teetered twenty feet in the air, suspended on almost a hundred logs, stuffed with bracken, kindling and anything else that would burn fiercely; including most of Clyde's Fighting Fantasy choose-your-own-adventure novels and Ma's cookbooks.

Erin dashed between the barn doors as the wickermen brought another cardboard box of her brother's books and dumped them unceremoniously on the pyre.

Hank grabbed Erin by the arm and lifted her clean off the ground.

Her legs bicycle-kicked in the air. "Put me down!"

The golem said nothing.

Shun clasped her legs in one hand and lifted her high above his head. Together they carried her towards the roll-top bath like a deceased soldier transported home on her shield.

"No!" Erin screamed. "You cannot! Not like this! Not now!"

The Patchwork Woman raised a hand.

The golems froze.

"Is my army complete?" she said, peering towards the barn.

"Yes. Almost."

"Then what further use do I have for you?"

Erin scanned the water and the blue-grey sky. The sun and moon were crossing paths as a billion stars watched on expectantly.

"I can make you more," she said. "Another dozen. A score even!"

"You said a dozen would be sufficient. You said that each would fight like a hundred hired hands. You said they would

239

love me. The Mother of Scarecrows!"

Signalling to the golems, they dumped Erin on the cobbles.

"Well," The Patchwork Woman added. "Are they alive? Are they prepared for war?"

Erin felt the world closing in.

"Do they love me?" the wretched woman went on. "Do they love me the way only a child can love a mother?"

Erin's eyes betrayed her.

"I knew it," The Patchwork Woman said. "Bring her!"

Erin braced herself, expecting the golems' clammy hands to snatch her up and toss her into the roll-top bath. But nothing happened.

Instead, the wickermen formed two rows along the cobbled path.

Hank stomped and Shun glided down the hill, wading out to *The Swarthy Stranger*.

The large golem heaved his thin counterpart on board who returned a moment later with a third creature. Erin squinted through her cracked glasses, struggling to see who they'd fetched from the schooner.

Two long legs appeared over the gunwale.

They slowly descended the rope ladder.

Erin's heart quickened.

She'd almost forgotten about her. Resigned her to a fate of confusion and mental torture on the Island of Trees, locked in the climber's lodge.

But she was no longer marooned on that desperate shard of rock.

Number Five had returned to Coldharbour Farm.

And she was *full* of spirits.

NUMBER FIVE

With her arms supported by the golems, Five tripped and scuffed her way up the cobbled path on electric-blue rollerblades. She stopped on the courtyard, the farmhouse to her right, the barn to her left, the towering bonfire and bathtub looming ahead.

Erin wondered what Five's addled, turbulent mind would make of this.

How long had The Patchwork Woman kept her locked away in the hull of *The Swarthy Stranger*? What effect had that had on the poor scarecrow?

Nothing good.

Erin knew that much.

She seemed well enough, however. In one piece. No visible signs of damage or distress.

The Patchwork Woman circled Five, nudging her towards the barn.

Erin darted across to intercept them, but Five sidestepped the girl and skated inside.

"What are you doing?" Erin said, trailing The Patchwork Woman.

"Finishing what you couldn't," she answered simply.

"Bringing my army to life."

"No," Erin whimpered, trying to get to Five. "Not with her. She's suffered enough."

The Patchwork Woman gave a quick hand gesture and the golems seized Erin again.

"You're quite the pest," she told her. "I ought to squash you like a fly, but I'd hate to see you miss all the excitement."

Erin struggled hopelessly in the golems' grip.

"You've given them a uniform," The Patchwork Woman said, walking down the line, inspecting the football jersey on each scarecrow. "How pointlessly quaint."

"I haven't armed them yet," Erin tried desperately. "I have weapons in mind, but I thought it best if—"

"What you thought is at an end. We have no use for your sticks and kitchen knives here. I have weapons for my warriors. Steel blades collected by Loren and her wickermen. The Mother of Scarecrows' army will be a lethal fighting machine, feared in every corner of The Endless Blue. All will perish or obey!"

The Patchwork Women spun to face Number Five. "Kneel," she ordered, rolling her shoulders.

Five sank to the ground.

"You remember what we discussed," The Patchwork Woman hissed. Five nodded slowly. "Then what are you waiting for?" she exploded. "I want scarecrow warriors and I want them now!"

Five's shoulders slumped, resigned. The scarecrow began to shake. Her hands grasped the edges of her eye sockets.

"Don't, Five," Erin begged. "Don't do it!"

The Patchwork Woman wrapped an infected hand across Erin's mouth.

"Begin!" she hissed.

The light inside Five's damaged basketball head started to glow. It expanded quickly, reaching into the corners of the barn, scaring spiders and bugs into deeper crevices.

Despite the vanishing sun, the barn shone brighter than midday in the height of summer. Five's head vanished, engulfed in a voluminous, pulsating orb of light. Her arms shook wildly. She steadied herself against the earth, fingers spread in the hardened straw. Stones and pebbles skittered away from her in perfect circles.

Number Five's body arched back as the orb shrank inside her head.

Silence descended.

Shadows took a peek.

Brilliant light shot out of Five's eyes hitting the first Redkite scarecrow—Number 18, the quarterback—pinning his arms and legs against the corrugated shell of the barn. He jigged around manically, as though strapped to an electric chair.

The Patchwork Woman screamed encouragement, egging the scarecrow on.

The light retracted.

Five re-adjusted her head like a ship's cannon training on a new target.

Hot vapour rose.

Number Five exploded once more.

"Yes!" The Patchwork Woman shrieked. "Live, my beauties. Live!"

The next scarecrow shook chaotically, engulfed by the shimmering white rays. On and on she went, from one Redkite to the next, until the entire team had been showered in her luminous phosphorescence.

Finally, it was done.

Five groaned and collapsed.

Her rollerblade wheels squeaked to a halt.

Darkness fell.

Erin struggled again, trying to help. "Please," she begged, pulling The Patchwork Woman's hand from her lips. "She's in pain. Let me help her."

The Patchwork Woman threw Erin to the ground, stepped over the stricken scarecrow and inspected her army. At first, the Redkites just hung there against the wall, arms and legs at jaunty angles as heat rose from them like boiled vegetables. But then, as if waking from hibernation, they began to move.

It felt like a scene from one of her favourite books.

A set piece from an elaborate stage musical.

Magic.

Each scarecrow had a strange, unfinished look to the way they moved. Metal joints screeched and groaned, helmets bashed into walls, gloved hands reached out, fingers coiling, hanging on to one another for support.

Seeing her creations come to life for the first time filled Erin with an odd sensation. One of pride and joy, and an overwhelming desire to protect them with her life.

Wickermen filed into the barn, fire-torches held aloft. Shadows danced across the walls. Shadows of scarecrows and wickermen, golems and The Patchwork Woman.

Erin recoiled at the fire. A mossy hand grabbed her chin and bent it skywards.

Loren stood over her.

She flicked the pistol towards the courtyard.

"It is time."

It was a beautiful night. The most glorious night since The

Many Years Storm. The dark grey sky was streaked with cyan and turquoise and mauve, dusted with twinkling, distant stars. But nobody noticed. Everyone's eyes were on the iron-clad, roll-top bath, and the ladder leant beside it.

Summoning what energy remained, Erin broke from Loren's grip, darting side to side. But the golems were there again. Shun caught her with one giant stride and dragged her across the courtyard. "Get off me," she screamed. "Get your disgusting hands off!"

Kicking and clawing, Erin tuned out everything except the gentle break of the waves on the shore. She scanned the skies and the horizon. Everything seemed so far away, so distant. Her hopes and dreams of what life could be turned to shadows and pressed against her, throbbing like a desperate heartbeat.

Everything tightened to a pinpoint.

Her vision clouded with black.

The golem stopped.

Erin jolted mid-step.

"I've been thinking," the woman said. "You were right. You're far more valuable to me alive."

The Redkite scarecrows had made their way out of the barn and shuffled into a rough circle around the bonfire, still holding on to one another.

"It's just as well there's someone to take your place."

Loren disappeared into the farmhouse.

She emerged with the pistol in one hand.

Marshall in the other.

"No!"

"You say that a lot." The Patchwork Woman laughed. "But nothing comes of it. I don't often change my mind. None of

my wickermen will turn to aid you. And, let me check—"
she glanced at the horizon "—there's no one coming to save
you. No birds. No mannequins. No scarecrows." She paused
wickedly. "No brother."

Erin whimpered.

"No one. You are utterly alone."

"You can't do this," Erin rallied, fighting a tidal wave of
emotion.

"Have I taught you nothing?" she said, brushing Erin's
tangled hair from her face with a repulsive hand and
straightening her wonky glasses. "There's no such thing as
can't. Just *will* and *will not*."

Loren muscled Marshall to the foot of the ladder.

"I hate you," Erin spat.

The Patchwork Woman snorted, grew to full height, and
stretched her arms towards the heavens.

"Put him in!"

RAINBOW DRAGON

Flames spread through the bonfire with a thunderous roar. Books and photo albums and kindling ignited inside the thick logs piled in the centre of the courtyard.

Marshall stood at the foot of the ladder, his hands tentatively wrapped around the iron rungs. "Erin?" he whispered, trying to turn away from the heat. "What's happening?"

But Erin's eyes were on the horizon. For a minute, perhaps two, she stared forlornly at the last sliver of sunlight. Was this the final time she would see it? Would it ever rise again for her? And, as its lower edge sank below the waterline, a dark shape shifted across the pale, smouldering orb.

"There!" She grabbed Marshall's arm. "Look!"

"I can't see a thing," he replied angrily. "What is it?"

Erin stalled, unsure.

As the shape grew, she squinted, trying to see who or what hurtled towards Coldharbour Farm at such a rate.

A thought occurred to her.

A wild thought.

Justice Raventhorne.

The blackbird had been missing for so long. Had he chosen this moment to return and save her from The Patchwork

Woman and Loren, the golems and the wickermen?

But the approaching shape had grown far larger than any blackbird. Bigger than an eagle or an albatross. It swooped low, rushing headfirst across the shimmering waves, before rising above the battlements of Coldharbour Farm, its mighty wings spread.

Erin gasped, her eyes wide in utter amazement.

"Erin?" Marshall bleated. "What is it?"

Cast against the moon, the enormous creature hung in mid-air. Feathered wings, dazzling with a thousand different colours, were edged with pale light. Upon the creature's head, two twisted horns pointed at the sky.

At first glance, Erin decided it was some kind of dragon. Something straight out of her brother's Dungeons & Dragons campaigns but, looking again, she saw the once-vibrant buttons on its pirate jacket, the dirty rubber-gloved hands, the cement-filled boots.

It couldn't be.

Scarecrows couldn't fly.

Could they?

Erin's heart somersaulted.

"It's...Twelve," she replied, her voice almost lost in her throat. "She's here."

"That's impossible," Marshall said, moving his head around hopelessly. "She died in the fire on BootHill."

"Twelve has come to save us," Erin said. "All of us!"

Twelve's boots crunched against the cobbles as feathered arms glided gracefully to her sides.

She strode purposefully up the hill.

Wickermen approached, weapons raised, fire-torches aloft.

Twelve held up a hand. "I come in peace."

The wickermen stalled, unsure what to do.

The Patchwork Woman screeched at them, knocking several aside as she tore herself away from Marshall and Erin. "What dark magic brings you here?"

Twelve and The Patchwork Woman came face to face at the edge of the courtyard, just feet from the graves of Erin's parents.

"I've come for the girl," Twelve replied. "And her friend. Marshall."

The Patchwork Woman laughed, sickly and bitter.

"And what makes you think I'll just hand them over?" She studied Twelve's feathered wings. "Just because you can fly does not give you any leverage. I have two hostages. I have a dozen wickermen. A dozen Redkite scarecrows made by the girl's own hand, brought to life by Number Five. You have nothing to offer."

Twelve's confidence faltered.

Erin saw it. Her heart fluttered.

"Five?" Twelve uttered. "My sister? She's...here?"

The Patchwork Woman clicked her fingers.

Loren emerged from the barn, the pistol buried in Five's spine. The scarecrow rumbled across the cobbles, struggling to keep herself upright on her rollerblades.

"What have you done to her?"

"She has given me an army."

The Redkite scarecrows moved around the bonfire. Their silver numbers shimmered in the firelight. They walked awkwardly, unsettled, as though their shoes were the wrong size, or their legs were uneven lengths, their backs unable to bear the weight placed upon them.

"Is this it?" Twelve countered. "Is this your *army*?"

"You dare to mock me?" The Patchwork Woman growled. "You? A scarecrow? A thing. A *nothing*." She ripped a handful of feathers from Twelve's arm, turning them over in her stitched fingers. "You're nothing but damp wood and rusty engine parts. One of your horns is cracked and your wings look as if they have seen better days. That jacket is burned and shredded and the insects that dwell in your eyes are riddled with fear."

Twelve took everything The Patchwork Woman had to throw at her. "Erin and Marshall will come with me now."

"Or what?"

"I will return with an irresistible force. A force that will engulf you all."

"The birds?" She snorted. "You mean to attack me with a handful of birds?"

Erin looked to the skies. There wasn't a single bird in sight. Twelve had come alone. Had she planned anything? Was this just an elaborate bluff?

Erin trembled, reaching for Marshall. "It's only me," she said as her skin brushed his. "I think something terrible is about to happen."

"Tell me something I don't know."

Twelve rolled her shoulders. "Birds? Yes. And more besides."

The Patchwork Woman stepped closer.

Her vile, stitched face hung below Twelve's. "I'm The Patchwork Woman. The Mother of Scarecrows. The last human woman. Empress of The Endless Blue!"

Twelve said nothing.

Instead, she thrust a rubber-gloved hand beneath The Patchwork Woman's cowl and grabbed the top of the repulsive head. In one swift movement, Twelve ripped the stitched flesh away.

The Patchwork Woman screamed, clawing at the scarecrow's arm. Twelve thrust forward, grabbed her shoulder, and ripped and tore for all she was worth. "I know what you are," she spat as The Patchwork Woman's hands beat her chest. "You're not the last human woman. You're not even a woman."

With one vicious movement, Twelve dragged the top half of The Patchwork Woman's skin away, wrenching it over her head and down her arms like a repulsive pullover.

The Patchwork Woman's dark cloak fell to the cobbles. Dust spiralled in miniature tornadoes as wickermen and Redkite scarecrows inched forward.

The Patchwork Woman was torn in two. Her legs and waist remained in black stitching and diseased human tissue, but a long red gash circled her torso. There was no gushing blood, just a thick line of coagulated, sore meat, like old steak sawn in two. Emerging from the wound was the woman's true form, the body she had concealed beneath her repulsive, cauterised quilt.

Dust filled the air.

Erin shielded her eyes.

"Hello, Number Eight," said Twelve, holding The Patchwork Woman's skin in her hands. "It's good to finally meet you. *Sister.*"

Number Eight!

Erin scanned the scarecrows in her head, whizzing through the pages in her *Book of Scarecrows*. What did Eight look like? What had she built her out of? Which field had she been placed on? What horror lurked beneath the patchwork skin?

Number Eight. Number Eight. Number Eight? What did I make—?

The wind dropped.

The dust settled.

Erin's eye caught the small escarpment of land, half a mile from Coldharbour Farm where Eight's cross stood, tilted and bent.

Bile rose in her throat, thick and burning.

Number Eight spun and glared directly at Erin.

"The skeleton," Erin whispered to herself. Her eyes wide as saucers.

Eight was almost upon her before the words left her mouth.

The scarecrow looked enraged, distraught, and confused.

Stumbling forwards, she pulled and ripped and tore at the skin around her legs with both bony hands, finally stamping and kicking the grotesque feet away.

Number Eight was a complete human skeleton. Skull, ribs, pelvis, arms, legs, feet, the lot. Each bone knitted together with wire and garden string, elastic bands, screws, nails and unwanted mechanical hinges—just like Twelve—but coated in chunks of rotten skin and smeared with blood.

But most disturbing of all was what filled her chest. Beneath the bloodied rib cage lurked a horde of dolls' heads, fifty or more, all bundled on top of one another; their faces damaged, melted, stained with grime and dirt, hair scraped back in tight buns or flowing in chaotic strands.

As Erin's gaze roved over the doll's heads, she took a sharp breath.

Her sickness subsided.

A fresh wave of terror seized her.

The heads were moving too.

Jostling around inside Number Eight.

Blinking, biting, *screeching!*

Their eyes burning blood-red.

The plastic skeleton had been acquired from Dr. Bonamorgan's Surgery after he'd retired and closed his practice. Erin had begged Pa to buy it for her. To begin with he wasn't convinced, but Erin was a determined young lady and, after weeks of running extra chores, baking his favourite cakes, and being exceptionally kind to her brother, the deal was done. She'd put Number Eight in a yellow dress decorated with blue flowers, a raspberry cardigan, straw hat, fruit picking gloves, and wellington boots.

Beyond the scarecrow, Twelve threw the top half of The Patchwork Woman's skin to the ground and stormed up the hill.

"You're a scarecrow," Erin told Eight. "You're one of mine."

"A scarecrow?" she said, pointing at Twelve. "Like this... *thing*?"

"She is not a thing!" Erin told her. "She's the same as you. She may look different—different in every way imaginable— but you are sisters. Scarecrows. Made of my hand."

"Lies!" exploded Eight. "These are my bones. My human bones. The Many Years Storm wrapped me in a monstrous hurricane. Sent me spinning across the world, high in the air and low against the water, until I landed on BootHill. The wind took my clothes and robbed me of my flesh."

She spun to face Erin.

"And I will replace it with *his*."

All eyes zeroed on Marshall.

"Those aren't bones. Not real ones," Erin said. "They're plastic. They're fake. Just like you!"

Number Eight roared. The dolls' heads in her chest screamed in fifty different tongues, gnashing their teeth like starving wolves against her ribs.

Erin backed into Marshall.

"Help me," he whispered.

In a fight, Twelve and Eight would most likely cancel each other out, but there were wickermen and Redkite scarecrows and golems and Loren to contend with. As Erin weighed the numbers, the wickermen hurried to Eight's side, forming a line. Jack and Tomas stood among them, their faces flooded with confusion at the blood-smeared skeleton.

"Twelve!" Erin screamed helplessly. "Do something."

But Loren slipped to her side, inches from her ear.

"It's over," the wickerwoman whispered. She drew the barrel down Erin's cheek. "You've lost. And soon The Patchwork Woman will be no more. She'll be reborn in his skin…or *yours.*"

Erin shivered as the cold muzzle pressed against her cheekbone.

Loren laughed, chaotic and unhinged.

"Climb."

Marshall slid his bare feet onto the first rung of the ladder.

"Don't try anything," Loren advised. "Or I'll put a bullet through your kneecap before you can move an inch."

"And what good will Marshall or I be to Number Eight if we're riddled with bullet holes?" Erin said sullenly. "It'd almost be worth it to see what she'd do to you."

Loren barely moved. "You're all words, Erin of Coldharbour. All words and nothing more."

Marshall reached the top, the sackcloth still draped over his head.

"Get in," Loren commanded, impatiently.

"Don't!"

Marshall manoeuvred himself over the lip of the iron-clad, roll-top bath and slipped soundlessly into the water. Erin closed her eyes and wrapped her hands over her ears, expecting to hear Marshall's screams, but there was nothing.

"Marshall?"

"I'm okay," he replied. "The water's lukewarm. There's still time."

"Bring wood and oil!" Loren screamed.

Half the Redkite scarecrows fled into the farmhouse. The others joined the wickermen and Number Eight on the cobbled path, forcing Twelve towards The Endless Blue.

The scarecrow stopped at the shore.

Her cement-filled boots squelched in the gunge.

"You're not welcome here, scarecrow," said Eight. Her plastic bones rattled in the gathering wind, the dolls' heads chittering darkly, echoing her sentiments. "Erin and Marshall are mine. Bring your army, if you dare. Bring your *birds*. Bring whatever you can muster. We will resist you all, for The Endless Blue is mine. And shall be forever more!"

Erin watched from the courtyard. Surely, Twelve would spring her attack any moment and overcome them all. But, as Twelve stood and scanned her opponents, Erin could feel the tears collecting in her eyes.

Twelve was outnumbered.

Twelve was outgunned.

Twelve was—

Erin dropped to her knees.

—*gone*.

The scarecrow had spread her rainbow wings and rocketed

up into the sky. She lingered there for a moment, casting a wearisome stare at Erin, before twisting her body and retreating across The Endless Blue.

"Twelve!" Erin punched the cobbles. "Come back. Don't leave us!"

But the flying scarecrow had disappeared into the waning moon.

PENNYBOMBS

Erin's tears fell. They came in shuddering waves, her body bent double. A twisting pain gnawed her ribs. How could Twelve do this? How could she abandon them to this fate?

She wiped her eyes and looked out to sea. There had to be more to Twelve's plan than simply demanding The Patchwork Woman—Number Eight—let them go. She must have known that would never work.

She blinked, her focus pulled to the graves beside the greenhouse.

"Ma," she said to herself. "What do I do?"

A bony foot shook the ground.

The accompanying body blocked her view.

"Crying, are we? How pathetic." Eight reached down and hauled Erin to her feet. "Tears are for children, the weak, and the broken-hearted." The scarecrow laughed. "Looks like you qualify on all counts!"

She dragged Erin through the barn doors and dumped her by the entrance to the hay-bale fortress.

"I want more scarecrows," she said. "I don't care what you make them out of. Dry your eyes and begin immediately!"

Erin crawled away. She wanted the universe to swallow her

whole. She wanted to fall through the cracks of reality and begin again in a galaxy far, far away.

"Twelve," she whimpered, hugging her knees to her chest. "Why?"

She rocked quietly.

Wickermen stomped back and forth.

Number Eight barked her orders at the Redkite scarecrows—who were still adjusting to the sensation of being alive—as the huge bonfire burned fiercely in the courtyard.

The bonfire!

Erin rolled onto her side and looked at the enormous pyre.

On top, Marshall sat in the bath still wearing the sackcloth. A sickly grey vapour bubbled over the edges, threading with thick columns of smoke.

Marshall seemed oblivious to all of this. Surely he could feel the boiling water, even if he couldn't see the rising steam.

Erin galvanised her fragile body and crept to the barn door.

Hank and Shun stood on either side. Their ruby eyes glittered in the firelight.

She dropped to her knees and crawled behind Hank's enormous legs.

Eight draped the dark patchwork cloak over her skeletal shoulders and disappeared into the farmhouse, screaming and yelling and barking commands.

To her right, Jack and Tomas argued animatedly in the lookout tower on the northern tip of Coldharbour Farm. Eventually, Jack dropped down and stormed up the hill. Tomas yelled something after him. Erin couldn't tell what he'd said, but it made Jack miss a step. The wickerman reached for the long, curved blade at his hip.

Erin withdrew behind Hank's legs again.

When she risked a second glance, Jack had gone.

Marshall had vanished in the torrent of vapour now billowing from the roll-top bath. Erin crawled forward, looking both ways. Redkites were stationed at the foot of the cobbled path, behind the stables and the greenhouse. Other than the golems, the courtyard appeared empty.

Now's my chance.

Run. Climb.

And be fast about it.

But if she made it to the top of the ladder and managed to haul Marshall to safety, where would they go?

The farmhouse? Nope.

The barn? Hardly.

The stables? Forget it.

It seemed so obvious when the idea finally came to her.

There was nowhere left to hide on Coldharbour Farm. Eight and her army would pull every building apart until they were found. No, the only safe place was away from here, far out to sea, across The Endless Blue.

They had to get to *The Swarthy Stranger.*

Erin shimmied to the scarecrow-building station and silently rifled through her drawers. At the back, packed in bubble wrap were the pennybombs.

Sixteen the size of golf balls.

Two considerably larger.

She placed them nervously in the pockets of her dungarees. If she were to slip and fall, igniting the bombs, the damage would be—well, she didn't want to think about it.

Taking two small pennybombs in hand, she crept to the barn door.

Redkite Number 82—one of the Wide Receivers—was within range. Even if she missed, the noise from the pennybomb might cause enough commotion for her to get to Marshall.

She paused. The pennybomb tingled in her fingertips. She waited, sweat building on her brow. And then, when the Redkite moved into range, she pulled her arm back and let fly.

Instantly, she knew it was going too high, so she launched a second before digging her hands into her pockets to retrieve more.

The first hit the cobbled path and exploded in a blinding flash.

The noise rattled her skull, far louder than she'd remembered. Her brother and his dorky friends had spent an entire summer constructing the perfect pennybomb, firing them from catapults or dropping them off multistorey car parks, but none had erupted with such force.

The explosion reverberated around the courtyard. The sound ricocheted off the farmhouse, blustering passed Erin and kicking up dust.

The second hit the ground behind her original target.

82 stumbled, his hands covering his helmet as the bomb burned fiercely at his feet.

She launched a third. And a fourth.

The third lodge itself between the layers of 82's shoulder pad, but did not explode.

The fourth pennybomb hung in the air.

The golems' eyes trained on it.

Erin darted beyond the barn door.

Hank's and Shun's arms flailed towards her, but she ducked and rolled, found her feet and pelted for the ladder.

The fourth pennybomb glided through the air on a perfect trajectory, rolling and spinning in the cool night air. It descended towards 82's head, striking the edge of the face guard and bouncing up inside the helmet.

The cap-gun explosives erupted with a blinding white light. Sparks bit into the sackcloth of the scarecrow's face and the gasoline laden balloon inside.

The fuel caught.

Head and helmet detonated into a thousand pieces.

Staggering, headless, the fire quickly spread to the cap-gun reel jutting from his jersey. The red reel fizzed. Caps exploded one-by-one. *Pop! Pop! Pop!* 82 shook wildly as though drilled by machine-gun fire.

Erin stuck her foot on the ladder and hauled herself skyward.

Her hands stung against the searing iron rungs.

A frenzy of cap-gun explosives caused the oil-soaked paper to ignite, turning 82 into a walking firebomb. He took a blind step. His flaming arms pinwheeled. The pennybomb lodged in his shoulder pads connected with the fire and exploded, ripping his poor body in two. 82's right arm and most of his torso went flying towards the sea. The rest collapsed in a smouldering heap.

Eight stood in the farmhouse door. Her skeletal jaw yammered up and down beneath her black cowl, screaming commands into the gathering dark.

At the top of the ladder, Erin shoved her hands under Marshall's armpits and lifted him from the scalding water.

"I wouldn't do that if I were you."

Erin froze, turned.

Loren perched on the farmhouse roof, pistol in hand.

"You cannot kill us both," Erin said.

The wickerwoman paused. Indecision flashed behind her stony eyes. The pistol weaved in gentle circles.

Marshall slipped from the bath.

Erin clung to his soaking, red skin.

Marshall moaned.

The ladder creaked, teetered.

Heat belched against Erin's skin.

The wickerwoman stood.

The pistol at her side.

Her mouth open.

Erin twisted her head as far as it would go.

Something enormous moved across the sky.

Birds.

Hundreds and hundreds of birds.

And flying at the head of the column was Number Twelve.

QUARTERBACK

The sight and sound of Twelve leading the birds into battle was something Erin would never forget. Wings beat, feathers rustled, squawks and caws and chirps of all kinds blasted a ferocious war cry.

Stirred by the spectacle, Erin left Marshall clinging to the ladder and launched herself at Loren. She took three quick steps and sprang from the roll-top bath onto the farmhouse roof. Her fingers dug into the wickerwoman's knotted grassy exterior, clawing and tearing for all she was worth. Loren stumbled on loose slates, scrambling to the top of the farmhouse.

Erin seized her chance and dived for the pistol. She connected sharply with the wickerwoman's arm, and the gun fell. It clattered against broken tiles and skidded into the gutter. With a swift kick to the midriff, and a hefty double-handed push, Erin thrust Loren over the top of the farmhouse and into the shrubs and shadows beyond.

Erin turned, dropped, slid. The pistol nestled on a bed of dry leaves in the metal guttering. She tucked the gun inside her pink belt, then returned for Marshall.

Wickermen and Redkites took positions across the

courtyard, in crudely built towers, behind farming equipment, amongst the piles of garbage and bodies on the shoreline. Number Eight stood among them wrapped in her patchwork cloak, the terrifying dolls' heads raging beneath.

A storm of birds circumnavigated the island.

Erin and Marshall clambered down the ladder and headed for the shore.

The Swarthy Stranger bobbed gently on the water beyond the walls and lookout towers, beyond the Redkites and the wickermen and Number Eight.

"What are we doing?" Marshall whined, as Erin faltered.

"Change of plan," she said, staggering towards the barn. "I'm going to hide you."

Hank and Shun barely bothered to apprehend them, their eyes fixed on the swirling dangers above. Erin steered Marshall into the hay-bale fortress. She led him into the furthest reaches of the cardboard stronghold, removed the sackcloth and brushed the hair from his reddened face.

"I'm hot and cold all at once," he told her. "I'm scared, Erin."

"You'll be okay," she whispered, dousing him in blankets. 'Stay here. Stay quiet."

Crawling as fast as she could, Erin returned to the barn doors.

Outside, Number Eight screamed.

Arrows sliced the air.

The massive cloud of birds moved effortlessly, avoiding the arrows as they cut through the night and vanished into the water beyond.

Twelve spun, her wings spread, encouraging the wickermen to open fire. As each prepared to take a shot, handfuls of birds broke off from the main group and sped towards them. Dozens descended on each wickerman. They grabbed their heads, shoulders, arms, and lifted them into the air. Screaming like terrified children, the wickermen rose above Coldharbour Island, legs kicking wildly. The birds tore and wrenched at the grass and moss and twigs, finally dropping what remained in dissected, motionless clumps.

Erin smiled.

It was almost unfair.

"Mark my words!" Eight waved her fists at the heavens. "I'll kill you all!"

The birds replied with feverous shrieks and hoots, jeering and mocking the scarecrow.

"I'll break your wings and make a crown from your bones!"

Jack, Tomas, and the Redkites rallied to Eight's side. Sharp blades and fire-torches gleamed in their hands.

Birds swooped, claws outstretched, searching for their next opponent. Swishing swords and searing heat kept them at bay. They made a second pass. Several birds took a tighter line, moved closer to their adversaries. Only half made it back.

Eight screamed with delight as birds fell at her feet.

Organising themselves into position for a third attack run, a sea eagle and horned owl dropped in beside Twelve.

Together, they turned from the circling mass and descended sharply towards the courtyard. The sea eagle and the horned owl zeroed in on Tomas and Jack, pursuing them in chaotic circles around the courtyard. Twelve landed inches from Eight. Long blades sliced the air around her. She ducked expertly, rolled forward, and kicked the legs of Number 39 away. The Redkite collapsed to the cobbles, spilling his weapon and fire torch.

Twelve whipped the blade into her red demon hand and sprung to her feet.

"Hello again," she said, raising the sword. "*Sister!*"

Steel sung through the gloom.

Sparks fell like rain.

Eight spun two elegant, curved blades in her skeletal hands. She drove Twelve towards the enormous fire. Parrying for all she was worth, Twelve kept her sister at bay.

Half a dozen Redkites emerged beside Eight, forming a semicircle.

"You can't win," Eight said, smiling gleefully.

Twelve held her sword vertically, the tip resting between her wriggling eyes. She turned from Eight to the Redkites. Their fire-torches burned brightly.

"You cannot kill me," Twelve said.

Eight approached.

Plastic bone clicked on stone.

"That's right," Eight replied. "What was it Erin called you? *Immortal.*"

She laughed, turning to the Redkites for encouragement, but they said nothing.

Twelve smiled.

"What's so amusing?" Eight said, prodding Twelve closer to the fire.

"These…scarecrows," she replied. "An army, you said. I count eleven. Oh, and that one over there, torn to pieces."

Eight growled. "They're perfect. And they're mine. *All mine!*" She glanced at her army of Redkites, then whispered, "Kill her."

Twelve spun and roundhouse-kicked Number 25 square in the chest. He flew, arms flailing, and collided with the base of the bonfire. His jersey caught light. The oil-soaked newspaper inside sparked into flames. The other Redkites turned to help.

"Leave him!" Eight screamed. "Attack!"

But the cap gun explosives rattled through his chest reaching for the gasoline balloon in his helmet. Number 25 ran, panicked, collided with the bonfire and exploded into hundreds of pieces.

The detonation shook the ground.

The bonfire groaned. Each precariously balanced log shifted. The iron-clad, roll-top bath shifted sideways. Boiling water slopped over the side, sizzling as it hit the inferno below.

"No!" Eight screamed.

The malevolent dolls' heads in her chest wailed sorrowfully.

"It seems Erin betrayed you," Twelve said, knocking 47 and 85 out of her way with a swift blow. "They're riddled with explosives and gasoline. She booby-trapped them all!"

Twelve strode across the cobbles, away from the disintegrating bonfire.

Eight blocked her path, poised between the shore and the courtyard.

"If the island burns, we all burn!"

The remaining Redkites surrounded the bonfire, prodding it with swords and rakes and pitchforks, desperate to stop the collapse. A gigantic log erupted from one side, sending 50 and 23 scampering for cover. The bonfire swung towards the farmhouse. The bathtub launched into the air, spun end over end and clattered through the front door.

Water fizzed. Steam rose. Scalding vapour choked everything. The base of the bonfire degraded, and the entire structure swung towards the shore.

Towards Eight.

And Twelve.

Hitting the ground with a meteoric thunderclap, burning trunks splintered, bounced, smashed against every building. Golden sparks showered both scarecrows. Jets of flame swept across the courtyard, discharging heat and panic in every direction.

Eight hurdled fiery tree trunks as they raced down the cobbles. Twelve hurdled one and sidestepped another. Her sister stumbled. A flaming trunk smashed into her skeletal leg, knocking her to the ground.

Twelve leapt, sword raised. The blade danced with amber fire. But, as Eight rolled over to face the oncoming blow, Number 18—the quarterback, now fully ablaze, his torso popping with Erin's cap-gun explosives—flew through the air.

He wrapped his arms around Twelve, tackling her to the ground.

Erin screamed, left the safety of the barn and ran in chaotic zigzags towards the fight.

Twelve struggled, desperate to escape. The quarterback's grip slipped to her waist as the scarecrow dragged herself away.

Erin sprinted. The smell of fire and motor oil and gasoline and panic filled her nostrils.

Twelve was almost free.

She was going to make it.

Erin was almost upon them.

Twelve was going to be okay.

And then—

Boom!

White light consumed Erin's vision.

A tearing, renting sensation washed over her.

Bits of 18's jersey and helmet bounced past.

Flames licked her dungarees.

The world turned over and over and over.

Something thick and hot muffled her hearing.

Voices sounded a hundred miles away.

Yelling.

Screaming.

Erin tried to stand, to run, to escape, but collapsed to the ground once more.

She could see Twelve across the courtyard. Amongst the burning detritus, fire licked her red pirate jacket and rubber-gloved hands. She looked down at the scarecrow's angular wooden legs and cement-filled boots but—they were no longer there.

They'd been totally blown away.

Eight materialised through the heat haze, her twin scimitars across her chest.

Erin roared.

Ground her teeth.

Stood to face Number Eight.

The skeleton marched towards her.

Smoke and flames rose from the collapsed bonfire.

Eight laughed demonically.

Erin's heart had never felt such darkness. A thing beyond pain, sorrow, grief. She wanted to kill, destroy, eradicate every memory of this monstrosity. She pulled the pistol from her belt and levelled it on the advancing scarecrow.

Eight laughed again. "You're not brave enough to fire that—"

Blam! The first shot threw Erin's arm back.

The bullet buried itself in Eight's ribcage. The blast knocked her backwards. Her dolls' heads screamed in terror.

Blam! The second made it home.

Eight flew back. One step, two, three.

Erin shortened the gap.

Fire danced in her eyes.

Blam! The third bullet tore through Eight's chest, burst her ribcage open, spilling dolls' heads onto the cobbles. The skeleton stumbled towards the roaring bonfire.

Blam! The last shot burst through Eight's left eye socket and out the back of her skull.

The scarecrow staggered. Unbalanced. Dolls' heads wailed their terrible fury.

The bonfire reached for her.

Erin raised the gun to eye level.

Gazed down the sight.

Click!

Her lip shook.

Click. Click-click.

Erin's finger jack-hammered on the trigger.

But nothing.

Click-click-click.

She opened the barrel.

Empty.

"No!"

Eight regained her balance.

Rooted her feet.

The scarecrow waved an admonishing index finger and shook the loose pieces from her damaged skull.

Fear erupted in Erin's stomach.

Cold and eager.

She flung the pistol at Eight.

It flashed harmlessly past the scarecrow and into the fire.

Erin raised her fists, ready for Eight's attack.

Whooosh!

Something tore across the sky.

Ka-Boom!

Everything turned to fire.

A mighty wave of heat swamped Erin.

She spun, squinted at the shore.

An almighty blaze had engulfed *The Swarthy Stranger*. The masts yawned and splintered. Sails billowed and turned to ash as though in the path of a solar wind. Balls of flame dropped to the water. The hull fractured, snapped, and started to sink.

Erin turned her eyes to the horizon and there, bathed in the light of the moon, glided HMS Fortitude, gun turrets smoking.

MANNEQUINS

Another rocket split the sky. The lookout tower behind the stables ruptured into flame and splinters.

A new cluster of shadows roamed the sky. They sped towards the island, dipping below the circling birds, and skimmed the water like a squadron of pelicans.

Erin dropped to the ground, eyes wide, watching the strange shadows approach. She smeared the dirt from her face and pushed her broken glasses up her nose.

Row upon row of mannequins soared towards the island. Their feet skimmed the waves as hundreds of birds airlifted them into battle. Landing like paratroopers, fifty or more battle-hardened mannequins stormed Coldharbour Farm in a chaotic frenzy.

The golems and the Redkites met the mannequins head on. The night exploded in a clash of metal and vengeful screams. Blades sliced the air. Flaming trunks barrelled downhill. The carcass of *The Swarthy Stranger* burned steadily by the shore.

The eastern lookout tower exploded in a ball of flames as another rocket from HMS Fortitude found its target. Erin squealed and crawled for cover. The pennybombs in her pockets pressed against her skin.

Mannequins went down under Number Eight's vicious swords.

A dark vapour swirled around the skeletal scarecrow, grabbing mannequins in a choking embrace. It reminded Erin of the icy fingers that had reached out to them on The Endless Blue. But these were something different, something darker. The mannequins hung motionless as the vapour smothered their bodies, coiling like snakes, before discarding them on the cobbles. Her dolls' heads howled with terrifying glee, their detestable eyes vivid red. Eight threw curses at the birds circling above.

"Cowards! Cravens! Come down and fight me!"

Flanking Eight, the golems created massive casualties too. Hank's enormous fists smashed the plastic mannequins to pieces, throwing them into the air and tearing them clean in two. As his arms swung back and forth, his mighty fingers scored huge tracks across the courtyard, uprooting flagstones and crushing them against his opponents.

Shun darted nimbly through the battle, taking off his adversaries' heads with a slim, elegant blade.

Spirals of glimmering white light rose from each mannequin as they fell.

Erin found her way to the barn door. She slipped the remaining pennybombs from her dungarees and launched them into the heart of the battle. One exploded next to Eight's foot, knocking her off balance. Another burst behind the scarecrow. Mannequins seized the advantage and dealt swift blows to her shoulder and skull.

Erin tossed another pennybomb at a clutch of Redkites who had singled out a wounded mannequin. Detonating on impact, Number 85's jersey flared into life, the explosives ripped through his innards as the motor oil ignited and his gasoline head shredded into pieces. The flames hurried to the Redkites and mannequins beside him, setting off a chain reaction that dissected both 11 and 47.

Erin smiled.

The rancid aroma of decaying foliage invaded her nostrils.

Her satisfaction quickly dimmed.

"Clever girl," Tomas said, grabbing Erin's hand before she released another volley.

He forced her into the barn while Jack retrieved the remaining pennybombs.

"Quite ingenious," Tomas added, dumping her in the hayloft.

"You've lost," she said. "The wickermen lasted minutes. The Redkites are all but defeated. You should surrender and beg for mercy."

"Surrender?" Tomas said. "The Patchwork Woman cannot be defeated. Her golems are making short work of your army. We shall be victorious. The Patchwork Woman will return us to human form, of that I have no doubt."

Jack didn't look as hopeful.

"The Patchwork Woman?" Erin scoffed. "She's nothing but a scarecrow. A scarecrow that *I* made with *these* hands. She doesn't have magic. She has blinded you with terror and fear and nothing more."

"You're the blind one," Tomas growled. "She leads the fight with two swords, while her magic reaches out and crushes the souls of a dozen more."

Erin kicked the wickermen away and squirmed against the barn wall. "It's not magic? It's...the dark spirits."

"Yes!" Tomas exploded. "She's riddled with dark, evil

spirits. The souls of BootHill—every murderer, thief, and psychopath—alive again in her!"

"The dolls' heads!"

"And no match for your pitiful little band," Tomas said cruelly. He flashed his eyes across the burning courtyard. "Especially without...Twelve."

"Don't."

"One of your Redkites exploded next to her," he purred. "Quite the mess."

Erin shook her head. "It's not my fault."

Jack couldn't look her in the eye.

Tomas chuckled. "Oh, but it is," he said, nodding. "Twelve is gone. There's no one left to help you now. It's just a matter of time."

A shadow descended over them. Even up here, in the hayloft, it would take someone of incredible height to cast such a shadow.

"Twelve?" Erin said, peering hopefully between the two wickermen.

"Sadly not," said one voice.

"Someone else entirely," muttered another.

A third added, "But no less fearsome."

"We are many, yet we are one."

Erin squealed as the scarecrow's battered basketball head came into focus.

Number Five snorted angrily and snared Tomas and Jack by the neck, lifting them clean off the ground. She spun, skating across the barn, through the doors, and into the belly of the fight.

Scrabbling to her feet, Erin followed.

Eight's wicked onslaught showed no signs of abating. She

laughed and screamed, hacking down mannequins with her blades. Five threw Jack and Tomas to the ground before her where they huddled together amidst dancing fire.

"Finally!" the skeleton yelled, dispatching another mannequin with the turn of her hand. "An adversary worthy of my time."

Two more mannequins dropped from the grip of Five's dark threads. Eight jumped through the flames and took a powerful swing. The sword embedded itself into Five's arm. Eight yanked the sword, fiercely trying to retrieve the weapon and strike once more, but it was stuck. Deep. She spun deftly, relinquished her grip, and seized Number 23. Kicking him towards Five, the disorientated Redkite tripped on a fiery log and fell, hands outstretched, into the ravaged bonfire.

Jack and Tomas clambered over one another, sprinting away from the time-bomb.

Five lurched aside as 23 was torn to pieces by the resulting explosion. Flaming chunks of shrapnel struck the side of her swollen basketball head.

She staggered, teetering as if to fall.

With both hands wrapped around the remaining scimitar, Eight lashed at Five's body, lacerating her arms and legs, splitting the staples wide open.

Five dropped to her knees.

White light oozed from the wound like treacle.

Strangled, terrified voices bled into the night.

Eight inched back, sneering victoriously. "The world is mine!" she screamed. "Nobody can defeat me."

Behind her, Hank raised a helpless mannequin in each of his massive hands and smashed their bodies together. Eight looked beyond him, at Twelve's legless body. "I'm the one that's *immortal*," she crowed. "I am the *Everliving*!"

Five planted her rollerblades, burst forward, and knocked the sword from Eight's grasp. She coiled her hands over Eight's shoulders, tore the embroidered cloak from her sister's bones, and wedged her fingers through the doll-infested ribcage.

Five raised the skeleton skywards.

Eight slashed wildly at her sister's head, digging her bony fingers into the widening gash. "What are you doing? Let me go!" she ordered. "You are done. Fire will do the rest."

Five did not listen. She pulled her close, holding her sister in a deadly embrace. Eight's dark vapours spiralled around them, mixing with the white light and helpless voices gushing from Number Five.

"Stop this at once!" Eight screamed. "Relinquish me!"

Five fell silent.

Calm.

The wails of anguish and torment from all of Five's voices were swallowed. Their light expanded. It poured through the vicious slice Eight had inflicted. It grew, suffocating her sister's dark vapour, thinning it until no trace remained.

Eight screamed at her golems.

Hank and Shun smashed mannequins aside as they stormed to her aid. But, in the glare of Five's ferocious light, they froze, arms shielding their ruby eyes.

Five shone.

Radiant and deadly.

Like a star preparing to go supernova.

"You are but a smattering of dark spirits. Treacherous and wild," she whispered to Eight, their foreheads pressed together. "But I am a million. I am darkness and light. I am turmoil and conflict and rage. I am love and joy and hope."

Eight squirmed helplessly. Her grotesque dolls' heads barked and wailed, gnawing on the scarecrow's plastic ribs, desperate to be free.

"You cannot resist me, sister."

Eight fought to escape Five's deadly light. "Help me, you fools!" she screamed. "I command you. Release me or my promises will be undone."

Nobody moved.

Not Jack.

Nor Tomas.

Not the last of the Redkites.

Nor Hank and Shun.

Five's light grew, folding into amber, gold, silver.

A blinding flash washed the world clean.

A box of pure sunlight, unlatched.

Five shook as it poured from her body, expanding across the courtyard, swallowing up the bodies of fallen Redkites and mannequins. The golems began to degrade. They hardened, cracked, then melted where they stood. Hot, thick clay sloshed to the ground, running in channels between upturned cobbles and broken flagstones.

A vertical beam punctured the sky like a gigantic searchlight.

"It is time, sister," Five whispered.

Shaking in the opulence of the light, Eight hissed, "You're no sister of mine."

A shockwave erupted.

Erin covered her eyes.

The light spread in every direction. It hurtled towards the shore, swarming around buildings, taking tree trunks and fallen Redkites, mannequins, and the last traces of the golems with it. The light expanded evenly across the water, thinning as it went, until all that remained was a pale glimmer on the crest of every wave.

Skeins of dark and white light marbled together, towering into the night, spreading and fading beneath the star-filled sky.

Where Five and Eight had once been, there was nothing.

No scarecrows.

No rollerblades.

No vicious skeletal face, patchwork cloak, or horrifying dolls' heads.

Nothing.

They were both utterly gone.

REUNION

Erin circled the courtyard, searching for Number Twelve. She found the scarecrow lying next to the farmhouse. Erin dropped to her knees and wrapped her arms around Twelve's torso. Her tears mixed with the burned crust on the pirate's jacket.

Slowly, Twelve lifted her head. "Did we win?"

"Yes, Twelve," Erin said, wiping her eyes. "Eight is gone. Her golems too. The Redkites and the wickermen."

"Jack and Tomas?"

Erin scanned the courtyard, but they had vanished. "I have so many questions for you," she started, then seeing Twelve's face added, "What is it?"

"I feel—"

"Happy?"

"Yes. Sort of. But also—"

"Relieved?"

"Even though Number Eight was riddled with the darkest, most evil spirits the world had ever known, she was still my sister. There were only a dozen of us to start with. Now, only eleven remain."

Erin's bottom lip trembled.

"What's the matter?"

"Number Five," Erin managed. "Her sacrifice won us this war. She had so many spirits inside her. Spirits that gave life to the wickermen and the Redkites. She used them all up to save us."

Whatever strength Twelve had slipped away.

She sank against the hard cobbles and stared up at the sky. Towards the horizon, the North Star shone brilliantly accompanied by a billion others, smiling down.

"I have nine others."

"What?" Erin asked, her cheeks wet with tears. Her fingers coiled around the lapels on the scarecrow's ruined jacket and circled the spot where her pin badge had once been.

"Sisters," Twelve replied. "I have nine more. We should go and find them. They may need our help."

Erin shook her head. "You cannot go anywhere. Not like this."

Levering herself up, Twelve stared at her missing legs. "Oh dear," she said. "You can give me new ones, right?"

Erin swallowed hard. "Of course. Maybe. I don't know," she whispered. "Remember what happened when I tried to give you a new head?"

Twelve nodded.

"Your original legs are…all over the place. I don't think I'll ever be able to put you back exactly how you were."

Erin turned away. Her shoulders juddered as the tears came hard.

"That's okay," said Twelve, her voice slow. "You're the smartest person I've ever known. You'll work something out."

The scarecrow smiled, but only for a second.

Behind Erin, two shadows approached through the fire and the flames.

Marshall came first, his skin red and sore.

The other crept behind him, one arm around the boy's waist, the other holding a pistol. Tilting her cowboy hat back, Loren sneered. "Don't move. Not even an inch."

"The war is over, and you've lost," Erin said.

Loren laughed. "Perhaps, but that doesn't mean I don't get what I want."

"You still think you can have a human body?"

"I know I can!"

"That's madness," Twelve said, shifting onto her elbow. "Leave the boy alone and we'll let you go."

"You'll *let* me go?" Loren scoffed. "I'll do as I please."

Erin inched towards them.

"Stop right there, missy! That's close enough."

The surviving mannequins made their way through the detritus, forming up around Twelve and Erin.

Loren shuffled back. "I will have a human body. I'll find a way." The wickerwoman flexed her trigger finger, pushing the muzzle harder into Marshall's temple. "I won't be trapped inside this body of damp leaves and mouldy grass and itchy nettles forever."

Erin smiled.

Loren noticed. "What is it?" she spat. "What are you smirking at?"

"There aren't any bullets left."

"What?"

"I used them on The Patchwork Woman. On Number Eight," she said. "And I nearly got her too."

"Lies."

Loren raised the gun into the air and pulled the trigger. *Click.*

Click-click-click.

"Also," Erin added, gazing over the wickerwoman's shoulder.

"What are you—?"

But it was too late.

Tomas grabbed her.

Marshall dropped to the ground.

Tomas ripped the pistol from Loren's grip.

Jack dragged the discarded top half of The Patchwork Woman's abominable skin. He thrust it over Loren's head and pulled the rotten flesh past her shoulders like a straitjacket.

Inside, the wickerwoman let out a blood-curdling scream.

"You wanted to wear human skin," Jack said. "Well, it's all yours."

Loren ran, blinded by the terrifying tapestry of tainted tissue. She slipped and stumbled, cursed bitterly, heading straight for the dying bonfire.

Erin jumped up.

Twelve pulled her back.

"Don't look," the scarecrow said, but Erin's eyes never faltered.

Loren thrashed around in the fire. Her tortured screams rang through the night for a time, before they faded into moans and whimpers, and finally silence.

Her body became still and lifeless, engulfed in fire and flame and death. Loren turned to ash in minutes, her body recognisable until the wind rose, pulling her apart, scattering grey flakes in every direction.

Cords of dark light twisted over the bonfire, ascending towards the stars.

The mannequins moved in on Jack and Tomas, weapons

pointed at their chests.

"Put the pistol down," Erin said.

Tomas slung it aside and raised his hands above his head. The mannequins secured the wickermen and led them to the stables.

Erin sat Marshall against the farmhouse next to Twelve. His face looked sore and scratched by the itchy cloth. His body was raw from the boiling water in the roll-top bath. Erin instinctively put out a hand and touched the side of his face, inspecting his wounds.

Marshall's skin goosebumped at her cool touch.

Erin blushed. "Are you okay?"

"Thanks to you."

Their eyes locked, searching for what lurked behind. Marshall's hand went to hers. A rush of excitement rippled across her skin. Their fingers knitted together.

"What did I miss? I heard so much, felt so much, but—"

"I don't know the half of it myself." Erin felt like crying again. "Part of me wishes I could go back to the day Twelve woke up and avoid all that talk of boats, and adventure, and looking for Clyde and her scarecrow sisters. We could have lived out the next fifty years alone on Coldharbour Farm in peace and quiet."

"But then you'd never have had such an adventure," Marshall said. "An adventure filled with excitement and wonder—"

"—and heartache and death."

Pa's words reverberated through her mind.

Brave the rain or die!

She saw the rain, the waves, the upturned rowboat. The weeks and months that followed. Long and cold. Sad and lonely.

But things were different now. She had Twelve and Marshall and Raven—

"Erin?" It was Twelve.

The girl blinked the memory of the blackbird away. "I'm okay," she said. "How did you do all this? How did you survive the fire in the chapel? How did you get your wings? The mannequins? The warship?"

Twelve smiled gloriously. "I got lucky," she wheezed. "As the floor in the chapel burned, it collapsed under my weight and dropped me into the concrete foundations. Down there I found such horrors, but also the answer to Eight's true nature. Amongst more than half a dozen discarded patchwork bodies and piles of naval uniforms, I found this."

Twelve opened the top pocket of her pirate jacket and retrieved two pieces of fabric. The first she'd found at the foot of Eight's cross—bright yellow with blue flowers. The other was much larger but made of the same fabric. Twelve placed them side-by-side, lining up the floral pattern. "I knew then that The Patchwork Woman was one of my sisters—Number Eight."

She returned the fabric to her pocket for safekeeping.

"Raven and the birds found me the next day and helped me to the beach. They graciously donated feathers to give me these wings."

"Yes," Erin said. "You can fly. How is that possible?"

"I do not know," Twelve admitted. "But I had to get to you. *Lazarus* was gone. My cement-filled boots wouldn't let me swim. The only way was through the skies."

"I guess none of us know what we're capable of until we're pushed to our limits."

"Until we face an unbearable choice."

Erin squeezed the scarecrow's hands.

"We returned to Clifftop and saw off Bavorski Beetlestone and his vultures. In the fight, Raven was injured, so he made me Governor of Clifftop. Just for the time being."

"Hang on a minute," Erin said, curling her fingers around Twelve's shoulder. "Raven's alive?"

"Oh yes," the scarecrow replied wearily. "He has a damaged wing, but I'll let him tell you of his adventures."

Erin felt lighter.

"We returned to The Scrapers and enlisted the help of the mannequins. Initially, I thought the birds could fly them all the way here for the battle, but it was too far. Only a handful of us would have made it."

The mighty sea eagle swooped in, landing on a charred tree trunk beside them.

"The victory is ours," she said, casting her eyes over the damaged scarecrow. "Will you survive?"

Twelve attempted a nod.

"I was telling Erin how we got the mannequins here from The Scrapers," Twelve prompted, slumping against the cobbles.

"A risky strategy by all accounts," the sea eagle said. "Twelve told us about a warship drifting about in the southern waters. If we could find a way to power it, we could transport everybody and have a battleship of our own."

More birds and mannequins gathered round.

"Initially, Twelve had the idea of dropping to the bottom of The Scrapers and searching for drums of motor oil, but Harunara had already plundered the depths for anything as useful as that. Instead, she thought of *Lazarus*. Twelve told us, *We need to give the warship wings!*"

"Sails," Erin whispered.

The birds chirped excitedly.

"She made sails for a warship?"

"We all did," the sea eagle said. "Huge great sails from bedsheets and clothing and curtains and anything we could find."

Erin spun on her knees and looked towards the horizon. There, on the ocean, sat HMS Fortitude. Dozens of colourful sails rippled in the brisk wind.

"*The Haughty Jinx*," Twelve said, tapping the side of her head.

"Yes, yes!" Erin cried in astonishment. "You created a mighty pirate galleon and took it to war!"

"I did," Twelve said, looking around at the birds and mannequins. "*We* did."

More birds descended.

The sea eagle ruffled her feathers as one landed next to her.

"We took a huge risk, putting our hopes and prayers on the fickle nature of the wind."

"Yes. It was all or nothing," said the new arrival.

"Raven!" Erin cried, cradling the blackbird in her hands. "It's so good to see you!"

"I have battled through darkness unbound to be here," he said morosely, and Erin laughed. "I'm also captain of a huge battleship, so it's Admiral Raven to you!"

An albatross, carrying a cumbersome cargo, came in to land.

"Oh, and somehow my first mate is a dog."

"Socks!" Erin and Marshall said together as the pale lurcher bounded towards them. "You rescued him from BootHill."

"Obviously."

"I'm so proud of you," she said, planting a big kiss on the top of Raven's head. "How's your wing?"

"I'll live," he said gloomily.

The sea eagle hopped along the burned trunk towards Erin. "The wickermen that destroyed Loren are secured in the stables. What would you have us do with them?"

Erin and Twelve exchanged glances.

"I don't know," Erin said. "What should we do?"

"No one deserves to die," Twelve said. "Despite all the horrid things they did, Jack and Tomas saved us in the end."

"But Jack betrayed us. Lied to us. Made us care for him."

"He was deceived by the promises of The Patchwork Woman," Twelve said. "I think he realised that in the end. They both did."

"Once Bavorski Beetlestone was overthrown, I exiled the vultures from Clifftop," Raven added. "I could have the wickermen returned to the Island of Trees and send scouts to keep an eye on them. They can do no harm from there—except to one another."

Erin angled her head.

Twelve nodded.

"Then it is agreed. Take the prisoners to the ship and prepare for departure."

"You're going already?"

Raven swivelled his beady eyes towards her. "Soon," he said, "but first, we need to help you clean up this mess."

NAME DAY

The mannequins and the birds worked tirelessly through the darkest night Erin could remember. They respectfully cleared the bodies of Redkites and mannequins and fallen birds, brushed away mountains of ash, stacked the scorched logs, and piled up discarded weapons.

Erin and Marshall carried Twelve into the barn. Removing the front wall, they settled her inside the hay-bale fortress, before making their way to the farmhouse to sleep until dawn. When they rose and ventured out into the courtyard, the horizon swelled with the most glorious sunrise. A vanilla and raspberry ice-cream sundae.

HMS Fortitude sat before the rising sun. Her patchwork sails billowed happily in the wind. A spiral of birds patrolled overhead.

Erin paced eagerly across the courtyard, signalling for Marshall to follow.

"Where are you going?"

"I have an idea."

In the farthest corner of the barn, Erin moved empty boxes and clutter until she came upon her mother's wheelchair.

"I fished it out of The Endless Blue during The Many Years

Storm. I was keeping it for—" She paused, absent-mindedly dusting the armrests. "Well, now I know why."

Erin opened the wheelchair. The leather seat folded down perfectly between the large rubber wheels.

"It's for Twelve," she told Marshall.

"I know."

Twelve peered over the top of the hay-bale fortress, watching the beautiful sunrise through the barn doors. "The world is changing," she said, as Erin and Marshall approached. "I thought I was imagining it for a while, but it's real, all of it. The dark last night, the colours in the sky this morning, the wind on my face. Are things going back to the way they were before?"

Erin wasn't sure, but she gave the scarecrow a shallow nod. "We brought you a chair," she said. "You'll be able to move around. Just like before, but, you know, on wheels."

"Like Number Five?"

"Yes," Erin said, biting her lip. "Just like Five."

Twelve considered the wheelchair for a moment.

"Looks perfect," she said sadly.

"What is it?"

"Is it the chair?" Marshall said. "You'll get used to it in no time."

"It's not that," Twelve said. "I love the chair. It's...I don't want to be the last scarecrow."

"The last scarecrow?"

"Five and Eight are gone. I keep wondering where the other nine are. Are they out there somewhere? Did they survive The Many Years Storm? Or were they drowned by the rain, smashed to smithereens by the ice storms, torn from their crosses and thrown around the world by the wind?"

"I don't know," Erin said. "But we're going to find—"

"No," Twelve said. "I'm in no state for adventure anymore."

"You shouldn't let the wheelchair hold you back," Marshall said.

The scarecrow sighed woefully.

"All this travelling and fighting has taken it out of me. I need to rest. I need to sleep...but I cannot. I don't know how."

Crawling into the hay-bale fortress, Erin knelt at the scarecrow's side.

"There's no rush. We've got our whole lives. I know exactly how you feel. I believe Clyde is out there somewhere. Your sisters too. All I want to do is find him and hold him and bring him home. But now is not the time. We'll stay here a while and then, when you're ready, we'll borrow HMS Fortitude and go in search of them all!"

Twelve nodded slowly. "Would you take me to the shore?"

Erin and Marshall positioned the scarecrow into the wheelchair and wrapped a dozen belts around her lap and torso. Marshall pushed the exhausted scarecrow across the courtyard as mannequins swept away the last of the feathers and ash.

Raven perched on Twelve's cross by the water's edge, the sea eagle beside him, cleaning herself.

"Finally," the blackbird said. "You slept so long I thought you were dead."

Marshall pulled the wheelchair to a halt and kicked on the footbrake.

"Thanks for doing such an amazing job with the farm," Erin said. "It looks as good as new."

Raven snorted. "It's not perfect, but it's a start. Several roof panels need replacing in the barn, the greenhouse has cracked panes, and the farmhouse…well, you'll see. Do you plan to stay here?"

"For now," Marshall said, looking at Erin.

"We need to rest, rebuild. And then we're going in search of Clyde, and Twelve's sisters."

"Is that wise?" Raven said.

Nobody had an answer.

"As you wish," he went on. "Remember, the birds and the mannequins are your allies. The power and might of Clifftop and The Scrapers will always be at your back should you need them."

"Thanks," Erin said. "That means more than you know."

"If you like that, then this will blow your mind."

Erin frowned.

Two albatrosses circled overhead transporting another item onto Coldharbour Farm.

"What is it?" Erin asked. "Everyone's here."

"Not everyone," Raven said.

The birds darted above Erin and released their cargo. She held out her hands and caught a blackened box, charred and split. Opalescent light reflected off the surviving mother of pearl shards. Erin's hands shook. The latch was missing but the lid opened easily, hinges intact.

Lucretia juddered, stood, turned.

Ma's music box played, slow and haunting.

A thousand memories seized Erin's mind, overwhelming and vital.

"Thank you, thank you, thank you," she said. "I cannot believe it survived the fire. I cannot believe I've got it back!"

"That reminds me," the blackbird said, fluttering onto Twelve's lap. "You have something of mine."

Slowly, Twelve lifted her heavy head. "I'm sorry?"

"My title. Governor of this fair isle and one true ruler of The Endless Blue. I believe I bestowed them upon you. And what an incredible job you did leading our forces into war. The birds of Clifftop owe you a great debt. We respect you as highly as any bird that calls The Endless Blue home."

Twelve levered herself up in the wheelchair.

"It was my honour," she said. "I return your titles, Justice Raventhorne, Governor of this fair isle and one true ruler of The Endless Blue. Your courage and friendship will stay with me forever."

"Have you put any thought into your name?" the sea eagle asked.

"Her name?" Erin asked.

"Yes," the bird replied. "Twelve is part of our colony now. Part of Clifftop. And should be named as such."

"I'm just Twelve," she said, tapping the space where her pin badge had been.

"Katherine," Erin said immediately.

"Really?" the blackbird croaked. "That's not very intimidating."

"It was my mother's name."

"Oh."

"And my middle name."

"No, Erin," Twelve said.

"I insist. It's a traditional...*family* name."

"Very well," the sea eagle confirmed. "And your closing title?"

"You fly like a mighty bird and fight like a dozen," insisted Raven.

"Like an eagle!"

"Or a condor!"

"A falcon!"

"Twelve's bigger and stronger and far more magical than those," Erin said, then glanced at the sea eagle. "No offence."

"Like a dragon," Marshall said.

"Like a dozen dragons." Erin smiled.

"Katherine TwelveDragons, it is," Raven croaked, his wings fluttering. "Lieutenants. It is time we departed for the Island of Trees."

He looked at Erin.

"Come and see us sometime. Any time. We'll be waiting for you."

Raven spread his wings and dropped off the cross. He arced into the air, the sea eagle and the remaining birds at his wingtips. He shot across the farm, swooped low to the cobbles, before skimming the water towards HMS Fortitude.

Erin and Marshall waved.

Katherine TwelveDragons sat and watched, her ghastly head resting lazily against her wonky shoulders.

THE LAST SCARECROW!

Two weeks passed.

Erin and Marshall spent their days rebuilding the barn, bricking up the back of the stables, fixing the greenhouse, re-laying the flagstones and cobbles, and tidying the farmhouse.

They organised the weapons and piles of broken body parts into Erin's scarecrow-creation station. By the time they'd finished she had enough to create fifty new scarecrows.

Perhaps more.

But she didn't have the energy for it.

Or the heart.

Well, almost.

In the evenings, they sat with Twelve by the shore and watched the sun set.

Every day the colours on the horizon were more amazing than the last. Raspberry and lemon were joined by jade and crimson and tangerine and gold. Fissures of colour sprayed on the inky blue backdrop like splatters of paint.

Slowly, the water receded.

Clouds filled the sky.

The cobbled path, that had once disappeared into The Endless Blue, was reclaimed.

Marshall wheeled Twelve down to the retreating shore, twice the distance from the farmhouse it had once been. But where sunflowers and corn had swayed gently in the cool summer breeze, there was sodden, ruined earth.

The cobbles met the water at an intersection where another path ran towards Eight's distant crop of land.

Erin followed, looking at the waterlogged earth, wondering how long it would take to recover. Twelve slumped to one side in the wheelchair. Her head bobbed gently.

Would Twelve recover too? Or was she like the farmland: spoiled, broken, and dying?

They took her down the path every day until the water level dropped low enough to make it all the way to Eight's island.

The air grew warm.

Swirls of sweetness found their noses.

Erin and Marshall wore shorts and T-shirts and sat on a chequered blanket, their backs to Eight's cross. Before them lay a picnic consisting of tomatoes, cucumber, and peppers that Erin had salvaged from the greenhouse. Out-of-date crisps and salted peanuts, scavenged from the depths of HMS Fortitude, were poured into bowls next to an utterly flat bottle of traditional lemonade.

Erin and Marshall ate and chatted and made plans for the coming days and weeks.

When they were done, they took Twelve back to the farmhouse and settled her in the living room opposite the painting of *The Haughty Jinx* and a pile of *National Geographics* discovered under Clyde's bed.

Erin and Marshall returned to Eight's island and removed her cross from the ground. They carried the awkward lump back to the courtyard and erected it next to Twelve's, facing

The Endless Blue.

Night slipped across the horizon.

Marshall sat with Twelve while Erin put the final touches to a surprise she'd been working on in the barn. A surprise she hoped would help Twelve turn the corner and rediscover her strength.

That night, Erin barely slept.

Excitement and worry kept her dreams at bay.

In the morning, bleary-eyed and aching, she hobbled down the stairs. Marshall snored gently on the sofa with Socks curled on his lap.

But Twelve was gone.

Erin bolted through the kitchen and out into the courtyard. She searched the stables and the barn, eventually finding Twelve down the hill staring up at the two crosses.

Erin circled Twelve and stood, with her back to the water, looking up at a brand-new scarecrow hanging on Eight's cross.

It wore one of her brother's Dungeon's & Dragons T-shirts, baggy blue jeans, a high-visibility life-preserver, and a Coldharbour High School Redkites Cap. Constructed from leftover mannequin parts, its head made use of the smiling medicine ball Erin had once tried to attach to Twelve's body.

"I'm calling him Thirteen," Erin said. "What do you think?"

"Him?" Twelve said.

"I suppose. I hadn't—"

"It's Clyde," Twelve said softly.

Erin's voice caught in her throat. "No, it isn't. He's called Thirteen," she said hurriedly. "I made him for you."

"No," Twelve said, smiling at the new scarecrow. "You made him for *us*."

Erin hadn't considered that at all. Perhaps, somewhere deep inside, she'd made a scarecrow in Clyde's image. Perhaps she needed a brother just as much as Twelve needed a scarecrow.

Swallowing hard, Erin said, "You're not the last scarecrow anymore. Thirteen is, or can be for now, until we find the others—"

Tears formed in Erin's eyes.

A deep yearning pulled her heart.

Twelve held out a hand and took Erin's.

"I love you."

"I love you too, Twelve. You're amazing."

"You created me. You made me what I am."

"Ma always insisted that our actions make us who we are."

They stood for what seemed an age, staring at the last scarecrow.

Thirteen.

Clyde.

"Is he going to wake up?"

A tear ran down Erin's face.

"No," she said. "I don't believe so."

They watched the shrinking oceans calmly lap against the shore.

"I'm tired, Erin. So tired." Her voice was slow, drawn. Despite the faint whisper of her words, the scarecrow cracked a smile. "Is this what it feels like just before you fall asleep?"

Erin looked at the exhausted scarecrow. Tears filled her eyes. "Yes. I believe it is."

"Good," Twelve replied, turning hers to the sky.

The faintest glimmer of starlight could be seen against the radiant blue.

"Finally," she said. "I get to find out what sleep is like. I don't have to imagine anymore."

"That's right, Twelve," Erin replied, her voice shaking.

Her vision blurred.

She felt hollowed out, empty.

"You can sleep now, Twelve. A good long sleep. You deserve it. And you can dream. Dream as big, and as wild, and as carefree as you dare. Dream yourself all the way to the stars."

Slowly, the scarecrow's chin dropped to her chest.

Her shoulders tipped.

A worm fell from her eye socket.

Skeins of crystal white vapour rose from the scarecrow's body, twisting and spiralling in the cool morning air.

A sickly shiver crept over Erin's skin.

"Mind how you go," she whispered.

Twelve was gone.

A NEW DAWN

Erin cried for almost an hour. Eventually, she felt Marshall's arms around her, pulling her close. Socks circled them, whimpering softly. The boy stroked her hair and whispered words of comfort. When she pulled away, his face was nothing more than a waterlogged, blurry mess, but she was happy he was here.

"She's—" Erin managed.

Marshall nodded, holding the scorched music box.

"Do you think—?" she said.

"What?"

Erin lifted her glasses and wiped her eyes.

"No, it's stupid."

"Tell me."

Erin summoned all her strength. "Twelve was fierce and determined like Pa. Kind and wise like Ma." She bit her lip. "And brave and adventurous like Clyde." They looked at the peaceful scarecrow. "I told you, it's stupid."

"Not at all," Marshall replied, slipping his hands into hers. "It's a lovely thought."

"We need to do one more thing for Twelve," Erin said. "I'll need your help."

"Anything."

Climbing the iron-rung ladder, they placed Twelve's lifeless body back on her cross. Her mighty bison skull drooped towards her fire-ravaged pirate jacket. Her rubber-gloved hands sagged by her sides.

They looked happy together—Twelve and Thirteen—two beautifully terrifying scarecrows on their weather-beaten crosses.

Just the way they should be.

"Something's missing," Erin said. "One last detail."

She grabbed a knot of rope and mounted the ladder one final time.

Taking Twelve's left hand and Thirteen's right, she lashed them together.

She kissed Twelve on the forehead, and pinned a new badge to her lapel.

Girls Rule The World!

Back on the wet earth, Socks nuzzled her feet.

Marshall cradled the music box.

Erin rested her head on the freckled boy's shoulder.

Their fingers intertwined like the two scarecrows.

Tears came.

Hard and raw.

Erin let them fall freely, holding nothing back, letting everything go.

The moon and stars paled into forever as the music box played, and Lucretia danced, and a magnificent sunrise bloomed across The Endless Blue.

Scan Me!

WHAT'S NEXT?

Thank you so much for reading *The Last Scarecrow*!
I hope you enjoyed it.

If you have the time to write a brief and honest
review on Amazon, GoodReads etc, that would help
me enormously to reach new readers.

I have a growing mailing list with exclusive news,
writing tips, and giveaways. Scan the QR code above
or visit **www.neiljhart.com/sign-up/** to get **FREE**
downloads including Erin's *Book of Scarecrows!*
You can unsubscribe at *any* time.

I'm also active on Facebook, Twitter, Instagram, and TikTok.
If you have a question about this book, or my writing, you
can get in touch with me there or follow for updates and
news about future books and promotions.

Once again, thank you for your reading *The Last Scarecrow*.
Best wishes, **NjH**

also by **NeiL j HaRt**

WATTY'S
2022
WINNER
FOR
FANTASY

Sadie Madison
and the
Boy in the Crimson Scarf

**Unlock the power of music,
magic, and memory.**

His Dark Materials meets *The Mortal Engines* in Neil J
Hart's award-winning urban fantasy adventure where the
fabric of reality is threatened by those who would give their
lives to glimpse the past and kill to see the future.

AVAilABLe DECemBER 2024

FACT FILE:
CLIMATE CHANGE

Climate change is the long-term shift in average weather patterns across the world. Human activity has increased production of carbon dioxide and other greenhouse gases that trap the sun's rays and increase the Earth's temperature.

In the past hundred years, the Earth's average temperature has increased about 1.5°F which has led to melting glaciers, drought, and coral reef bleaching.

Rising temperatures lower many species survival rates due to less food, less successful reproduction, and critical changes to their natural environment.

Global sea level rose about 40cm since the year 2000 and is accelerating every year.

The number of record high temperature events are increasing, while the number of record low temperature events are decreasing.

Climate change has serious implication for human life and the natural world.

FACT FILE: SCARECROWS

Scarecrows go by many names including Jack-of-Straw, Scarebird, Tattybogle, Hay-man, Gallybagger, Showy-Hoy.

The Egyptians were the first to use scarecrows. They placed them along the Nile River to protect their wheat fields.

A long time ago in Britain, scarecrows were burnt during Pagan ceremonies as sacrifices to bring a good harvest.

Kuebiko is the Shinto god of folk wisdom, knowledge and agriculture, and is represented in Japanese mythology as a scarecrow who cannot walk but has comprehensive awareness.

In Germany, wooden scarecrows were carved to resemble witches.

There are many famous scarecrows throughout popular culture including Dorothy's brainless sidekick in *The Wizard of Oz*, the fear-toxin obsessed supervillain in DC's *Batman*, and the friendly but chaotic scarecrow with changeable heads *Worzel Gummidge*!

SCHOOLS QUESTIONS

In chapter two 'After The Storm', Erin describes the farmhouse as looking like it had been ransacked. Why do you think this is? Provide evidence to support your answer.

What is The Endless Blue? What information can you find to justify your answer?

Using evidence from chapter two 'After The Storm', summarise how you think Erin is feeling?

In chapter three 'Number Twelve', find and copy the word that means wicked or evil.

At the end of chapter three 'Number Twelve', Erin knocks a frying pan off the wall and alerts the scarecrow to her presence. Predict what will happen next.

In chapter four 'Hay-bale Fortress', find and copy the evidence that suggests Erin is frightened.

In chapter five 'Medicine Ball', Erin describes her books as being dog-eared. What do you think this is?

On a boat, what is a figurehead? What information can you find to justify your answer?

Using evidence from chapter five 'Medicine Ball', summarise how you think Number Twelve is feeling?

In chapter seven 'Lazarus', find and copy the word that means scrap or fragment.

In chapter four 'Hay-bale Fortress', Erin explains that Number Eight's cross beside the mineshaft is empty. Predict what happened to Number Eight.

What visual clues did Twelve and Erin use to help them build *Lazarus*. Find and copy evidence to support this.

And finally...

Who was your favourite character, and why?

What was your favourite part of the story, and why?

What was the scariest part of the story, and why?

What do you think happens to Erin and Marshall next?

ACKNOWLEDGEMENTS

A huge thank you to my friends and family for their endless support and encouragement. It's been a long road. Thank you. I could not do this on my own.

Special thanks to Jen Moss, Winter Simpson, Chris Jenkins, Nicki Cater, Josh Morton, Deby Goodyear, and Scarlet Frost. Your feedback, criticisms, and praise have truly helped shape this book and breath life into every scarecrow, wickermen, and mannequin!

To my editor, Manda Waller. Thank you for your forensic dissection of my manuscript and genuine excitement about this project. My book is infinitely better from your deft touch. Can't wait to work on future projects with you.

What can I say about the Wattpad community? You guys are incredible. Before *The Last Scarecrow* won a Wattpad Award in 2021 I received tons of amazing comments, encouraging me to write every day. Since the award, hundreds more of you have found and read and liked and commented on this story (many of you in tears!) and continue to do so. Some of you even sent me fan art! I'm blown away every day. Thank you.

ABOUT THE AUTHOR

Neil J Hart has won awards for his haunting fantasy novels *The Last Scarecrow* and *Sadie Madison and the Boy in the Crimson Scarf.*

Neil also works as a graphic designer.
He fosters for Cats Protection. Relies on coffee.
Adores cheese and cucumber sandwiches.
And collects Tomb Raider memorabilia.

More info and links to Neil's social media at
www.neiljhart.com